The Enbalan Dilemma

The Enbalan Dilemma

by Isaiah Cox

Isaiah Cox in Newberg
MMXX

Chapters

Proverbs 10:19 (KJV) –

In the multitude of words there wanteth not sin:

but he that refraineth his lips is wise.

Everything Changes

The Jeep was a rusty, ugly, outdated piece of junk. It needed a tune-up, ten years ago. But Nick didn't know that. Perhaps he had some vague inkling that something was amiss, but mostly Nick didn't concern himself with the mundane. In a testament to the manufacturer, it still rambled on, leaving in its wake a fragrance of half-burnt oil. It was the unmistakable aroma of Nick's vehicle... and it was the smell of Nick, if he travelled anywhere in it.

The red sun burned a crimson hue across the Western desert sky as the open topped Jeep scrambled towards the Pacific Coast. The weather was perfect, and only a roll bar was between the pilot, Nick, and the vast painted sky where the planets were slowly beginning to burn through the red as it swept East, as fire sweeping through a field, leaving behind hues of dark purple; this time of year there would be little temperature difference between night and day, but there was the welcomed relief from the direct rays of the sun.

For Nick it was all blurring together, a combination of black asphalt, faded road paint, and black cinder shoulders framed by steep desert canyon walls. The wind roared past his ears and the pleasing smell of desert brush (mixed with ½ burnt oil) filled his nostrils. His senses were having a hard time taking it all in; there was a blurriness that didn't exist in this rugged landscape, only in his overtired and chemically altered mind.

Only an hour earlier he'd been beside a camp table, enjoying friends and music, with plenty of beer aiding the festivities. The conversation, friendship, temperature, music and buzz had been ideal when a painful thought struck him, "Tomorrow I'm scheduled to work."

He'd snuck off several hundred yards to make a phone call, but it wasn't far enough. His boss' reply, to calling in sick, had been, "Do I hear music in the background? Nick, you've already missed five days this year. Our sick policy states that on the fifth absence you can be fired. We had this discussion after your fifth day. Unless you can provide a doctor's note for tomorrow, I'll be forced to let you go. Either that, or show up."

Now the desert was blurring past his tired eyes, and he struggled to react to the corners in a timely manner. Only a burning anger at the memory of the phone call kept him alert enough to respond to curves, although in this wide-open desert they seldom appeared, which almost made them harder to negotiate due to their unexpected occurrences.

The sky darkened from red, to orange, finally turning to dark purple as the stars joined those early peeking planets in the heavens. Far to the North the horizon disappeared into the faint black outline of a towering storm cloud, and at its base flashes of lightning could be seen. A faint smell of the rain that accompanied the lightning drifted into the Jeep. The late summer desert sky was wondrous to behold, if only Nick had the wherewithal to recognize it.

A single light came towards him and Nick thought it must be an approaching motorcycle. It was on a long, deep, straight stretch, where the end of the road wasn't visible, being found on the

3

distant side of the curvature of the Earth; difficult for those that don't live in the desert to imagine, but these roads exist and can be found leading in and out of vast deserts.

Five minutes later the light suddenly began rushing at Nick. Nick's vision was tired and the contrast of the bright light against the twilight sky made it difficult for Nick to perceive where the road was. He aimed his vehicle to the right of the light. As it drew closer Nick perceived something was wrong. He was aiming to the right but he could feel the wheels on that side of the vehicle bouncing on and off the edge of the road.

Trying to focus, Nick squinted his eyes, and struggled to make his tired mind perceive where the edges of any vehicle behind the blinding light might be. He flashed his bright lights at the apparition, in an attempt to get the onrushing vehicle to dim their light.

It was to no avail. The light seemed to grow bright as a stage spotlight, and Nick could see nothing but the light. He took his chances with the desert bushes and committed to falling completely off the right side of the road. His wheels began to bounce up and down in a pounding fashion, as he tried to apply his brakes on the slick undulating roadside sand swales. His vehicle thundered roughly into the desert and his eyes vibrated within their sockets.

Worst of it all, the light was still coming at him. There was no escape. If he had all his senses, Nick might have offered a prayer, but his mind wasn't quick enough to respond verbally to the confusion and chaos he suddenly found himself in.

And it only became worse. As the light swallowed Nick he felt his body torn from the vehicle. These things happen fast, but your

4

mind takes them in at such a rate they seem to be in slow-motion; words cannot attempt to keep up with the turmoil, but the conscious mind still breathes in the events, and Nick realized he was ripped from the vehicle, his limbs beating against unknown obstacles as he flew.

But there was no windshield frame that Nick would see, no seatbelt, no steering wheel. Nick was only in the light.

And then it was over. From calamity to silence, Nick had fallen. His bruised, broken and beleaguered body would not respond and a darkness, so very different from the light that previously enveloped him, dropped its shades down on him. His eyes slowly closed and his body tried to rest and reset. And Nick heard the static hum of deep silence as he faded out of consciousness.

Nick's heavy eyelids cracked open to reveal little more than what he saw with them shut. The world was grey. Dark grey. And it seemed colder than his dream. It was as though he was laying on wet stones. Did he smell the sea? Surely it was humid. And in one lucid second he thought he saw a building, next to an enclosure, away in the distance, but it was ethereal, as if growing from the very stone it sat upon.

But these were momentary lapses in consciousness.

These glimpses at his new reality lasted only until the visions began.

Strange visions. They were moving him. He felt a lightness when they lifted him off the rocks. There were uniforms, that much was to be expected, ambulance drivers probably, but the uniforms were odd. And there was no siren or flashing light.

And once he struggled for clarity, only to capture an image of eyes within a helmet which were much too large. And black. So black.

They were moving him.

But then he was lost again.

As his body temperature returned his mind began to revive, but his memories were so convoluted and intimidating that his body seemed to force returning to sleep whenever wakefulness appeared too near.

Eventually his body's need for sleep was completed, and Nick's eyes opened.

He was lying in a hammock, strung from one corner to the distant corner of a square, green, glistening cell. The walls seemed organic, vegetable plant-like in hue.

He was covered by a silky material that was thicker and warmer than any silk he'd previously experienced. His hammock was made of the same material.

The ceiling appeared to glow lightly, in an iridescent way, reminding Nick of the glow-in-the-dark stars he'd applied to his bedroom ceiling as a child.

And there was the smell. It all smelled heavily of the ocean, the unmistakable pungent smell of seaweed combined with cool salt air. Cool being the operative word, he could see his breath in the moist air above him.

He tried to rise but he was wrapped, his efforts restrained by the warm silk-like material cocooning him.

Near his feet the wall began revealing an opening, as the organic material folded inward and away from the rapidly gaping hole.

Nick heard a muffled grunt and he focused on the opening, wondering who his visitor might be.

Through the door shuffled a seal creature, wearing what was unmistakably a uniform. Its eyes were nearly five feet above the floor, making the creature nearly nine feet in total length, considering the flipper behind him.

As Nick's eyes met the black eyes of his invader, he knew the creature recognized his newly awake status. It was as though he heard the word "wake", in his mind, but the word wasn't said, only a seal noise had escaped his visitor.

Terrified, Nick yelled, and thrashed in his hammock, as best his battered body could, but it was fruitless. The silk bindings were as strong as they were soft. Soon he was left tired and panting, and mumbling "Do you understand me?" to the seal.

The confusion of the seal was apparent, and Nick gave up.

The seal had a black device in his mouth, which he pointed towards Nick's stomach region and head. Nick realized the seal was scanning him, and it seemed the diagnosis was acceptable, hearing, or perhaps only realizing, "OK" the same way he'd earlier recognized the seal's realization of his waking state.

And then he was alone again, in the moist room for, what felt like, an eternity.

Nick started freaking out. His breath was fast, his heart pounding. He tried to escape the cocoon a second time, but with the same luck. Giving up on literal escape, he determined that sleep might also provide escape. He'd close his eyes and try his best to sleep, but whenever he opened his eyes, he was still right there.

Eventually Nick gave up on his efforts. His mind drifted, as real sleep came near.

He had the wherewithal to remember that it was likely a crash in the Jeep that instigated this.

As he passed the time, his thoughts went to the Independence Day celebrations earlier that summer when he'd returned to his hometown. He thought through the chain of events after he was found in jail the morning of July 5th, for an intoxicated driving offense.

His father, Mark, had taken him to breakfast when they left the jail. He hadn't yelled, or even appeared angry. As Nick gobbled his breakfast, his father clearly informed Nick that unless he changed his ways, Nick's life was going to suffer painful and long-lasting repercussions for the lifestyle he was choosing. He spoke of Christian repentance. After they left the restaurant the discussion was over, his father hadn't brought it up again.

But Nick hadn't found his dad's sermon particularly relevant because he didn't share his parent's faith, so he had no need to justify himself before an omnipotent being.

He considered this fate and denial invaded his psyche. Nick thought that his current predicament couldn't possibly be real, just as his father's divine being couldn't. This must be a coma, or a terrible dream, and he tried to recall intense memories that might cause a person to wake up.

But, lying in his hammock, he could not reawaken to the reality he imagined existed elsewhere. But his delusions were strong, and

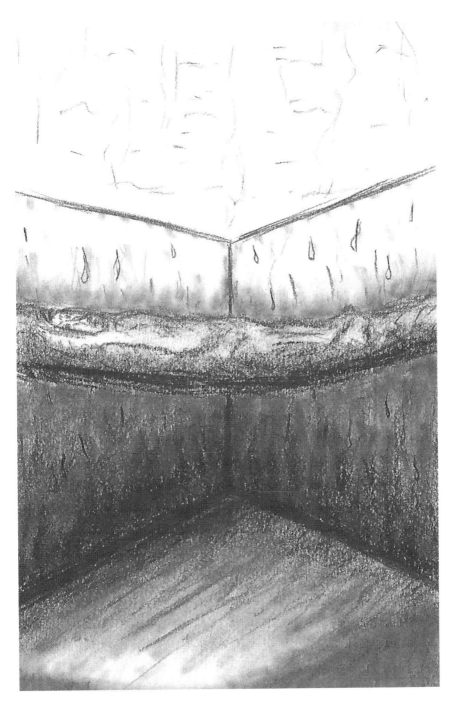

rather than face his current reality he chose to view his predicament only as a temporary sickness of his mind.

Then the hole gaped open again and a squadron entered the room, with the seal who earlier inspected him. The squad members were also seals, but wearing uniforms that seemed somehow harder and military.

He tried talking, yelling and screaming at these seals, but the same looks of confusion appeared.

He could hear in his head the concept of words never said.

One of the sternly dressed seals was communicating that Nick was very foreign and must go somewhere.

The evaluating seal was replying that Nick had recovered and a trip would be acceptable.

Nick guessed that this non-verbal communication was the form of speech his mind was inventing for creatures of his imagination. They didn't talk as men do, with vocal cords vibrating airwaves, but telepathically; minds could understand concepts conveyed by others.

The strange communication reminded Nick of his college Latin classes: clear and direct, despite being somewhat general and using fewer specific words than English chooses to employ. Was this an embodiment of the confusion he'd felt during that class? Latin nightmares?

The ends of his hammock were released by the harder dressed seals, but he was still trapped within the wrapping. He was pulled through the yawning portal to the world beyond his cell. If the scenery didn't make it odd enough, the sensation of being moved through a foreign place while being horizontal and unable to move compounded the oddness of the experience.

Only pulled wasn't the right word. He felt a ripple of energy floating him just as a surfboard is pushed along. One of the soldiers held a device that appeared to be directing forces that were holding his cocoon aloft, and moving it.

As he moved through the corridors, he passed a speckled black, long, red-eyed slithering eel, being escorted by a seal into the room he'd just left. A long gash was down its side. The eel's eyes regarded Nick with equal curiosity in the second they met, and Nick was left frightened almost into a catatonic state. He wanted to escape so badly.

Then the squadron passed through another opening and they were outside.

Although he was being hustled along, his flying carpet ride was smooth and he opened his eyes to the world around him.

First, there was the cold and wet entering his lungs and lapping at his face. It wasn't raining, yet, but it smelled humid, like the moment before the rain begins. Not the warm desert rain either, but the rain that is just several degrees from turning to snow.

The smell of the sea was stronger outside; fading memories of laying on the rocks returned to him with the sea smell.

His eyes were slow to capture the visual scenery because, as he passed through the opening leaving the structure's brightly glowing ceiling, the sky outside was dark, requiring his eyes to adjust.

It was grey, to say the least. The word gloom sprung into his mind. The sky was filled with clouds, and whatever sun might be above had much between it and this land. At the horizon the grey of the sky and earth met with no discernable hard transition. It might not be raining, but mist floated in the air. He was looking into a never-ending horizon. His heart jumped into his chest for a brief second, as "Is this hell?" passed through his mind.

The terrain was the same surface he'd lain on after the accident. He recognized the black, wet, stony surface he'd previously inhabited (if there'd been any doubt when the smell, cold and humidity had returned to his senses).

He realized they were walking between portions of the structure he'd spied in the distance during his semi-conscious post-accident period.

What a cruel joke his mind was playing, Nick thought.

What was consciousness? It was apparent that he still wasn't conscious in reality, he thought, so what would a period of semi-consciousness within a dream state be called? He realized that it all seemed pointless, but that somehow gave Nick reassurance. It was then that he began to not be as frightened; if this was a dream he didn't have to be scared of it.

Through a gap, Nick spied within the enclosure they were now next to. It seemed as though the wall was also made of organic growth, thick and dense, but grown resembling prison bars, with gaps between vertical supports so that what was inside could occasionally be seen. Through the brief gaps Nick glanced into the enclosure and he thought he saw the same eyes that the slithering eel in the corridor possessed, staring back at him.

But his glimpse into the enclosure was short, and he was soon back in another section of structure. And shortly thereafter he was in another cell. The seals attached the corners of his hammock, just as they'd been in the previous room, using a technique that resembled a form of organic growth welding. When a certain device was pointed at the wall it suddenly gushed growth from that place.

Then the seals began exiting the room. Except for two seals.

One took a position guarding the exit and the smaller approached Nick. Fear invaded Nick and he began to fight in his cocoon, but an idea formed in his mind that resembled "freedom" and he realized it was the seal communicating. Nick took a deep breath and ceased his pathetic thrashing.

Whatever bound the silk-like wrapper was released and Nick felt the entombing pressure on his body release. He didn't dare jump up though, not while the seals were still in the room. But they left after completing his unbinding.

Slowly and cautiously he swung his legs out of the hammock and placed them on the floor. He was weak and terribly sore. But he was capable of standing. He stood and examined this room. The walls and lighting were the same as the previous, the only difference being that this room had a clear shelf upon one wall and a small floor hole in the opposite corner. Nick was again reminded of his Independence Day adventure, and realized that he was incarcerated, in a room with a bench and toilet.

He ambled to the shelf and sat down. And he waited. And waited. And waited.

Suddenly a small gap opened at the bottom of the wall holding the entrance, and he saw a bowl of water and a second bowl, with a mysterious material, pushed into the room by flipper.

The water was delicious and he drank it gratefully. It bore the faintest hint of salt, but it was clear.

The food, for Nick knew that was what it was meant to be, tasted heavily of fish and seaweed, but a sudden realization of a deep hunger overcame any quarrels his taste buds might have raised.

And then Nick resumed waiting. He wondered if he would wake up, or if this "dream" might continue.

The phone call, for Mark, came at his work. He was finishing his fourth day of swing shift at the steel mill, when late in the evening a control room worker yelled out onto the foundry floor, "Mark, you have a call!"

"I'll be up in a minute," he yelled.

Few calls ever came for Mark. They were never good. Hospital trips, deaths of family members, etc.; those were the reasons Mark received calls at work. No one called a steel mill at 1 a.m. to chat.

He sighed as he made his way to the upstairs enclosed office. Mark didn't like going up there for any reason, much less a phone call. The office was the place of judgement, gossip, and malcontent. Leave me to my steel, thought Mark.

He climbed the stairs and picked up the crusty old brown land line phone laying on the front desk for foundry floor employee use.

"Mark here."

"Uh huh. Yes. I understand... Where?... Ok... I'm several hours away... Thank you."

Now he had to ask for time off. He shuffled towards the shift manager's office. If Mark didn't like going upstairs, he really disliked the dreaded Black Door of Death, after all, that's what they called it on the floor.

Soon he was on the road. Heading for a city of poor regard, deep in the desert, and its aging hospital.

And he was tired. Tired after a long day of work, but also tired of these circumstances. A deep tiredness settled in his bones. Here he was responding to Nick's latest escapade.

Mark stopped into a dirty road-side mini-mart and bought a black coffee. He needed it.

Mark felt waves of sorrow and anger as he drove. Hadn't they just talked about this? But now his son was lying in a hospital. Mark wasn't sure if he hadn't gotten any of his points across, or if it was simply unheard.

Could he be angry with himself? He didn't think so but it was hard not to. Nick was old enough to be responsible for himself, but still a father hopes he can, and does, influence his decisions.

A DUI accident in the desert? Really?! The anger burned.

But then he thought of his son in the hospital and he was brought almost to tears.

It wasn't that long ago that Nick had been happy to hear Mark come in the door after work.

"Daddy!"

Do you ever forget that sound? Mark knew he certainly missed it most days, when the door thunked shut to only silence.

How do you go from "Daddy!", to wrecking Jeeps in the desert in such a short time?

Was it a short time? Mark was beginning to realize that people he'd always considered young no longer qualified. Had it been a long time but Mark just hadn't noticed?

Life was short.

And no one wanted to be driving to a desert hospital for their son's accident.

There it was, the pain, sadness and anger rolled into one emotion. The pity train had arrived. And Mark sighed, whispering, "Thanks a lot Barbara."

After all, if she hadn't passed, he'd at least have company now. And she was halfway responsible for Nick too.

A New Friend

If it was a dream, something was wrong.

Too much time had passed in terrible monotony. Nick had no idea what time it was within his sheltered glowing green confinement, but he was sure days, if not weeks, had passed.

After he was placed in this cell, coverings resembling clothing were passed in, made of a similar material to the hammock and its covering. They fit Nick surprisingly well and seemed to repel the moist atmosphere in entirety, remaining dry despite the dampness of the cell.

The only thing Nick had to judge the passage of time was the arrival of water and food. He regretted placing his used stone bowls back by the door, he might be able to count them if he hadn't done that. But he'd worried that if he didn't return them it would encourage visitors to come in, and he'd had enough interaction with the inhabitants of this dream. Now he was simply biding his time until he returned to consciousness, on Earth.

But his futile hopes were for naught.

The opening of the cell gaped wide, withdrawing the wall panels to the outside, resembling a strange four petal flower when contracted; it was obviously a door, but there was something far more organic about it then the doors Nick was used to.

This time there was a seal wearing a stern uniform, but also a crab accompanying him. The crab stood at about the same height as the seal, but his eyes set taller upon his countenance giving the illusion that he was taller. His pincers were folded across what might be considered his chest, in much the same way soldiers hang their weapons across their chest, at rest but quickly accessible. The pinchers were also decorated in a manner that reminded Nick of tattoos. The crab's front legs seemed to act as arms.

Nick was laying in his hammock, but the strong thought occurred to him that his visitors desired him to sit and face them from the bench.

There was no doubt this was to be an interrogation. He slid his feet from the side of the hammock opposite his visitors and walked along the far wall to the bench.

The seal slid forward. The crab moved to guard the exit.

Nick's mind heard the seal ask something to the effect of "Do you know our way?"

Nick's words broke into a torrent, "No. I don't know why I'm here. I don't know where here is. I was driving and then I wasn't. You brought me in from the cold wet hard stone. Where is this? Who are you? Is this a dream?"

The seal's black eyes stared quizzically at him, the muscle that shielded his eyes from fighting prey slid slightly forward, and then back again into his head.

Nick realized that although the seal heard him, there was no recognition of his words. Or perhaps it was his manner of speaking. Was it possible that Nick could engage in thought sharing? Nick thought of how he'd heard the seals before. Dwelling on that area of his thought, he tried to imagine the word, the feeling, "No".

And he was successful. The seal slid noticeably back and turned his head to look at the crab.

Nick heard (always in his head) the crab intone, "Done".

The seal seemed to argue, "More".

The crab replied roughly, "Why? Pointless."

Nick was stunned. He realized he could, in some way, understand the communication of these beasts. Secondly, he was surprised his captors were not of one mind, being all of the same imagined dream.

The seal seemed to pause, and then intone, "Ok, done".

The seal didn't move but the crab sped to Nick. The front legs skillfully grabbed and wrapped Nick's arms before he had time to take in what was happening. One pincher had come off the chest and was now in striking position, obviously to discourage Nick from arguing his situation.

And then the crab was pulling Nick out of the cell, back along the corridor he came in through. The crab moved with a skilled and practiced technique, always keeping Nick within pincher range regardless of the corner, door or other obstacle they might traverse past.

They went outside, to the place where Nick had seen the eel eyes, and he realized he was being taken to the enclosure. As they approached, Nick saw camouflaged crabs at intervals along the wall. The camouflage was a natural black, matching the hard, cold rocks he now stumbled across.

They came to a place that Nick now recognized as an opening. The crab's free front leg rapped the opening, and Nick realized the word "Now."

The opening sprung wide and another black clad crab reached its pincher through, grabbing Nick by his binds and in one deft motion pulling him through the portal and into the enclosure while cutting the ties that bound him.

As the entrance retracted into the wall, a crab stepped between Nick and the opening, and folded his pinchers back into the at-rest position. Nick was sure the crab was watching him, but it reminded him of the time he walked in front of the Beefeaters while on vacation in England. This crab was on guard, and Nick would get no interaction from the crab.

And then Nick heard a wet, soft, slide behind him. He turned to see red, deep, dark eyes returning his gaze. He was among the eels in the enclosure.

The enclosure walls stretched far to the left and right, extending and circling out from behind him. In front of him Nick saw that, although large, the enclosure was something of a pen. Towers holding caves, made from the rock he was standing on, extended awkwardly from the ground, struggling to remain standing. In the distance he could make out that the land fell off into water, although the pen continued into the water, providing barriers to both land and water exit.

And directly in front of him were a bed of eels, slithering, intertwining, gaping their mouths, exposing jagged teeth, and glowering. Their eyes were squinting as they curiously took in Nick.

Nick thought they might be considering eating him.

The largest, and possibly ugliest, peeled from the fray and sped to Nick. Nick turned to run but was confronted by crab and wall.

The eel was behind him. He could feel its breath on his damp hair and exposed neck. He could smell the fishy diet of the beast. Nick dropped to his knees and turned his head to meet his fate.

It was within striking distance, mouth gaping, but nothing happened. His eyes met it and he heard, "What?"

Realizing it meant, "what are you?", Nick replied "Man" but he also tried to force it into that word into the form of thought communication these creatures used.

Fast as a cobra, the eel spun and told the horde that the new arrival was "confused (or "stupid", it was unclear to Nick)."

When the eel spun, his tail came around and struck Nick, knocking him flat on his back. The slam on the black cold rocks took the air out of him and he couldn't breathe for several moments. He wasn't sure if the action had been willful or accidental, but pain surged through his body. He bled a little from his cheek, where the rock had given him road rash.

The eel glanced back and took in the sprawled figure and returned his gaze to the others, "and weak" Nick heard.

The eel slithered away. It was as though Nick had been quickly dismissed as entirely worthless to all the eels.

Well, at least they didn't want to eat him.

Nick eventually rose to take in his surroundings. He was still imprisoned, but now with others, and not in a cell. Shelter would

be required if this world had rain, night, or even just to regain some repose from the wet, cold, inhospitable weather.

He noted most of the caves were near the water. The eels slithered in and out of the caves and water, as though no rest was to be found in their confinement within the enclosure. Some of the caves were even partially in the water, and Nick was unsure if there were others below the waterline.

Near the wall farthest from the water, the one he'd entered through, there was an old shelter, different and dilapidated. Perhaps Nick wasn't the first non-aquatic being to be imprisoned here. It was auspiciously far from the eel's shelters also, and Nick couldn't see it ever belonging to the teeming mass that had just confronted him; this little abode was different, and thuggish groups don't appreciate things that don't conform.

This all was temporary anyways, only lasting until he woke up, he reminded himself.

Entering the structure he'd seen, Nick found bones. Unsure if they were the meal of the last inhabitant, or the last inhabitant, Nick cleared the bones to the outside. Inside was only black rock but it seemed dry. And there seemed much value in having a little privacy.

A crab scuttled across the hard deck to his shelter and delivered the hammock and sheet from the last cell.

Later, the thought "food" came loudly to him, and looking out his doorway he realized that it must have been a call because the eels were fighting, sliding, flipping, hopping and writhing to reach a wall of the enclosure.

Unfortunately, this also meant they were coming straight towards him, for his habitation was near this wall.

Unwilling to join the fray, from the safety of his hole Nick watched them fight for substances flung over the wall. Eventually the fray settled, and the worst offenders moved back towards the waterfront. Eventually all the frenetic eels left.

Nick realized there were still bits of substance laying among the rock, the eels had not eaten it all. He was contemplating exploring the gleanings when he realized motion. Smaller subdued eels were slowly edging up from their dormitories. Accompanying these were little eels, and Nick realized these must be the females and children, smaller in number and stature.

One of them passed near his hole and he heard, "Eat" in a tone that seemed to have the slightest sense of civility. The female eel paused and looked in at him.

It somehow seemed confirming, as though saying, amongst this group you are "ok."

Nick ventured out of his hole and the eel began slithering towards the scraps of food. Nick struggled to keep beside her, not being sure the others would be as willing to share.

As they approached the other eels a few heads swung in surprise at the new attendee but hunger trumped curiosity, and his notice was short lived.

The scraps appeared to be meat, but Nick couldn't see himself eating them. He watched as the eels and their children cleaned up the last of the scraps. They seemed very hungry.

The crab guard nearest Nick appeared to be watching him, Nick thought.

Nick also noticed the side of the eel that had invited him to the feast was moving in an odd way. She looked back at him, and catching him looking at her side he sensed her communicating, "babies."

She began to move back towards Nick's hole and he accompanied her. Approaching his home, Nick noticed that his hole sat near the back corner of the enclosure, and a guard stood on each wall looking down on him. There was also a crab positioned in the corner, where the back wall and side wall met. It was as though the previous inhabitant had built at this location strategically, providing themselves the security of crab oversight.

His friend communicated "safe", although his concept of this communication seemed to be improving because he imagined, "This is safe", not just the concept of safe.

She slithered off to return to the eels, and Nick found his way into his hammock.

Shortly, another crab appeared at his entrance, and (although he couldn't be sure) Nick believed it might be the crab that had watched him at the feeding. In its front claws it carried the same bowl of water and food that he had received in his cell with the bench.

He sensed the crab communicating, "Your food is different", before it scampered off.

The days again began to pass, much as they had in the cell. The days on this land seemed longer, and the sun seemed obscured, as though the atmosphere was less opaque than Earth's.

Although Nick couldn't be sure, because the sky was always cloudy. At times Nick could see lightning in the clouds, but it wasn't as on Earth; this lightning moved as waves approaching a shoreline, flowing and undulating across the clouds in a hypnotic way, turning the clouds brilliant reds and purples as their wave crests passed through the dips and furrows of the grey ceiling.

The same eel and crab began to visit Nick with reliability. And as they did so Nick's ability to communicate continued to grow. Nick wasn't sure how this non-verbal communication worked, but he had a feeling it had something to do with the greater energy in this atmosphere (as evidenced by the cloud lightning waves) and perhaps, as vocal chords rattle the air, the focused thoughts from that part of the mind might shake the energy in a way that transfers across spaces.

Not all thoughts transferred, only those that were pointed and focused; it took extra effort to communicate and thankfully not all thoughts were put forth. HIs eel friend seemed unaware at his occasional repulsion to the writhing bulbous slimy eel skin covering her brood of snake-like shapes within her midsection.

Nick often travelled his end of the compound with his eel friend, during daylight. Her flexing side was growing, and perhaps it was the maternal instincts that extended favor to this strange human being. She communicated little but Nick gathered that she was not a favored member of the eel society. The males seemed to group and move together in a way that reminded Nick of plotting bullies, or Catholic priests; he thought it strange that those two could be alike in consideration. The male eels conveyed disdain for Nick and his female companion, without ever speaking to them.

Occasionally one male eel would break from his mates and quickly overtake Nick's companion and entangle with her, as she fought them off. When he'd leave Nick would hear her communicate the concept of "unwanted" and "anger". He was shocked when it dawned on him that the attacks might be the cause of her pregnancy.

When Nick would ask "Why?" she would respond, "I am nothing".

His companion spoke little but it was clear she accepted his company, and perhaps even enjoyed it a little.

The crab visitor was also open to talking about the enclosure.

At first their interactions were simple, and the crab responded to Nick's enquiry of "Why am I here?" by stating that the enclosure was for "Invaders".

It wasn't that the creatures spoke simply, it was just that Nick struggled to grasp the fullness of the concepts. Eventually, as Nick's skills grew with this method of communication, he learned more.

"I'm not a criminal, why am I here?" said Nick.

"You are held until we know your goals; you are not a prisoner".

On a later date Nick asked, "How do the eels get here?"

"They are prisoners of war. They came from the deep and they invade our border settlements".

Nick asked, "Even the women and children are prisoners?"

"The children are with their parents, and when they mature they are released to the deep. They are not criminals."

Their meal time discussions continued from day-to-day.

Once Nick asked, "Why are you here?"

"My family was killed by invading eels. The seals cannot be trusted to protect us. They don't understand why we value our remote homes. They also struggle with morality. It is my intention to protect others from the eels".

"The seals don't understand?"

"They lack empathy and understanding. They are curious, regardless of consequences. They care little for others, and if the eel invasion hadn't begun reducing some of their shoreline food supply, they would never have joined others in fighting the eel invasion."

"At first they watched, with little regard to our pain and suffering. They didn't understand that the invasion might affect them, until it did. The seals are unable to look ahead because they will not accept that there are consequences for bad decisions. They only know if something is hurting them or not. Any form of judgement is looked down on."

"Selfish?"

"Greatly. Their teachers only seek and teach personal happiness."

"Crabs are different?"

"We are simple, happy to live on one shore all of life. We care for the shoreline because we are not content to move on if it is destroyed, and we are likely to be destroyed with it. The seals call us small brained, assuming their ways are better".

"Why do the eels invade?"

"There had always been shore eels, but these are different. They believe in a God, the Shark of the Deep, and that all the seas should resemble the Shark of the Deep's home, to make all waters welcoming to him."

"What is the Shark of the Deep?"

"They claim that he is an ancient shark, the father of all sharks, and who lives in the great depths still. He will come out when the shallows are ready."

"It is a God of forceful control. All sharks are his princes and are served by the eels. The eels are lowly, but adopt the faith and work for the sharks in hopes that after death they will be re-born to this world as a shark."

The crab continued, "The eels attack our homes and move in. They build structures to direct strong cold ocean currents to shore; this allows the sharks of the deep to venture higher and closer to the shore. If structures can't be used, the eels will infect the water so that bacteria grows, blocking out the sun's warmth."

"The seals don't care about this?" Nick asked.

"The eels lie to the seals about their motives, but the seals can't see it."

"So now you guard the enclosure for captured eels?"

"Exactly" said the crab.

"This place was built by the seals for eel prisoners; the seals wanted a comfortable place for the eel criminals to live in; an attempt to show friendship to the invaders.

This place is near the end of our country, and is almost as cool as the deeps. We black crabs inhabited this area since creation, and we became ideal guards due to our ability to withstand the cold and our experiences with the eels."

The crab continued, "Your arrival was a great surprise and is suspicious. Only invaders and crabs find their way here. That is why you are in the enclosure. The crabs don't trust that you are not from the deep, and our captain negotiated with the seals to have you watched within the enclosure".

"I'm not from the deep sea!" Nick said in his best attempt at mind shouting.

"So you say", said the crab, "but the Great Shark honors misleading enemies. We are still evaluating who you are," the crab said.

Yelling, voices and noises from the water side of the enclosure reached them and the guard headed for them.

In his next meeting with the pregnant eel, Nick asked, "Invaders?"

She replied, "The Great Shark is supreme. We do his will."

"You?" asked Nick.

"I am a settler, my mate helped conquer the crabs; he died in the fight," replied the eel.

They had ambled down near the water and it was later than usual. The sky was beginning to turn black and the dark shadow of the enclosure wall was pronounced with the sun low in the sky.

"Hurry," she said to Nick.

Suddenly, from out of one the largest caves, a teeming cord of eels slithered and reeled out, headed straight for Nick and his companion. The atmosphere was loud with their shouts; it sounded of terror and frenzied excitement in a primeval way.

They both did their best to escape but the brood was on them momentarily. First Nick went down. He was pinned under a large slimy beast.

Soon after Nick's friend was caught, wrapped and entwined by several eels. Another started pulling her towards the cave. Nick too was grabbed by a gaping eel mouth and dragged into the cavernous black hole of the main hangout of the male eels.

Inside ferocious sharks were painted across the ceiling of the cave, and it was lit by the same iridescent material that had lit Nick's first cell.

Nick was nipped, bumped, rustled and thrown into a recess at the edge of the cave. His female companion was dragged into the middle of the room.

An unearthly humming filled the cavern, a rhythmic hissing sound reminiscent of rattlesnakes warning their enemies. The largest eel began adding periodic throaty "blarps" while he swayed to the humming and hissing of the eels. And then he moved in on his prey.

She was held on her side, the protrusion of her wriggling embryos exposed upwards.

The crowd parted to make way for the large eel to approach his victim. As he slid up to her Nick wondered what he would do. He lifted his head slowly; his sharp teeth seemed to be smiling. Then he slammed his snout down brutally. He bit into her embryos and began eating the slithering slimy baby eels within, tearing through Nick's friend's flesh.

Nick screamed at the horrific scene, which surprised the eels and they spun on him. The creepy hissing chant lost its time in the commotion.

Nick rushed towards his friend but his courage was short-lived. Like a striking cobra, an eel popped him with its nose as he passed, knocking him to the ground. Another slapped him with his tail, and still others tried to drive him into the cement-like rock with their tails, like steel hammers upon a brass nail. Not only was his courage gone, so was conscious thought.

It was surprisingly warm when Nick came to. Wet though, and with a strange smell. Nick's eyes opened to discover he was laying against the body of his friend, the maternal eel. Her breathing was labored, and she too was unconscious, with a gaping oozing hole in the side of her body. They had been deposited mid-way between Nick's opening and the caves of the eels.

Nick rose, and struggled to the crab on duty at the wall.

"MURDER" he intoned.

The crab's eyes didn't even appear to take Nick in, and it responded, "The seals say, 'It is not murder; the babies are not yet alive if they are unborn.'"

Nick could only think, "How is that right?!"

The crab responded, "It is a seal law, not mine."

"She is almost dead," said Nick.

"She is not dead. And what you saw is the official eel procedure for procreating without a mate".

And then the crab looked at him, "Do your's not do this?"

Nick suddenly realized this might be one of those times that he was being tested, to see if he was of the deep dark world. He said, "No, that is horrible!"

But in his heart he wasn't sure he was telling the truth. The abortion ceremony of man was hidden behind closed doors, witnessed by few, but how did the number of witnesses or lack-of-ceremony change what happened during the procedure? A writhing baby was still killed.

He felt the crab's steady gaze upon him, studying him. He realized that there would be no help from the sentries.

He moved away, back to the convalescing mother. He tried to pull her to his hole, but she was too heavy.

Nick retrieved his hammock cover, and placed it over her body. He then laid against her and tried to share warmth with this creature of the deep.

Nick woke to a crab prodding him with its front legs.

"Come with us," it said.

As he rose, he looked to his companion. She was no longer breathing.

The crab said, "This is now murder. We will find the eels that did it."

Nick said, "I know who! It was the largest eel."

But the crab replied, "Two witnesses are needed. And he is the leader of the eel's Great Shark worship."

Nick began to realize what the crab was insinuating. But then it got worse.

"They have blamed you. Their witnesses are numerous."

As before, Nick was led away by a crab holding his bound hands with one front leg, while one pincher was extended and posed ready to sever Nick's neck swiftly.

He was led to the gate. Would his escape from the compound be as a condemned murderer? Was there a worse place to go to if he was found guilty? What could be worse than the eel enclosure at the end of this world?

And on top of these thoughts, Nick's heart hurt for his dead friend. Why hadn't the crabs aided her medically? And now there'd be no justice?

The crab led him through the wall, to the courtyard between the enclosure and the buildings, and then pushed him to another squadron of crabs awaiting his arrival.

Freedom

Nick's first indication that something was different was that no crab had a pincher drawn to potentially strike him. There was no imminent threat of pincher snapping his neck if he chose to run or fight.

The crabs scuttled along at a quick pace and Nick struggled to keep up.

They entered back into the structure where Nick's first cell was located. Nick was bathed in the green iridescent light and his eyes adjusted to the corridor in time to see his previous dormitory's entryway as they rushed past.

The hallway opened into a larger, high vaulted corridor. Nick now understood that his old cell, the hallway that crossed past it, and the door to the enclosure were at the rear of the building, not designed to be seen by the majority of those that entered into this main part of the structure. He'd been stowed in a back room.

Nick saw crabs, seals, lobsters, sea horses, and a diverse variety of rarer shallow water sea creatures roaming the halls in an array of creatures and clothing. En masse, the seals seemed to be wearing matching uniforms.

They entered a corridor that passed along the public front of the building; large arched openings revealed the barren bleak black rock and grey ocean that encroached upon it outside. The material that should be glass seemed to shimmer, and Nick imagined it was a form of energy barrier.

Nick's considerations of his surroundings were short lived; he was ushered into a room with a number of uniformed seals and crabs present.

He was dragged to a corner where a stool stood, made of green material that smelled of seaweed.

"Sit."

Nick dropped into the seat. The organic material gave a little and was not entirely uncomfortable.

The room was loud with thought and Nick had difficulty understanding and pulling apart jumbled conversation.

Suddenly one seal barked loudly twice.

"Rarf! Rarf!"

The din of the room slowly dimmed, and then fell largely silent as Nick's captors stared at him, seals and crabs alike.

A large, obese, old seal, with grey splotches on his muzzle and grey whiskers protruding struggled to shuffle in front of Nick.

"You witnessed last night's Eel ceremony?"

"Yes," Nick conveyed.

"You objected and ran to protect her?" asked the seal.

"How do you know?" Nick asked.

"There are eels that provide truth for favor," the seal replied.

"Why did you not help?" Nick asked.

"It is their way, they have practiced it for ages. Who are the seals to dictate wrong?" said the seal.

Nick heard several crabs around the room yell out thoughts that were along the lines of "trash", "academic refuse" and "fool seal."

The seal began to growl, he swung his muzzle toward them and his countenance showed utter contempt. "Silence!" he transmitted, in a way reminiscent of the eel's snake-like hissing.

His focus returned to Nick.

"We are watching you. You are not of the deep?"

"No," replied Nick, "I am of Earth; which I've decided is another world entirely".

That started another round of turbid discourse around the room.

"Silence," hissed the old seal again.

"You are not a water creature; you only use the water to bathe, and you did not submerge to do so."

Nick replied, "It is too cold to get in."

"You cannot swim?" asked the seal.

"Not as you can," said Nick.

"Thank you... wait here... silently," said the seal as he backed away.

Several of the crabs broke away from the crowd, including the one that had led the party to the room. Also, a number of seals from the far side of the gallery also moved out from their brethren and towards the wall farthest from Nick. The crabs, the old seal, and his seal compatriots gathered together in what appeared to be council. Little could be heard, and the whole room seemed to go silent, hoping for a preview of what was to come.

Eventually the council broke, the crabs steaming away irritably. The old seal returned to his position in front of Nick.

"It is decided. The enclosure is not right for you. Our world is mostly water, and mostly aquatic creatures, but one group of creatures live on a warm spit of land called Enbala. They follow a god, The Creator. Their society has adapted, and it is mainly land based. Like you, they swim little and smell poorly. We want to send you there; to determine who you are, and how you can add value to our world."

He continued, "The crabs believe you must be of the deep. They have encouraged the council to leave you in the enclosure, but the seals outnumber them in council. We are curious of you, and will continue to observe you to see who you prove to be."

"Prove to be?" a confused Nick responded.

"Who are you? Maybe you are too simple to understand me. Seals are complex beings."

Nick realized that wasn't the impression he'd gathered. Stuffy and prideful, maybe. Not complex.

"There is a transport bringing supplies today. You will leave on it, and they will provide your passage to Enbala. We have arranged a place for you to stay there."

With that, the crabs and seals on either side of the room again erupted.

The crabs seemed frustrated and Nick picked up on considerations like, "Why must harm occur before seals recognize invaders are bad?"

The murmuring seals seemed more curious and several times Nick picked up on the concept of "another world" in their discussions.

The old seal withdrew from Nick, and the room. He did not excuse himself, for he had no need or consideration to ask excuse.

Nick was unsure what to do. For the first time he felt some sense of freedom in this alien world, and he had no idea how to use it. A world was before him and he was only comfortable with the chair he sat in.

The crab that brought his food, and on occasion conversed with him, approached.

"Come with me," he said.

There was no rope, no claw ready to snap. Nick went willingly just the same.

As Nick passed out the front of the building structure it struck him that he was free. True, he still had an escort, but without one he would be entirely lost.

As the damp air enveloped them Nick realized there was little outside the front doors.

The landscaping of the building extended several hundred yards to the sea. The finishing on the black rock made it smooth, giving an appearance similar to concrete, but entirely natural and harmonious to its surroundings.

The sea beyond was grey, and it slowly frothed up onto the finished rock. The waves were small but faster in frequency than what Nick was used to. This caused a frothing stripe at the water's edge that undulated up and down. Farther out, the color of the water turned to black, fading to grey as it disappeared into a grey horizon.

To the right of the courtyard there was a canal that extended inward from the sea to the side of the building. This, Nick was sure, was where the supplies must arrive. Structures that resembled docks were hewn out of the black rock at the edge of the canal.

The crab communicated to Nick that he was glad to see him go.

Unsure exactly what that meant, Nick only replied, "Thank you for your kindness."

The crab swung his eyes towards Nick oddly and replied, "Kindness?"

There was a silence.

The crab then said, "It was required I provide sustenance for you."

Nick asked, "Do you believe I'm from the deep?"

The crab replied, "I'm not sure. But unlike seals, I don't want to risk another family's safety for a strange invader's freedom. The seals don't respect that our homes and families are being destroyed by the ideas out of the deep. I would have left you in the enclosure."

Nick was quiet after that. On one hand, he was able to understand these creatures better now, but it seemed he was friendless.

It had initially appeared as only a slight dot on the horizon, but soon it was clear a vessel was approaching. As its stature grew, Nick came to the conclusion that it was much too large for the canal beside them. Expecting it to moor at sea, and a smaller craft approach the shore, Nick was terrified to see the large vessel continue bearing down on them as it approached the shore and canal. Nick turned to run from the collision of the boat with the rocks, but the crab grabbed his clothing and picked him up. Nick's stomach rushed into his throat as he watched the monstrous vessel fill the sky above him.

Instead of metal sheeting, the vessel's skin was the maze of a circuit board. As it loomed nearer the side came into view and Nick realized the entire vessel was covered in the same circuit-like material, with shimmering energy view holes for windows. A pulsating glow came from the rear of the ship. It was apparent this ship was at a higher level of technology than those found on Earth.

When it reached the canal, Nick realized why it was able to approach the narrow slip at great speed; much like his cot had surfed along when he was transported in it, the ship was levitating above the waters. The water directly under it bowed and took on a suppressed look, implying there was great force on it. Dark grey steam trails rose up at the edges between the pressured water and the free water of the sea, giving the impression the ship was held aloft by ghostlike spirits, Nick thought.

When it stopped at dock, Nick was surprised that a causeway extended and dropped from the front of the ship into the water. Seals, crabs, water-spider like creatures, and other denizens of the ocean rushed down the ramp and into the water before exiting a ramp at the far end of the canal that allowed them to come up onto the black rock. The travelers looked delighted when they reached the water; it must have been relief from extended dryness on board, and it reminded Nick of the airport public

restrooms after a long flight. Perhaps the short dip into the water served that same purpose.

The above-water docks that Nick had earlier noticed were used mostly for unloading supplies and luggage.

Who were the passengers? Nick guessed a mixture of workers and management.. He couldn't believe anyone... or thing... would voluntarily visit the enclosure after what he'd experienced.

The crab and Nick rested in silence, taking it all in.

The crab spoke, "You go in through the dry route."

The crab walked towards the docks with some supplies for Nick. Nick walked to the docks silently, wondering what he'd find inside the ship. The crab deposited Nick's supplies in a pile where others were doing the same, and then he turned and left. He didn't so much as look at Nick as he returned to the black land at the far end of the dock.

"Well, goodbye 'friend'," thought Nick.

Left alone, Nick was unsure of what to do. He knew that he was meant to be on the ship, but how to go about it eluded him. Waves of questions flooded over him as he wondered where he'd go when he got on, how would he eat, would he be able to communicate, was there a toilet, and would he know where to get off? These questions, among others, weighed heavily on him, and he felt as though his feet were locked into the dock he stood on.

Unable to move, he stared at the ship. Octopi were unloading and loading the cargo bay in front of him. Their tentacles were mesmerizing to watch in action, but the foreignness of the visual only added to his feelings of alienation.

A scratchy, small "bark" next to him startled Nick.

The smallest seal he'd seen was standing next to him, pulling a levitating box. Nick heard, "Your food and clothes. Also, I will now accompany you."

"Who are you?!" Nick asked.

"Geran" said the seal, and continued, "I'm returning to my father's land after being stationed at the-end-of-the-world for a time. I was hoping to rest, but I have been tasked as your custodian until we reach Enbala."

The weight Nick had felt left his body, and relief washed over him.

"Thank you, Geran".

"Come along, Man", said Geran, and he lunged forward down the pier. Obviously, he'd somehow been briefed on Nick.

When they reached the Octopi, Nick was sure they'd pause their loading endeavors to let them pass but the octopi kept working, with tentacles reaching in front of and behind Nick as he pressed forward to an opening into the ship's hold. One tentacle even impatiently grabbed Nick and pulled him quickly forward to access a box behind him. The tentacles sucking wet grasp had felt like he'd been momentarily attacked by a vacuum cleaner.

They passed through the storage hold and found themselves in a seating area, with the windows he'd previously noticed providing light from the outside. Despite the light passing through some form of shimmering energy field, the room retained the moistness and dull green shade he was becoming used to. The notable exception, there seemed to be flourishes of color resembling ocean corals swishing along, and through the walls. Nick suspected that the color was energy pulsing through the walls.

Geran situated himself next to Nick and brought out some sustenance. They ate in silence as a variety of shallow water sea creatures boarded the ship. Several others were snacking as they awaited the ship's departure, and Nick was forced to take notice that intensely aromatic shellfish were a common food for these beings.

Nick was surprised several eels had boarded the vessel, but there was a different look in their eyes, compared to those in the enclosure; at a glance, Nick could tell they weren't of the same culture. These eels carried themselves with some humility, respect of those around them, and conformance.

Eventually almost all the seats were filled and Nick sensed a voice initiating a departure. The doors opened out to the far-flung prison world were closing and Nick realized he was very happy to leave.

Unexpectedly Geran said, "Must you wear your emotions so visibly? All the females looking out of the administration office were sad as you stood staring at the boat. They imagined you as a lost child. That was when I was drafted to be 'custodian', since I was already on the trip."

Nick couldn't help but laugh. It felt great to laugh. He couldn't remember the last time he laughed; his laugh erupted, a dam had broken. Tears came to the corners of his eyes he laughed so hard. What Geran had said wasn't that funny, but Nick allowed himself to go with the emotion.

"A lost child"... well that was exactly what he was, it seemed.

Geran seemed appalled that his request for stoicism seemed to have elicited the opposite reaction. His little muzzle seemed tense and almost jeering, the whites of his teeth just visible under his sneering upper lip and tight black gums. His protective eye coverings slid partly forward to complete the image of a sullen little seal getting ready to snap out.

Nick thought it best to cease conversation with Geran. Was everyone in this world so tightly strung?

The ship began to move. Unlike an Earthen ship, the first shudders of movement were upward, not outward. The boat seemed to hum with charge, and the translucence of the windows changed from golden to an almost imperceptible hue of blue.

Nick's curiosity regarding the windows overcame his will, and he reached out to touch the blue hue. It took him several minutes to muster the courage. Would he be shocked? Finally his finger touched the blue hue; it felt solid, just as glass.

Geran, who had been eyeballing him, said, "What did you think would happen?"

Nick responded, "I wondered if I'd be shocked."

Geran chuckled this time. "Window fields haven't shocked in 400 years, since the nascence of the technology."

The ship elevated several feet, and then the walls increased, pulsating the fluorescent waves of energy, increasing in frequency until the ship seemed to glow in the color rainbow. The light was almost too much for Nick's eyes, and he realized that the other passengers had simply closed their's. Geran's grey lids were closed, and he was likely attempting that rest he had planned before the ladies forced his custodianship.

When the ship began to pull away, the sensation was unlike any boat experience Nick could recall. The forces were more reminiscent of a sports car on a charged takeoff, than that of a passenger ship embarking into deep waters.

There wasn't any wave-like motion. Nick remembered the small and frequent waves, and realized that the hovering must eliminate all bobbing effects produced by them. What Nick picked-up on, although far from understanding it, was that the surface of the vessel drew energy in for the use of the propulsion and hovering system.

Out the window the view was negligible. Grey approached grey, and a gentle mist coated the window. If they had painted the window grey the effect would have been the same. The only information the window conveyed was a high rate of speed, because the mist droplets passed across the window horizontally, streaking quickly in their course.

Nick returned to spying on his sometimes-slumbering bunk mates. He recognized some of that had been present in his trial. Perhaps they were authorities, reporting from an unknown world. Would that be Enbala?

After long hours the grey outside the windows lightened. While still moist and cloudy, the grey had taken on a warmer tone, indicating a latitudinal difference from the location of the enclosure. They must be getting nearer to this world's equator.

Geran's eyes eventually fluttered back open. After giving the location of the toilets to Nick (who had a hard time perceiving the alien portal locations in the omni-green walls), Geran and Nick discussed Geran's world further.

"Is everyone going to Enbala?", asked Nick.

"No", said Gerard, "Only you. It is a pointless place. A relic of bygone days".

"What does that mean?"

"Thousands of years ago, the creatures that harvested wood for dens realized a religion centered on the creator of our world. Over time, a faction of them became permanently tied to the worship of this deity. Enbala is the center of worship for the Creator, and there this faction remained, largely abandoning non-religious activities. This religion was strongest about 500 years ago. Now a small fraction of land dwellers follow the old religion on Enbala, hoping the Shark's followers don't become too great a threat."

"Why has the religion lost its followers?" Nick wondered.

"The moral obligations to a creator were too great a burden, and eventually we threw off this obligation. The seals were the first to question the need for such beliefs, I'm proud to say".

"Ok. Well, what 'moral obligations' do you have now?"

"We, the seals, are at the forefront of searching that out. It's unclear at the moment, but these are exciting times. Ever we draw closer to the fullest truth. I feel honored to be alive in a time when morals are being re-established, or perhaps I should say, redefined. We are realizing our true importance."

Nick thought of the Crab and their conversations.

"The crabs seem to think the seals are selfish, not caring for the plights of shoreline creatures different than themselves. Does this new moral norm not include empathy for the crabs, your neighbors in this world?"

"Empathy… for our neighbors?! What a strange way of putting it! The seals focus on what brings inner health. What's good for me, is good for all. The externalities of a random world, and their consequences, are too burdensome to place upon my back".

Garen continued, "The crab's have, in large, stayed devoted to the old religion. A visit to Enbala is a high honor for their type. But their old-fashioned ways have left them unable to adjust to the eels joining our society. It's a great example of how the old Creator religion is archaic; it provides little room to accommodate the needs of the followers of the Great Shark."

Nick asked, "And the seals follow a great shark?"

"Of course. We follow everything if there's value. We follow some of the Creator's religion too. We accept and adapt to all externalities, embracing the random. After all, the only responsibility we have is adaptation of self. The Eel's religion is similar to the seal's beliefs in a number of ways. They too believe in adapting and changing the world, and because their deity, The Great Shark, is so intent on conquering, the followers are convinced that they might achieve greatness in a similar manner. Although they believe, as the Seals, that they are looking out for themselves. This inherent strength of the sharks lends credence to their ability to rule".

"Ok, but what about their morals?"

"That's an externality I don't have control of, so I refuse to bother with it. Their morals are their responsibility alone" replied Garen.

An eel seated nearby responded harshly, "The Shark religion has been leading my kind astray for far too long. They are harsh and brutal rulers; in their kingdom you would only be considered food. You are a fool to think you could co-exist."

Garen replied, "In this theoretical situation you suggest, I've failed to adapt and preserve my life. If overrun from the deep, most seals would embrace the religion of Shark to save ourselves. We must do what is best for us. Just as we have humored those who gathered at Enbala since ancient times".

The eel shook his snout angrily at Garen and hissed, "Only when seals die do they realize the error of their ways. There is no comparison between the peaceful followers at Enbala, and the feeding frenzy of a Shark 'religious' gathering."

"Absurd", replied the seal, "they are both a religion and should be treated equally".

The exasperated eel glared at Garen for a moment before whispering, "Hopeless, all of you". She turned her gaze away from them.

Nick asked Garen, "Where are you going?"

"My father is a leader of the seals, managing those who presided at your trial. You may recognize some of the seals from your trial around the boat, they too are returning to civilization. I'm returning to serve on my father's team. My trial of distant service is complete".

"So those in your world's leadership know of me?", asked Nick.

"Ha, know of you?! You are big news. An undiscovered race! Our world is brimming with rumors of your arrival. You may think Enbala is freedom, but it's an island where you can continue to be monitored. You are being watched. Especially after the eels accused you of murder. At the time of your acquittal the Shark followers invaded another reef area; their delegates say that it was in retribution for the seals finding you not guilty."

Nick fell quiet. This was a lot to take in. Unbeknownst to him, he had fame. Or infamy. He found himself thinking about this conversation for several hours. Eventually he drifted off, falling asleep as the boat sped towards Enbala and his future.

Nick felt weightless. Not the comforting weightlessness of pleasure, but the odd feeling that he was hurtling through space without any control.

Something was suddenly different. Something had changed. He opened his eyes, only to brace them shut again as he was hurtling toward the wall of the ship at great speed.

The collision was hard, and Nick lay dazed on the floor staring up at the wall that had just accosted him. Everything was in disarray. Fellow passengers were lying next to him, along with much of the baggage that was in the compartment.

Alarms were sounding, "Horrmmm, horrrmm, horrrrmmm".

Nick struggled to his feet among the debris he was scattered in. He fell back to his knees as the boat lurched forward. A bright ripple of energy pulsed through the vessel's walls, turning red and rebounding back, as it failed to propel the boat forward.

Nick heard explosions and the ship shook. He hurried to the window portal. He heard an announcement broadcast throughout the boat, "Protect yourself."

In the tinted, and now flickering, view out the window, Nick could see the water burbling as though things were passing quickly through it. Then he thought he saw the unmistakable momentary glimpse of an eel's eyes as they sped past in the bubbling water.

Nick ran towards the portal at the end of the room, jumping over the bodies of several seahorses and other passengers that were oozing their version of blood into large slippery puddles. The room convulsed with the repercussions of explosions, and the lurching pulses of energy passing through the ship.

As he approached the portal it blew open, lifting him off his feet and carrying him onto his back ten feet from where he'd left the deck, sliding in a sticky puddle of seahorse blood.

An eel flowed into the room, vicious and snapping. Nick saw several additional behind him.

The eel spied Nick's seal companion, Garen, first. Cowering next to the wall, Nick's custodian was doing his best to bare his teeth and growl but the effect was negated by his meager size.

The conscious passengers, those still capable of movement, quickly dragged themselves to the farthest corners of the room, away from the eel attack.

The eel was upon the Geran in a heartbeat, reminding Nick of the attack his eel friend had endured at the compound. The two eels that followed the first joined the scene and it became a flurry of seal fur and leathery eel skin.

Suddenly a high-pitched screech pierced the din and flowing sparks began flowing from the ceiling as saw-like blades pierced through, flailing dangerously into the room.

The eels instantly stopped their attack and regarded the blades wildly stabbing through the ceiling. Two of the eels retreated back through the portal, but the third eel snagged Garen with an atrocious bite to his flipper, and started dragging him towards the portal.

Nick was conflicted. His hatred for the eels was great, but Garen had been a smug little bastard and Nick was unsure if he should act. But a sudden memory of the Great Shark ceremony flashed through his mind and his hatred for the eels won over this short-lived internal struggle.

Nick ran forward and punched the eel squarely in an eye. For a second the eel was dumbfounded and he released Garen. The eel had not expected that Nick might be capable of inflicting pain.

At that moment a blade from above passed directly in front of them, spilling a shower of sparks between Nick, Garen, and the eel.

The eel turned and fled out the portal.

The roof in the passenger compartment was beginning to crumble, and Nick, Garen and the rest of the survivors were forced to follow the eels to avoid being smashed under the crumbling ceiling.

When Nick came out onto the deck he was again confronted with an image of great confusion.

A yellow glowing energy orb seemed to encapsulate the ship. The deck was strewn with blood and slime from the eels, walruses and octopi that were tussling across it. Contrary to the green of the compartment below, the ship's deck was dark black and circuit-like. The black contrasted with the glowing scars caused by the electric saws the octopi and walruses were brandishing; these were what Nick had seen cutting through the ceiling when they'd been downstairs.

The eels were also taking great notice of the saws, and seemed to be retreating into the water in response to them. As the last eel dove from the ship, an octopus cut the rear quarter of its body off.

The eel landed in the water with a thud, rather than a splash, and a putrid purple cloud surrounded it in the wavy tossing sea.

After a moment the yellow orb surrounding the ship cracked, in a loud snap, and released the ship.

There was an odd silence across the deck. Octopi and walruses stood at attention near the edge of the deck, staring into the water, awaiting any second wave of attack.

The passengers began to murmur. They talked of why, most finding it unbelievable that a ship of this status would be attacked by eels.

The murmurs grew to a loud din as it became apparent the eels were not returning.

An old walrus, with the bearing of a captain, ordered everyone to gather to him mid-ship. His crewmen kept their saws at ready.

"Attention! Attention!" he barked.

"Now the majority of you here are associated with our illustrious government, who banned us from carrying weapons, ending our ability to defend ourselves. This was in response to complaints from the eels, who claimed they felt threatened by our traversing their depths armed. I hope you all see the truth now. Those of us that make our living upon the sea know the danger presented by the eels. If we had not stored these construction saws, with the intent of using them as make-shift weapons, knowing the possibility of this very event, you all would likely be dead. Take that back to your seal leadership, and tell them to rescind the weapons ban."

There was some murmuring of dissent among a few of the seal survivors, but the Walrus was quick to address them, "Speak up seals, do you have something to say?"

Nothing was said.

"That's right," said the Captain, "Even when confronted with truth a seal will refuse to see it. Your hardened hearts will be the death of us all. You'll likely go back and ask that these saws be banned, as that reeks of your mode of operation; a complete lack of common sense".

"Now we must press on. We have four hours of travel to Enbala, and another six after that to the mainland. Everyone will take a position along the ship's deck and stand watch for any future efforts from the eels."

Nick looked over at Garen, who was laying with his snout upon the deck, blood oozing from jagged holes in his tail. "Captain", Nick spoke up, "My companion Garen requires assistance".

The captain snorted in contempt.

"Your companion?! You mean your jailer! You'd help his kind after all they've been putting you through?"

Nick briefly registered that even the Captain knew his plight, though he responded, "Yes, he's done nothing that would make me want him dead".

The captain looked surprised and motioned to a nearby octopus who squabbled forward and began addressing Garen's wounds.

The captain had stationed the survivors around the deck of the ship, and members of his crew disappeared below deck to repair damage to the propulsion system. After some time the visible flow of energy began to pulse through the deck below their feet again, although not with the same seamless smoothness as before. At the open scars the energy would crackle, pop and arc with a smell of burnt ozone wafting about the deck.

It was determined that two seahorses and a seal had lost their lives when the ship initially crashed headlong into the forcefield erected by the eels to start their attack.

The crew's quick thinking had prevented any further loss of life. They'd immediately went to the saws as they knew an eel attack was under way. The bubbling water Nick had seen next to the ship was an ancient eel technique of eliciting fear in their prey before the attack, but in this case it had worked against them as it had given the crew time to access their improvised weapons.

Garen was given food, his wounds dressed, and soon he was alert again, and ordered to stand watch near Nick.

The ship continued on towards Enbala, at a greatly reduced pace.

Enbala

Nick and Garen were within speaking distance, at their retrospective perches, but Nick found that he had little to say, and Garen made no attempt to communicate either.

Within an hour the outline of an awesome peak pierced the horizon. The sun was beginning to set, and this massive jagged mountain first appeared as a fang tooth extending from the purple gums of the sunset.

As they neared the island the sharp peak rose to awe inspiring heights above the boat, requiring Nick to tilt his head back to look up at it.

With nearness, Enbala's features begin to reveal themselves through the purple, but with the falling darkness everything remained cloaked in light grey shadow. Still, in the twilight Nick could tell there were three main areas on the island. At the lowest levels the island was surrounded by rolling hills, obviously agricultural, with structures dotted throughout. Higher up, the lower levels of the mountain were dark with trees, taller and narrower than any Nick had seen before, with thick trunks and fewer leaves and branches than their Earthly relatives. Towering far above the tree line was the snow laden peak, framed in the now purple-grey twilight of a fading sun. This was the most striking aspect of all, the severely sheer nature of the mountain; it was higher and steeper than any mountain Nick had seen before.

Beautiful music drifted out to the boat.

The captain yelled, "There she is, we've made it to Enbala! Hear the beautiful sound of evening worship!"

59

The heights of tone, length of notes, and crystal-clear nature of the music seemed to pair with the island's grandeur perfectly and in the warm air Nick realized that for the first time since he woke up in this strange land he felt comfortable and at peace. Nick believed they were now safe from eel attack, he was warm, and the sight before him was beautiful.

The warm fresh sea air, the bright receding colors of the evening, and the soothing sounds of the island's worshipers settled on Nick like a favorite childhood blanket, and as they approached the island he began to feel very tired.

At one-point Nick's head drooped, and as his chin hit his chest it woke him. The captain, noticing Nick's head snap back upright, laughed, "The peace of the Island is on you man. It will fade, but it lays heavy on all at first."

Garen snorted.

They sailed into a river, perhaps even creek, much smaller than any waterway an earthen ship could sail, but the unique propulsion and flotation system of this ship allowed it to flow inland on this small ribbon of water.

The low-level hill lands were the most similar to Earth Nick had yet seen. Hills of green grass rolled away from sandy beaches lining the water way.

But the structures they passed by were impossibly tall, obviously built from the trees growing on the higher slopes. These structures loomed over the water, and with the sun just peeking out from the horizon, the shadows they cast engulfed the ship as the structures' spires pierced the atmosphere above them, the small light of stars beginning to float outward from their peaks.

It was dark when they reached their port. Torch-like lights floated ethereally in the air, likely using the same energy the ship harnessed to cast their glows. This glow revealed that the boat was small among a village of towering structures; the lights only revealing the very bottom of the tree trunks used to build the structures which disappeared into the now black sky. Only a few stars could be seen in the sky above, most being blocked by the tall structures.

Garen turned to Nick, "This is your port, Man".

Nick, taking it all in, was barely breathing as he stared at the island.

A figure was striding towards the ship, with small forceful steps. He was dressed in a costume Nick knew to be the dress of a religious man, otherworldly or not.

Garen stated, "I believe your escort approaches. Be careful what you say Man, you are now among the free, but your words may change that."

"What do you mean?", asked Nick.

"While you think you know what happened, when we were attacked, it is far more complex than you fathom."

"The eel attack?", Nick responded in surprise.

Garen snarled, "You do not know that it was an eel attack! They were eels, but they may have been pirates, or eels otherwise engaged in their own motives. My father is in negotiations with the followers of The Great Shark, and that attack could have serious political ramifications. You have captured the interest of the world, be careful what unfounded words you say if you are approached by any asking questions."

The Captain yelled, "Man, come over here," from an extended walkway near the side of the boat where the figure from shore was coming aboard.

Nick left his post, glancing to Garen, wondering if he should offer some form of "goodbye". Garen was staring out into the blackness, obviously intent on dismissing the man without formality. Reminded of how the Crab left him at the dock, Nick decided it must be the way of this world.

As Nick neared the Captain, he said, "Man, meet Eanmund, your guard."

"Guard?" asked Nick and Eanmund at the same time.

"Call it what you will, I have a schedule to keep. Gather your belongings, get off the ship, and get on with whatever life it is you will have," said the Captain. Then, to both their surprise, he winked at Eanmund and Nick. It was as though he realized he'd spoken harshly and was attempting to apologize.

An octopus scampered up, depositing the box the officials at the enclosure assigned to him, presumably filled with articles of clothing, food, etc..

Eanmund gathered up the box, using the energy field to slide it along behind him as he tersely stated, "Come, Man".

While they were still on the ship's ramp it began to roll back onto the ship. They hustled to land before they were dragged back to the ship, having to jump the last step. The ship began to retreat back towards the open ocean. Eanmund asked Nick, "Is Man your chosen name?" as the ship began to pulsate and move. An electric charge filled the air with the smell of ozone as the ship's bulk pressed forward from berth.

"Stinky old junk heap", Eanmund muttered.

"No," replied Nick, remembering the name question, and watching the ship pulse away.

Enamund looked sharply at Nick, thinking he was disagreeing with his condemnation of the boat.

Nick continued quickly, "No, when I told them I was of the species 'man', they found that easier to say than 'Nick'."

Nick realized he hadn't really taken anything in about Eanmund, except his clothing. Up close, an otter-like head appeared under the hood, with whiskers and exposed yellow teeth protruding from under a black button nose. But his fur was thin, blond and Nick could see skin.

"Ok, Nicth it is".

"No, 'Nick'".

"Hmmm... Ni...ck.... perhaps 'Man' will do. Come quickly now, Man, it is late and my family will be expecting you."

Nick's eyes squinted as he struggled to follow Eanmund down the paths past the immensely tall structures surrounding them. "I'm surprised, you have a family?"

"What an odd thing to say! Why?" Eanmund replied, slightly winded from their walking.

"Well, where I'm from, often 'men-of-the-cloth', those that wear clothing specific to their faith, don't take wives," stated Nick.

"What a terrible system! Do they have no passions? Is your world cold of romantic and familial relations?"

Nick, slightly defensive, responded "No, of course not", as their pace increased as the structures seemed to become slightly smaller, with some space between them.

"Well then, how, possibly, can these so-called, 'men-of-the-cloth' exert their passions?"

The words 'men-of-the-cloth' and 'passion' made Nick think of the scandals that plagued the Catholic church, and his only response was, after a pause, "Often, where they shouldn't."

"Well, why does their belief system call on avoiding normal, healthy relationships?" asked Eanmund.

Nick tried to think of what Sunday school and his father had taught him of Jesus. It had been many years, but Nick couldn't seem to recall Jesus ever condemning marriage, or families; in actuality, he remembered Jesus celebrating a wedding with wine. Nick couldn't remember why the Catholic leadership didn't marry.

"I'm not sure," said Nick in reply.

"Then why would anyone do it?" asked Eanmund, as they approached his domicile, still made of wooden columns, but smaller in height than the buildings the ship had unloaded next to, likely only around 30 feet tall. It was almost tee-pee in shape, with the poles leaning against a large central pole, at which point there was a glow from inside and smoke escaping from ports at the junction.

Before Nick could respond to Eanmund's further probing on the church's marriage stance, he was through a door made of wood,

unlike the living and moving walls at the enclosure. These doors were hung on the hinges Nick was familiar with. But unlike Earthen hinges, there were three braces attached to the outside, the top and bottom of which swung in, but the third rotated the door, allowing it to spin inward, and rotate out of the way, onto the wall beside them as they passed through.

In front of them was an effeminate otter-like creature, and three smaller otters, standing to greet them in the middle of a great-hall room with several floating balls of energy illuminating the well-kept interior. Decorative features graced the walls, and the floor was made of a decorative stone, with beautiful alternating patterns impressed upon the stone.

"Welcome!" she said, and quickly followed it with, "You poor soul, when I learned that you were being kept at the eel camp my soul pained for yours."

The children also expressed greetings.

Eanmund stepped in, "This is my wife, Murin and my children…", at which point the children exploded in a cacophony of overlapping questions.

Eanmund shouted, "Ok, ok, you have met the Man! Now to bed with you all! I'm sure he is tired and we have many long days ahead of us, introducing him to the island. Man, you have the guest room, there, on the far end of the hall."

Eanmund escorted Nick to a small cell, with a bed-like area made of wood and grass, and said, "Get rest, tomorrow I must introduce an entirely new concept and culture. That is, if you have truly never been here before and do not know of Enbala. Most know of Enbala, even when they claim they don't."

Nick plopped down on the bed-like platform, thinking that the foreignness of everything would surely keep him from sleeping. Eanmund scurried away, somehow extinguishing the orb in the room, and closing the door behind him. Nick stared at the door for a short while, but the length and excitement of his trip quickly overcame him, and the bed, being surprisingly soft, quickly lulled him to sleep.

Nick though he had only just closed his eyes when he felt Eanmund pulling him up.

"Man... Man!... It is time to go to morning revelries."

"Revelries?" Nick asked groggily.

"Yes, we thank the Creator for the morning he gives us, every day."

"Why am I going?"

"Visitors to Enbala are required to attend the ceremony; it is the law of Enbala".

"But I don't know your beliefs?", Nick parried, hoping to talk his way into longer sleep.

"Your beliefs are irrelevant; to be on Enbala means that you are acquiesced to the founding beliefs of the Island. If you are unwilling to participate, we will be forced to ask you to leave. If we allow visitors who are not willing to adopt the island's core beliefs, they can change those core beliefs, and we are happy with our ancient identity and beliefs. We have no desire to conform to the rest of the world."

Nick, feeling slightly flustered, replied, "So you will force your beliefs on me."

Eanmund laughed, "You are a feisty one. It is not possible to force a belief, but we can require you to honor our customs. If that is done, it really matters little what you believe of the Creator. But those that don't honor the customs and laws of the Creator, make themselves God. Their will is subject to their shallow conscious, and that is not the way of Enbala. This is a place of order, not mindful dalliance, or the making of small gods."

Nick realized he felt anger rising in him, and he was unsure why.

"You're assuming my thoughts are nothing but 'mindful dalliance'", he almost shouted.

"No Man, I know that your thoughts, when compared with those of the one that ordered our world, are simple dalliance, no matter how profound. When you create a world, you might persuade me to think otherwise. And you seem to be assuming you have a right to be here; your time here is with our privilege, and you may return to the eel encampment if you can't integrate here."

The thought of returning to his previous home quickly silenced Nick. Regardless of his ever-shifting postmodern belief system, successfully programmed during his college attendance, he realized he was likely in a better place than the compound, and that it wasn't too difficult to rise from his sleep and attend a ceremony for an un-flexible deity who required a morning "Hello".

As Nick exited the room he saw the rest of the family gathered at the fire, and smelled the unmistakable aroma of breakfast. Murin called him over and as he approached he was surprised how cheerful the entire family seemed to be, despite the early hour.

He mentioned his surprise, stating "You all seem so cheerful for such an awful early hour."

The children stopped their eating and glanced quizzically at him.

Eanmund also seemed surprised. "Awful?" he asked.

"Yes, isn't it hard to rise so early?"

There was a long pause.

Murin was the first to respond, "Man... you have seal-like concerns. Here, on this island, we recognize true difficulties that make rising early seem a pleasure. Was your ship not attacked by the eels? Can you not see that you are on an island surrounded by the eel's sea? Are you not aware that we worship a creator that is not the Great Shark? Our very existence is a gift, and each day we wake without attack is a miracle from the Creator. To thank him for a new day is a pleasure, and comes from a grateful heart. Rising early is a silly concern, if it can be considered a concern. Besides, the entire island rests quite early in the evening. I imagine you were quite alone on your trip here late last night?"

Nick considered his surreal walk from the wharf, his host's words, and, feeling slightly convicted, responded, "Yes... it was surprisingly quiet."

A silence settled on the dining room as breakfast commenced. At the conclusion the family gathered belongings, and Eanmund led them all out the door and into the street. Surprisingly, dawn had already broken, and a beautiful golden sky framed the mountain of Enbala as the sun struggled to break free from behind it.

Noticing Nick looking at the mountain, Eanmund said, "Due to the mountain, each morning we have several hours of twilight; it is symbolic of reflection, a time for considering the Creator and the coming day. It is joyfully begun with revelries."

As they walked through the looming timber structures, the residents of Enbala joined them. Many of the families looked strikingly similar to the Eanmund's family, but Nick noticed there were numerous crabs joining the throng as they made their way to a mysterious (at least to Nick) gathering place.

Nick asked, "Do the crabs live here also?".

Eanmund glanced at the crabs, and replied to Nick, "No, but they enjoy visiting here. Their territorial wars with the eels are tiring. They find solace in an island dedicated to the worship of the Creator. Also, the weather is temperate here, and the steep terrain is easy for them to traverse, unlike some of the water-bound worshipers of the Creator. So, we often have crabs joining our services, and exploring Enbala's ancient treasures."

Nick's ears perked at the word "treasure."

"What treasures?"

"For thousands of years Enbala has been a place of worship. We are attending a modern sanctuary this morning, but throughout the island are places that were built to reflect on our Creator, and the builders, wanting to offer their best to Him, poured all of their energy, worldly wealth, and creativity into these places. Even the very trails to access them are works of art, infused with a spirit of love. They are treasures, and we are blessed to live near them."

A nearby otter, wearing a different colored tunic than Eanmund, overheard him and responded, "Indoctrinating the man already, in the old ways, huh, Ean?"

Eanmund, in a tone Nick had not yet heard from him, shortly replied to the interloper, "It is best to have 'ways' Aelred. Have you discovered the 'ways' that you want to follow yet?"

Aelred laughed contemptuously and replied, "Of course, unlike you I'm willing to adapt to a Creator who is still talking to his children."

Eanmund snorted, "By embracing the long-standing ways of gods that are not, and were never, our Creator. They are not new ways. Your ways, and the ways of old, don't align Aelred. They never have, and sooner or later you'll discover that they are in conflict and cannot exist together."

Aelred had begun to outpace the family, being alone, and obviously caring little for Eanmund's opinion. He just managed to throw back, "You're a dying breed, I'm embracing our world and our future. I will join in harmony with all."

Eanmund said lowly, "Family stop."

The family stopped and turned to him.

Eanmund, looking to his children with loving care, said, "Listen closely. Aelred speaks platitudes. While it sounds wonderful, 'harmony with all', is not attainable without the Creator breathing into all. While there are forces living contrary to his laws on this world, they will be forces diametrically opposed, and they cannot rest in harmony. It is impossible. If the Creator could exist along with their evil ways, then he wouldn't truly be good. Only when all of the created bow to the Creator's will, then harmony can be found".

"Is 'harmony' boring dad?", the middle child asked.

Eanmund's arm flashed towards the center of Enbala, and said, "Look! Look at that creation! His harmony is not boring, it is amazing, beautiful and imposing, with worlds upon worlds to discover."

And at that he looked to Nick, "Consider the man; there is always something new, unknown, and interesting that the Creator can produce. For thousands of years we have no known record, that I've found in the records yet, that tells of a creature such as this man."

Murin spoke up, "We must hurry my love, if we are to find seats together".

Nick gathered that Eanmund's lectures were familiar to the Otter family, and that they'd been late for revelries before.

As they approached the meeting hall Nick was struck by the sheer magnitude of the hall, especially when he realized that the walls were made of timbers incredible in height and straightness. Across the top of the hall, the same beams had been curved into arches. There were no doors, but the shimmer of energy barriers provided windows, light and shelter from the elements.

To Nick's surprise, although he might have expected it, the otters walked right through the energy barrier at the front door. Nick followed; as he passed it felt like a light wind gust.

Energy pulsated through the trunks of the walls, through veins within the tree trunks, providing light to the hall; it was needed since only dim light from the twilight sky filtered in from portals set high in the walls. Floating balls of energy provided additional lighting to busy areas that the walls didn't sufficiently highlight.

Nick commented on the height of the timbers, while the children raced to take their place at the front of the hall. Eanmund was directing Murin and Nick to a seating area towards the middle of the space, and he said, "The acoustic design of the hall provides the best sound here, in the middle. And yes, the hard woods of Enbala are an amazing blessing in their height and straightness. The trees used in the construction of this building were sourced and shaped over a period of one hundred and fifty years; you are lucky, we've only had a completed roof for ten years now. When I was young we would often enjoy the elements, even the coldest, wettest ones, as we brought in the day with praise and reflection."

Murin added, "I do miss the excitement when the perfect trees were found and brought down. And that feeling when the roof was almost completed, that was so fun to be a part of".

Eanmund replied, "Yes, but we still have the finishes to consider and complete".

To which Murin quickly replied, "The finishes, which have been in committee for twenty years?!"

At this Eanmund only chuckled.

The children at the front of the hall began to sing. It was remarkably loud and beautiful. The song was similar to that which Nick had heard in the boat the previous evening, but this version was louder and brighter. There was a note of expectance that had been missing in the retiring evening tune; this song spoke of what was to come, and even without understanding most of the words, Nick still knew that a concept of arrival and dawning was being conveyed.

He leaned towards Eanmund, "Why don't I understand the words?"

Eanmund quietly explained, "Many years ago we found a way to use the energy in the atmosphere to decipher language before it reaches the ear, based on energy patterns, both in the ear and in the mind's response. But the ancient language of Enbala is used little, and there was no cause to clutter the bandwidth of the atmospheric energy with its translation requirements."

The revelry continued on for a comfortable time, and the children concluded with a rousing tune that filled the chamber with bright and brilliant voices. The acoustics of the hall were ideal, highlighting each note, both high and low, with just a little pleasing echo.

When the music went silent, the sound of the crowd stirring to their feet filled the room, alive with voices and happiness. It felt as though everyone was, for a moment, greeting the day together in strong cheer. The children came back to the family and, as a group, they made their way back through the shimmering portal onto the island of Enbala.

As they passed out of the hall, they found that the sun had risen above the mountains and beautiful sunlight bathed the mountains, tall forests, rolling hills, dwellings, and the village in golden light. Enbala's avian population was also welcoming the dawn with their form of canticles.

Nick glanced out towards the sea and saw white foam washing the black sand at the sea edge. The blue water blended out into the darker sea, and finally disappearing into the horizon of the sky, meeting together in a blend of similar blue.

Nick noted the sound of buildings being opened, and a general buzz of population, the unmistakable sound of commerce he had not before heard on Enbala. He noticed much of the crowd was dispersing into the village rather than returning to the homes.

"What do we do now?" Nick asked Eanmund. "Do you have a business?"

Eanmund laughed, "No, man. Do I seem like a creature of trade? I am one of the keepers of the repository."

"What is the repository?"

"It is where we keep the written records of our culture."

"Oh," Nick said, "We call that 'the library'."

"As I understand that word, there is a connotation of 'free'. The repository of Enbala is not a library, it is a repository of utmost importance. Its continued success ensures the probable transmission of our beliefs and culture into the future, if the Creator is willing."

Eanmund embraced his family, and then the family retreated back towards their domicile. Eanmund turned to Nick, "Come, we will go to the repository now. It is the perfect place to introduce you to our world further."

But instead of heading towards the village buildings, Eanmund selected a trail leading through the grasslands towards the nearest strand of tall forest trees on the distant hills. What mystery lay in the deep depths of those far tall arbors Nick could only imagine.

The trek through the lower grasslands was relatively easy, the trail well-groomed and where steps were needed, supporting understructure was used to reduce erosion and slipping.

But, about halfway through the head-high grass, a huge beast stepped across the trail in front of them. Nick froze in terror. Eanmund only paused. The beast had gray skin, resembling an elephant's, both in size in color, but with a horse-like head and a large, slab-sided body.

Eanmund made a shooing noise and the creature reluctantly finished crossing the trail.

Nick was still frozen. Eanmund looked back curiously.

"It's only our main livestock animal, the santor. They're large but mostly harmless, unless angered."

After about ten minutes of walking across the field the tall trees dominated their path forward.

"Is the repository inside the strand of trees?"

"In a way; these trees serve as a natural fortification for the repository. It is located beyond them, but you shall soon see it. Come, I'm excited to show you our greatest treasure".

Nick was aware that there were other travelers along the path, heading to the same destination.

Standing at the base of the mighty Enbalan trees made Nick feel very small; he imagined an ant staring up at a redwood, although the comparison was slightly exaggerated.

They passed in, among the massive trunks. Some of the trees growing next to the trail oddly bowed to the trail, and their trunks had been worn smooth by the passing traveler's paws and garments. It was as though the many travelers had

successfully withheld the trunks from growing into the trail as the years passed. A twilight enveloped them quickly among the shadows of the giant trees, but a few strategically placed floating orbs provided illumination of the forest trail. The ground was coated with the leaves from the trees, but the covering was sparse, and patches of deep dark soil showed through. Soil that Nick cold smell.

Suddenly the trees were clear and Nick's eyes fell onto the most amazing building he'd seen.

He was standing at the edge of the tall trees, on a bank looking down into a valley that could easily hold most Earthen small towns. But instead of a town, Nick saw a living building of monstrous proportions. There was a center shaft extending from near where Nick and Eanmund stood, to the distant end of the crater. Protruding at 45-degree angles were branches, living, but clearly hollow, with shooting lights of energy pulsating throughout the entire structure, emanating from the central hall. The central hall had pipe-like protrusions shooting into the dark soil, likely rooting the behemoth, and they seemed organic. Taken together, the structure looked rather like a giant V-shaped engine, with a half-dozen, or so, individual cylinders on each side of the V, each roughly ten stories in height. There were openings in the cylinders that could only be windows, and on occasion a large sheet of energy would buffer an edge of the structure in a flash of undulating light.

"... What is this?..." an awestruck Nick asked.

"It is The Repository. The oldest living structure on Enbala, produced by manipulating the Foli tree with energy barriers to produce... well, this", and Eanmund motioned to the structure before them.

"The energy you see as a flash of sheet light are energy barriers guiding the growth of the structure. Once the peak of biological technology, when the initial hall and two wings were begun hundreds of years ago, but the entire system has become exponentially more complex as the spatial needs of the repository have grown. There is a village of native warm-blooded Enbalan creatures that have looked after the repository and their skill have increased greatly through the centuries."

Flashes of energy periodically sparked around the structure, eerily lighting the valley in the trees nesting the structure. The bio-fiber of the Foli tree was red in nature, and in the flashing light of the barriers, and the pulsating inner energy veins, seemed to cause the structure to glow like embers within the dark browns and greens of the inner forest.

At the near end of the main hall's tube was another shimmering barrier of energy, similar to the door at the morning worship hall. As they approached, after Nick had spent several minutes staring at the wonder of the outside, Eanmund said, "I must touch you as we pass the energy shield. We have programmed it to recognize the biological signals of those that work inside, and visitors must be accompanied through the entrance."

As they went through Eanmund laid his paw on Nick's shoulder.

Within, the red walls glowed in a manner similar to Eanmund's hospital cells at the enclosure. It was apparent they were reaping the atmospheric energy, in the same way, to illuminate the building.

Just within the entrance, the walls were decorated with portraits of otters in religious garb, but unlike earthly portraits these were three dimensional in nature, with some form of depth added to each.

They made their way past this first corridor, through a transition point, into a second corridor. At the edges of this room Nick could see that two columns came up from either side of the corridor; they were the building's towers. The room and towers were similar to an earthly library, the walls of the towers were filled with the unmistakable form of books. Only these books were larger than what Nick was used to, and stored flat, with labels painted onto their page edges, which faced outward towards spiraling, smooth paths which wound their ways up and around the columns.

Eanmund motioned him towards the tower on the right.

"The two towers that protrude from this gallery were the first towers; they house our oldest records."

By this time Nick was standing in the middle of the base of the tower, and he could see all the way up the column. Towards the top he could see that the volumes were protected by another energy shield, but still visible through the shield's blue hue.

Suddenly the energy shield opened, allowing an otter out, before instantly snapping in place again.

Eanmund growled, then watched the figure slowly make its way down the spiraling path. It was holding an old volume, but it looked different from those that surrounded Nick and Eanmund in the nearby gallery, as they looked up.

When the figure was close enough, Eanmund loudly addressed it, "Well Aelred, you're back to studying your favorite work, are you?!"

Nick realized that what Aelred appeared to be holding was a rolled-up eel skin, up, tanned with age and dust. The head of the eel had been left intact, and the front fangs were being used to latch the skin into its roll shape. The unmistakable characters of writing began between the eyes and continued back onto the rolled skin, in a manner similar to Earth's scrolls.

Aelred ignored Eanmund, but as he reached the bottom of the spiral, Eanmund blocked his path.

"Get out of my way old man", snarled Aelred.

Eanmund snapped back, "Why do you devote so much time to the scroll of the Shark God? Wouldn't your time be better spent studying the theology of Enbala?!"

Aelred, looking annoyed that he would have to address Eanmund, quietly said, "There is one Creator, and we have studied Enbala's interactions with him for centuries. I am choosing to further our knowledge of the Creator by studying what he's revealed of his nature to all cultures."

"Enbala was here, and had long been sharing the Creator's works and words, when that imaginative record was produced. It does not speak of our Creator, it speaks of an entirely different power and dominion of the deep," Eanmund countered.

"And that is why I call you old.'" Aelred said. "Your opinions are outdated, close minded, and lead only to divisive rhetoric."

"There is division between us and the denizens of the deep because our values don't align, and they cannot exist together!"

It was clear Eanmund was angry. But it was also clear that Aelred cared little for Eanmund's opinion.

Aelred sidestepped Eanmund, saying only, "Don't you have more pressing concerns than my studies, with your 'man' project?"

And then Aelred shuffled off to an unknown (to Nick) recess of the structure, likely to study the scroll and beliefs of the Great Shark.

Eanmund looked to Nick, and Nick recognized Eanmund's facial expression was the same as when he began the morning lecture at his children.

"Aelred thinks that he will find added enlightenment, more than centuries of Otters before him, by studying the works of the Great Shark religion. He wants greatness, by finding previously unknown characteristics of the Creator. He's mad! Our Creator is not found in those words he carried; the Great Shark is a hateful, capricious deity. His mind cannot be known, mainly because his written words are foolish, and when they are found to be consistent, they are hateful, vengeful and stupid, bucking against anything our Creator has revealed of his nature. Just look at this beautiful island! From the smallest seed of the grass of the pasturelands, to the peaks of our trees and mountains, even to the energy that surrounds us in the atmosphere, our Creator has revealed that he is caring, beautiful, giving, and wondrous in deeds. The Great Shark only cares for the wet and dark deep, and that which doesn't resemble his dark enclave, he wants to destroy, to bend to his will. The eels love this because they flourish in dark, cold waters where they can reap their feudal system to wring every source of life from those they can enslave."

Nick remembered what Aelred had said about "harmony" in their morning meeting. Could there be harmony with the eels? Nick remembered his internment at the enclosure with mixed emotion; he had an eel friend, but she'd met a terrible death at the mouth of the eels. Could she represent what a harmony with the eels looked like? But was she a follower of the Great Shark, or at the time Nick had known her, was she only an outcast?

Nick pondered these things as Eanmund drew out a dusty, huge, tome, and made his way to a protrusion in the wall, clearly designed as a platform for reading the records.

The pulsating energy in the walls seemed to follow them and provide just the right amount of illumination for the task at hand.

"What is that made of?" Nick asked, when he realized that he was looking at a sheet stronger, greyer, and more translucent than the paper he was familiar with.

"Our records are written on the skin of the santors, the animal you saw in the pasture."

Nick looked up into the tall column, filled entirely with similar records.

"How many santors do you harvest per year?!"

"They shed their skin before our hottest seasons. Only the finest, and most important records are put on the skin of a dead santor. A tradition the eels stole from us, as you witnessed by seeing one of the earliest records of their Great Shark religion in the paws of

Aelred. Only we make our records on agriculture, not the skins of fellow otters. That alone should give you a clue to the nature of the Shark god."

Eanmund then began to tell Nick the history of Enbala, their beliefs in its creator, and the interpretation of the Creator's revealed character, that led to the traditions and customs of Enbalan culture. Largely, it sounded like the God of Nick's parents; a caring, loving, compassionate, giving Creator.

Nick didn't feel that the religion of an otter on a far-off island really had any bearing on his life, but a curious thought had occurred to him. Nick thought about his Sunday school teachings and then, speaking, cut Eanmund off mid-lecture as he'd long ago stopped being able to focus on Eanmund's multitude of words.

"Eanmund, your Creator sounds like my world's supposed 'creator', but you haven't told me how your creator deals with sin."

"'Sin?' I think I know what you're saying, but please elaborate Man."

"Well, what does the creator of Enbala do when you are disobedient? You know, do something that breaks his rules?"

"What a fascinating question Man. Remarkably perceptive! Why, this very thought is my business, and the work of most of the others engaged here at the repository. The portraits of those that you saw in the entry are otters that have guided our thoughts forward on these matters. Your question could be discussed for hours, but I'll try and answer it as precisely as I can."

"It's obvious, because the followers of the Great Shark haven't been wiped from the planet, that he's patient towards those against him. But for how long? And to what degree? And what will their just rewards be in the end?... So many questions...."

Eanmund started to stare off into space, in deep consideration, a mindful stare that Nick could tell was familiar to Eanmund, but then he snapped back to attention.

"But what does your creator do man?!"

Nick didn't think he'd ever seen Eanmund pay so much attention to him before, in the brief time they'd been together.

"Well, this is kind of my parent's religion but... he sent his son to take the punishment. And if we put faith in his son, as God, we are saved by him."

"Why would they accept him as God, if he was the son?"

Nick tried to remember what he'd been taught, and the trinity came to mind. "Well, he was the son, but God at the same time. He's also a spirit, throughout the world."

Eanmund stared quizzically at him. "These are fantastical thoughts man, please continue. I need to know how this God, but also a son, could take the punishment of sin."

"Well, he was perfect, is the theory. And a perfect God can accept a perfect payment for sin."

"Fascinating. What did he pay?"

"A horrific death. Nailed to a cross... well, you probably don't know what that is. A tree, basically. The stuff of nightmares. Betrayed by a friend, hated by his countrymen, then nailed up in a tree and left to die."

"If he died, how could he be God?"

"Well, he didn't stay dead. He came back alive. His believers celebrate this every year with a holiday."

"A holy day? Hmm. These are fascinating things man. You said, 'his believers', are you not among them?"

Nick thought, and then responded, "No, I've been unsure. His believers say the son's death is the only way to come to our creator. I've been unsure that good deity could be so stringent. It seems so limiting. Shouldn't there be different paths that lead to a creator?"

Eanmund's deep attention and almost awe-like wonder suddenly disappeared, and his next words took a frigid tone, "Take care man! The things you just told me of your Creator's reconciliation resonate with Godliness, even in the half-hearted way you shared with me. But what you just said about 'paths' reeks of Aelred's spirit."

He continued, "If there is a Creator of the beauties of this world, he is an ordered God, and the path to him shall be ordered, but awesome to such a degree that it will overwhelm understanding. The dalliances and uncertainties of many 'paths' doesn't fit with a God who set planets, nature, and seasons in perfect order and balance. This is logic, and it must be applied!"

Nick, feeling flustered, was preparing a rebuttal when something very unexpected happened.

Throughout their discussion there had been creatures entering and exploring the records, walking past them. But at this particular moment a crab ventured near Eanmund and Nick and began to stare at them, without moving, from approximately ten feet away.

Nick instantly thought of the guards at the camp, and he shut down, returning the stare. Were there still crabs watching him here?

Eanmund, noticing that Nick had no return for his statements on the character of God, realized that the crab's stare had stalled any response from Nick.

He chuckled.

"It is our custom, as official record searchers, to read the records we study out loud. It helps with memory, and the visitors have a long tradition of listening. The crab is simply waiting for me to recite from the volume we have open before us."

The crab, realizing something different than a reading was happening, scampered off.

Mark sat next to the bed, listening to the now too familiar, and ever-constant, "beep… beep… beep…", of the machine helping his son breathe.

They'd placed Nick in a medically induced coma after the accident, to fend off brain damage due to swelling of the brain. Nick still hadn't come out of that coma. It'd been six months. Six long months.

Mark had been at the hospital almost every weekend of that six months. There'd been the one where his truck broke down… damn old thing. Someday he'd figure out which newer model he wanted… but for now it was comfortable, even if he had to fix it all the time. And there was the weekend his own mother had fallen at the nursing home.

But those two were it. Other than that, he'd been here. His heart hurting and heavy. Thinking. Thinking.

Too much thinking.

He knew it wasn't his fault. Nick had made his own choices.

One weekend the chaplain had come in; asking Mark how his relationship with God was.

It was a fair question. Mark knew and loved his savior. God was good, and Mark knew that. But Mark also knew that life, and the sin that plagued it, was hard on this world. He wondered if Nick's decisions were, in some small way, repercussions for any of his sin. The chaplain reassured him that the world was fallen, and these things would always happen until Jesus returned; what is important is to remember the awesomeness of Jesus' ongoing forgiveness for those that love him.

Mark had his own temptations. Especially after his wife died. The evening beer to relax had turned into several beers. And then more. It'd become a habit, and he'd ballooned seventy-five pounds, looking unlike the fit man of his youth. He'd seen old acquaintances in the grocery store who didn't recognize him.

He told his friends he was trying to quit for that reason. It was part of it; but Mark had realized there was a darker pull. Call it the devil, spiritual warfare, or what you will... the release a drunken "high" brought, or at least the idea of it, was causing real problems for Mark. Whether it was the want of it, or the stupid things he did when he was "achieving it", or the plaguing hangovers and health effects, Mark had realized it was something he needed to get away from.

And he had. Mostly. And it taught him. Taught him the frailty of man, and the consequences that frailty can bring.

Now here was his son, a casualty to that same frailty.

The chaplain was certainly right; it was miraculous that Jesus still loved them, and he was grateful for it.

Still, Mark worried that the example he set when he was drinking had somehow encouraged Nick to drink.

What could he do now?

He prayed. He thanked God again for getting him through the temptation to drink. He apologized profusely, if it had affected Nick.

And, of course, he prayed often that Nick woke up. But not that he just woke up. No, that wouldn't be enough. He needed to wake up and understand. He needed to take in his mistake, and turn. The pastor, at Mark's church, called turning away from your mistakes true repentance. Mark prayed that Nick would have repentance. Nick's current choices couldn't continue on. There could be no more of this.

And in six months Mark had thought often on this. And prayed. Oh, how he wanted Nick to wake up. He missed his son. And how he wanted him to repent. Mark wanted the best for his son. Always would.

Eanmund gave Nick a very thorough tour of the repository that day. And the next day. And for five days he continued to find texts and locations within the repository to lecture Nick. Finally, Nick, fearing he couldn't take more, asked why Eanmund continued to introduce him to the repository daily.

"This is my work," Eanmund said, "and because I suggested that we bring you here, it's been appointed to me to train you in a vocation. I doubt you'll ever be a Keeper of the Texts, unless you find yourself compelled to our beliefs, but I do believe you can be a Keeper of the Repository, perhaps aiding the woodland natives in their care of this resource. As such, I must first introduce you to the importance of this place, and that means understanding what it contains."

Nick responded in a whisper, "Ahhh, that makes sense."

It was true, in the last five days Nick had seen texts older than he could imagine, which seemed to be of great importance to the inhabitants of Enbala. There were texts from long before the repository existed; Eanmund explained there'd been earlier structures in this very valley and some of their remains still existed.

The skins of the santor seemed to weather time better than Earthly paper, although the ink had often eaten through the skin, producing a surreal effect of ghostly text present only in its well-defined absence, the voids left behind retaining the shape of the original ink characters.

The surrealness of the situation suddenly weighed down heavily on Nick's soul. He still wasn't sure that he accepted this world as a reality. But the passage of time, and familiarity, had begun to breed a comfortableness with the situation that surprised even him. But the thought of menial labor hit him hard, as it didn't seem the substance of dreams. Was a job to confirm that this world was reality? The concept of working was certainly grounding.

After following Eanmund's endeavors for several hours, traversing across the repository, Eanmund and Nick retired to a small room to enjoy some sustenance. Santor seemed to be a meal of choice in the repository, a staple food for the island, and with little wonder. The taste was good, slightly softer than beef, but not quite as light as chicken. It paired well with grain creations, which tended to be slightly tougher than what Nick was used to. Nick also realized that Eanmund's teeth and jaws were stronger than his.

The thought occurred to Nick, and he questioned Eanmund, "When do I meet my future coworkers?"

Eanmund, still seeming thoughtful and distant this day, said, "All will come Man. You have nothing but time; you should have nothing but patience."

He continued, "Today we have a somber task, which bears additional explanation and weight beyond my usual tour discussions."

Nick tried to hide a smile at the term "discussions", but Eanmund duly noticed, responding, "I am no fool, Man. I am well aware that my communication style is one-sided. But don't dismiss my knowledge as foolish; poor communication skills do not lessen the gravity of the truths I speak."

"Today we will visit the room where we keep items like the Great Shark eel roll you saw Aelred accessing several days ago".

Nick, slightly confused why this was a somber task, responded, "I don't understand why you seem to be concerned about that?"

"The teachings in the Room of Shadows are contrary to the values that make Enbala a beautiful and peaceful place. The Room of Shadows contains war, impurity, crime, lies, indulgences and hatred".

Nick laughed a little, and flippantly said, "Well, that sounds like most of my world's libraries."

Only Eanmund didn't smile. He sat pensively, staring at Nick for a long time. The next thing he said shocked Nick.

"Sometimes I fear that I made the wrong decision, offering you refuge here".

He quickly continued on, the stern look fading a little from his eyes, "Dangerous words must be treated with care. You can't ignore the existence of a sedition that is sure to destroy you, and you can't handle it light heartedly either. Words have power, especially the written word. Regardless of how your 'libraries' are sharing this information, if insipid ideas are flippantly transmitted there will be those that adopt their ways simply because they were introduced to them."

"You mean... desensitization?"

"In essence. It's a much greater concept though. It's about giving ideas that are wrong the respect they are due. It's understanding that there exists the weak of mind, and ill-willed, and giving them access to harmful ideas and information is not wise."

"That being said, during our visit today we'll only talk about the physical aspects of the Room of Shadows, rather than the documents. Come on, let's head that way."

Nick was relatively certain he'd just been insulted, but he wasn't sure. He followed Eanmund towards the first tower, and at its apex, the Room of Shadows.

The Room of Shadows was aptly named; the energy orb, floating centrally, was small (seemingly an afterthought), and the room was arranged in rows, with a small round portal to the outside world high on the wall at the end of each row letting in the natural Enbalan light, although tinted as it passed through the green energy field blanketing each hole. Eanmund and Nick entered through a locked hatch in the floor, and this was the only flat floor in the entire tower, the rest of the records lining the walkway spiraled their way up the tower.

Nick noticed that each record was chained from its binding directly to metal bars mounted above the shelves. The rods ran along to a locking mechanism at the end of each shelf. This obviously prevented removal of the records, except by those that possessed a key to the rod mechanism.

For reading, there were long dark tables in a corner of the room. Several were v-shaped, to cradle books, and others were canted at a light angle so scrolls would naturally remain open.

Eanmund said, "As I told you, this is our oldest tower, and the Room of Shadows is much the same as it was the day it was established. We've found that there was little need for addition, the seditious teachings have since changed names, but

their central concepts are much the same today as they've always been. The foundational records selected by our forefathers in faith, to establish this room of counter-intelligence, still serve well to remind and educate the citizens of Enbala of what those counter to the Creator believe."

With no thought of their earlier discussion, Nick responded, "What do they believe?"

Eanmund only answered, and slowly, "... Mostly a love of self, Man, mostly a love of self above all consideration of the Creator, and the other created beings."

He continued, "The Keepers mainly access this room to clean the settling dust, or maintain the light. An occasional oiling of the locks serves to keep them operational. The dust also has acidic content, and can't be allowed to build up on the records or it will degrade them."

Suddenly the hatch in the floor of the room creaked open on its ancient hinges. It was behind several rows of records, so Eanmund and Nick could only wait until the new arrival revealed themselves.

The eyes and head of an eel presented themselves as the creature slithered forward. As the eel and Eanmund spied each other, both reacted in fear. Eanmund grabbed Nick and yanked him behind a dark row of records. Frenetic sounds from within the room confirmed that the eel was taking similar evasive actions.

A familiar voice spoke up, "What is going on?!"

Eanmund's features darkened, and he rose from his place of retreat, venturing forward to meet the voice.

"That's what I was wondering, Aelred!" said Eanmund, his voice dripping with contempt.

Nick peered around the corner to find a smallish eel slithering beside Aelred, who was responding to Eanmund.

"You haven't attended the last several meetings of the island council?" asked Aelred.

"No, I was busy attending to the details of bringing the man here. And since, I've been introducing him to the island... Why? What have you done?"

"Me?" laughed Aelred, "It's you that opened this door."

"Explain." said the icy Eanmund.

Aelred growled, his disdain at answering to Eanmund grossly apparent, as he contemplated whether it was necessary at all.

After an uncomfortable pause Aelred said, "The eel, Vian, is here in just the same way your man is. After you successfully argued for having this man here, I simply reiterated your arguments. Vian is here so that we can learn from each. We will teach him what we know of the Creator, and he will teach us what his society believes are the attributes of their creator. After all, if there is one God, he must be the same being, despite our differing worldly terms for him."

Eanmund exploded, "They are not the same God! They have different origin stories, they have different values, they have different aspirations! This is utter foolishness; we already knew what the Eels and their ilk believe, you've simply confused yourself by looking into theories and conspiracies that are baseless. You cannot coexist with beliefs diametrically opposed to yours! The Great Shark isn't the same, at all! We had no idea of Man's beliefs, and we have an opportunity to learn. With your eel, you are simply bringing an enemy into our cradle."

Aelred responded, "It is this hatred that has divided our world too long! You are simply a bigoted being, Eanmund and I'll have no more of you! Now move out of our way, hate monger!"

At this Aelred blew past Eanmund, commanding the Vian to follow. They went to the Great Shark manuscript, instantly recognizable by its eel shape, and Aelred unlocked the document from the shelf.

Eanmund looked shocked at Aelred's dismissal of his concern, then, turning to Nick, he said, "Let's go, now!"

That evening, as the family & Nick ate, Eanmund regaled Murin and the children with the outlandish decision of Aelred and Enbala's leadership.

"Have they lost their minds?!" he yelled, questioning no one in particular.

The flickering firelight cast long, warm shadows around the home. The food was delicious, and the children happy, despite their father's dark mood.

The oldest asked, "Dad, why does it matter so much?"

"The religion of the Great Shark hates us. Specifically, us. Because we fail to recognize the Great Shark as God, and give all to him, it is their belief that we are free to be eaten. But we're not special. If illegitimate children are born to them, they will be eaten, because they can't be reconciled to the Great Shark."

The children's eyes grew large, and the youngest said slowly, "ewwwww."

This seemed to break some tension, and there were chuckles from around the table.

Mother otter, between bites of a delicious stew (produced using the meat and marrow of the santor) said, "The ladies and I will be praying on this Ean. The eels and their violent attacks have always been a threat to our families and island. To invite them here seems disastrous."

Nick was enjoying the meal, but he was beginning to wonder if he would tire of the taste of santor; there seemed to be few protein choices available to the islanders. Probably because many of the creatures of the sea were sentient, he thought (only he didn't know the word sentient, but recognized the concept).

Murin had developed a bond with Nick, after all, she fed him and was largely responsible for his living conditions. She turned to him and asked, "What do you think of all this Nick?"

Nick, surprised (because Eanmund would never have asked this question), responded, "Well, I don't think it's my concern."

"That's nonsense!" she responded. "You've seen their dark ceremonies, you've experienced their abhorrence of outsiders, you've been attacked by them, and now you live in a land despised by them. How do you possibly conclude they are not your concern?!"

Nick took her words in, but felt them conflicting with his school trainings of "co-exist", and that there is no clear wrong.

"I... I guess I don't know. I'd like everyone to get along, but I'm starting to realize that may not be possible. I'm not willing to give up yet though."

Eanmund only sighed. He then looked to the children and said, "We'll discuss the man's thoughts at this evening's fireside studies."

Fireside studies were an almost nightly discussion of the Creator's attributes, works and deeds. Nick had been encouraged to participate, since his arrival, in an effort to instruct him on Enbalan beliefs.

Tonight the lecture was on co-existence, and peace. Nick had difficulty focusing due to the long length of days on Enbala. He was very tired at evening time, and the warm, orange, flickering firelight's rhythmic cadence upon the walls further lulled him. For fireside discussions the energy orbs in the home were extinguished, further casting the room into a peaceful state.

Nick's main takeaway, tonight, was that the Enbalan religion held co-existence and peace in the highest regard. But, Eanmund stressed, co-existence is not possible with beliefs violently opposed. He told a parable involving ill-fitting clothes:

An otter was given a robe once worn by his stately father, who had been of high importance in Enbala's councils. The father had been considerably larger in size, and the robe was tailored to his specifications. The son was confident he could fill his father's robe, but the son found that when he wore the robe he struggled with bunching and often tripped over it. But the son wanted the robe to fit, and he was sure he could force his will upon the situation. But the chaffing robe opened sores that became infected. And the tripping was sometimes at risk to life and limb.

After some time, trying to force the robe to comply, the otter was left with three choices; die from infection and falling, alter the robe, or throw the robe away.

Eanmund lectured the family that those three choices are all that eventually remain when foundational beliefs are at odds. When two modes of operation are fundamentally opposed, they will fight until the other is changed or destroyed.

Nick thought the story over-simplistic but he was having trouble pinpointing why, as he lay in his room trying to sleep.

He tossed and turned for some time on his mat. He was conflicted; were the cares of the Enbalans becoming his own? Were his beliefs aligned with theirs? Were the eels truly an enemy that must be fought? Was Vian a threat to Enabla?

Frustrated, he suddenly rose. The room had become hot, and there was little chance of sleep.

As he passed through his room door and into the hall, he was surprised to find Eanmund still awake and sitting by the fire. He'd grown accustomed to Eanmund as a tutor and guide so it felt very odd when Eanmund barely acknowledged him. When Eanmund looked towards Nick, his glazed eyes seemed to look through Nick, saying, "It is a good night for reflection."

Nick fumbled for words, "I... I... need a walk."

Eanmund said, "You are not a prisoner. There is the door, I may not be awake when you return."

At that moment Nick realized he wasn't a prisoner, or a responsibility of Eanmund's; Eanmund was choosing to tutor him.

Eanmund's tutelage had seemed a given, but as Eanmund pointed to the door, Nick suddenly gained respect for his situation.

He stumbled into the cool seaside night air of Enbala, his head whirling with thoughts of his fate, the island of Enbala, and his beliefs.

The low slow murmuring ebb and flow of the pulsating sea beckoned him, and he turned his path to the sea.

The air was chilly, and there was mist rising from the island's wet grass. The tall village structures were engulfed in the gray mist, suddenly jumping out at him when he came near them. He rushed past them, disliking the transient nature of their appearances, which matched his thoughts.

At this late hour the sea was little more than a horizontal ribbon of black, slowly evolving out of the grey mire. The shore break was scrubbing the colorless sand in small undulations of the only perceptible hard line. Down the shoreline the straight line of the shore break was overtaken and erased quickly by the covering mist.

Nick was following the sound, smell and humidity of the air to the waterfront. He almost stepped into the water when he reached it, as it formed suddenly out of the grey.

He walked alongside the shore for some time until he came to a cold, hard, and wet stone, the right height and shape for sitting on.

And he sat in the dark grey mist, listening to his thoughts and the light, but constant, sound of lapping water.

Then there was the loudest splash he'd ever heard. It wasn't loud if it had been measured, but compared with the light and soft sounds emanating from the grey blanket of mist and island, it was as startling as a gunshot.

He stared into the black. Searching. Fear rising as the seconds moved forward. Was it an eel?

Moments passed. His eyes began to see the black and grey the same, and just when he thought he would be unable to see anything anyways something passed through the black ribbon of water just in front of him, an undeniable presence.

He yelled, "Wh... What?!", not knowing what to say to a figure in the dark oceans off Enbala late at night.

The calmest, sweetest voice he'd heard yet in this land said, "ppppeeeaaacccceeee".

Then, oddly, he felt compelled to explain himself, his existence, to this form in the dark.

"I'm... I'm sorry... I'm just thinking."

Near where the grey shore and black waters met, he kept seeing a shape and movement. The part of his mind where the words were stored couldn't verbalize what he was seeing, but a different part of his mind recognized feminine form.

The voice asked something which his mind recognized as, "You are different." Although, he wasn't sure that was what was said.

"Yes", he said into the darkness, "I am new here.... I don't know how I got here.... I'm not even sure I am here."

A feeling of reproach instantly weighed upon him at those words. He thought, "Oh no, an eel!".

But, he realized that the shape... she... was telling him that she was not an eel. And he felt her hatred for the eels. A deep passionate hate, and it made him afraid.

He said, "I am alone", not knowing why. He didn't mean alone in this place; he meant the greater alone, when one feels lacking in friendship. As if the creature couldn't perceive that. It seemed to know his every thought and emotion.

The hate he'd felt at the mention of the eels disappeared, melted even, as it was replaced with a warm feeling of empathy. And briefly, Nick thought he saw, through the mist and the grey, the torso of a beautiful woman. But the vision was gone with the slightest sound of stirred water.

And then he could feel that she was gone. The presence was no longer with him. He was alone again, in the grey, cold, and wet. And he missed her.

That brief moment of empathy was warmth he hadn't experienced since he arrived in this world. Perhaps Murin's efforts approached empathy, but there had always been a perception of duty. This was the first time Nick had felt the free gift of empathy, and he wasn't sure why.

Eventually, the cold and dark grew too much for Nick. His thoughts had stopped swirling since the strange visit. For a long time he'd just been searching the unsearchable, hoping for another encounter. But more than anything, Nick was hoping for additional emotional interaction.

But it didn't come. And Nick had to give up. Returning back from where he came, he stumbled through an even deeper fog than on his walk down. For some time he couldn't find his way back to the Otter's home. Lost, in the early morning dark, he felt ridiculous. Gone were the earlier thoughts of right and wrong, Nick replaced them with feelings of pity for himself.

When he found the Otter's, the living area was free of presence; Eanmund had retired.

Nick fell into bed, relieved to have found the home; at times he'd wondered if he'd spend the entire night wandering the village searching.

It was while they ate lunch, at the repository, that Eanmund began quizzing Nick about the previous night's events. Eanmund was expecting, even hoping, to hear a narrative of Nick's thought process. Eanmund was hopeful Nick was beginning to process and understand the Island's history and tribulations.

Instead, Eanmund was surprised and disappointed to hear that a pensive Nick had been interrupted by an unexpected presence in the sea. It was a double let-down, as his goals for Nick hadn't been met, and there was something in the near waters of Enbala that he wasn't aware of.

But as Eanmund listened to Nick's tale he became intrigued.

Just as Nick came to the part where he was telling of searching the waters for the vanished apparition, Eanmund began chuckling.

It was Nick's turn to be disappointed. He wasn't sure what reaction he'd hoped for from Eanmund, but it surely wasn't laughing. He'd felt this encounter so deeply, and to hear the retelling of it laughed at annoyed Nick.

Eanmund said, through the chuckles, "So it is true, they are your kind and you've found each other."

Confused, Nick, rather abruptly and loudly said, "What are you laughing about?!".

Eanmund clammed up a little.

"Relax, Man, you don't know what I'm talking about. I have something to show you. Come with me, we need to go back to the Room of Shadows."

This time they were alone in the old tower. Eanmund was searching among the records, lifting, pushing and re-organizing the older records; a haze of dust floated through the greenish afternoon light seeping in from the room's tinted portals to the outside sun.

Nick sneezed, which seemed to startle Eanmund, as if it reminded him there was another presence in the room.

"I know it's here somewhere... It's our oldest attempting to catalog the creatures of creation. It was moved to this room due to its errors; there was still much to be learned about the natural world when it was created. Whether the uneducated but well intended mistakes of the past should be condemned to the Room of Shadows is another ongoing discussion." Eanmund said, from out of his dust cloud.

Nick started thinking of other things. The sun and dust brought to mind the desert trip he enjoyed before he was violently inserted into this world.

"Aha!"

Eanmund lifted a dusty thick tome of records.

He brought the tome to a stand, ancient, and obviously designed to hold these types of records. Its wood darkened with age, flakes of crazing paint were peeling from its richly decorated legs, and deep dark cracks ran through parts of the structure where the stand had endured the weight of records upon it for hundreds of years.

Nick approached and watched the turning records over Eanmund's robed shoulder. The stand creaked.

He saw illustrations of creatures strange, and some familiar; there were variants of the crabs, eels, seahorses and various shallow water dwellers. But among the familiar were some wonderful, and some monstrous creatures, with odd numbers of appendages, rainbow colored bodies, elongated mouths, and shimmering scales. The images resembled the woodcuts in Earth's earliest printed books; the shapes were recognizable but inaccurate because the artist had only read a description, or seen the disfigured carcass of an example dead for quite some time.

Then Eanmund rested on a specific record. The illustration's profile was raised with a material resembling papier-mache'. The raised figure, and relief of its surrounding outline, brought a recognizable shape to Nick's eyes; he was looking at a mermaid. The mermaid's womanhood wasn't as exaggerated as a lonesome

19th century sailor's description, but its form, and some sense of beauty, was unmistakable.

"This is an Aenenya, an almost mythical creature now, their sightings have become so rare."

Nick replied, "Yes, we have a similar legend in our world".

Eanmund said, "The Aenenya are no legend. Perhaps there is more to your world's legend than you are aware of. But since the resurgence of the Great Shark and its followers, the Aenenya have largely disappeared because they inhabited much of the territory the Shark's followers have overrun."

"Where did they go?" asked Nick.

"That's the thing, we don't know. It's one of the last mysteries of this world. We know that they survive at huge depths, but so do the sharks. There are rumors of underwater caves housing cities and subterranean aquatic worlds where they live and thrive. But these are legends, even if their existence is not."

"How do you know they aren't purely mythical?", asked a disbelieving Nick.

"They have a strange funerary practice. They send a raft of seaweed, with their dead wrapped among it, to the surface near Enbala. When it reaches the surface, chemicals they've placed on the raft react to the air and cause a violent fire, cremating the raft and its occupants almost instantly. These brief flares from the deep are how we know they are still out there. I used to occasionally see Aenenya flares off Enbala. Always in the corner of my eye, for the fire is so brief that by the time you've turned to look it's no more. Either my eyes have degenerated, or there are far fewer Aenenya deaths now. I haven't seen one in years."

Nick reached out to a round diagram mounted on a pin near the middle of the record, obviously designed to be spun. As he turned it, an arrow pointed to various symbols on the parchment, while a window in the spinning piece revealed various life stages of the Aenenya; and the last symbol revealed a haunting illustration of an Aenenya wrapped in seaweed on a blazing raft.

"An intriguing volvelle. Only our older works have these learning tools. Shame we don't still use them," said Eanmund.

Questions formed in Nick's mind, "What did you mean when you said that I was of a similar 'kind'?"

"The seals, deciding that there is nothing they can't know, declared that you are a mutant Aenenya."

Now it was Nick's turn to chuckle. "So I'm a merman am I?"

"Officially, if that's your term for an Aenenyan, then yes, you are a mutant merman."

Eanmund then let a small smile come through, and added, "It does have a fitting sound to it when I say, 'mutant merman'."

They both laughed. It felt like a step forward in their relationship, to laugh together. Nick couldn't remember doing that with Eanmund before. Were they getting along, or was it simply the absurdity of the seals arrogance that had struck a note with both of them? It didn't matter, they were laughing, and that was the best thing for them.

But there was also sadness. Something about laughing with Eanmund made Nick think of his father. He missed him.

As they left the repository that night, Eanmund and Nick found themselves alongside Aelred and Vian, as he slithered through the grass to wherever it was that Aelred was housing him.

Aelred, with an air of gloating in his voice, asked Eanmund if he was attending the lecture that evening.

Eanmund sighed, and asked, "What lecture, Aelred? What lecture?", his voice trailing off in exhaustion as he trudged through the grass. Although Eanmund didn't know what Aelred was referring to, he could tell he was not going to appreciate the answer.

"Vian has been giving lectures, every 10th day, on the beliefs and culture of the Great Shark followers."

Eanmund's voice was no louder as he queried Aelred, "And why have I not heard of this lecture series?"

Aelred laughed, "Probably because everyone was scared to tell you; who wants a lecture on your perceived rights and wrongs?!"

Eanmund's pace increased, and he withdrew from Aelred without response. Nick struggled to keep up. He looked back at Aelred who was positively beaming. Vian seemed to be smiling too.

Conflict

That night, at supper, Murin asked Nick and Eanmund if they'd heard of the protest. When she realized that they were in the dark on the matter, she enlightened them to the undercurrent pulsing through the village.

"The mothers of the city are protesting at the lecture."

"Why?!" asked Eanmund.

"The ceremony, of course!"

Eanmund grumbled, "Shall this day get worse?". Then he looked squarely at Murin and asked, "What ceremony?"

"Oh no, you haven't heard? Well, in a way that pleases me. Ignorance is better than the apathy many husbands are displaying."

"No, rest assured Murin, I'm not apathetic. What ceremony?"

"Vian has agreed to invite several prominent members of the Great Shark religion to demonstrate one of their ceremonies. Aelred, several of Enbala's doctors, and several Council members are going to watch the disposal of a female eel's fetuses of an unknown father."

"WHAT?!" Eanmund yelled, as his paw slammed down on the table.

"Oh good", said Murin, "In talking with the other wives, many of the Otter husbands are entirely uncaring at the thought of baby eels dying. There are some wives that fear their husbands appreciate fewer eels entering the depths."

"That's ridiculous!" Eanmund yelled, "Everyone knows, or should know (because it's what our records reveal to us) that each beast is responsible for their own actions, and not the actions of their fathers. Even if they are born eel, they are still without fault. This ceremony has long been the murder of voiceless innocents."

Nick thought back to the last time he'd witnessed the ceremony, and he found himself agreeing. It surprised him to agree wholeheartedly with Eanmund.

"So why are the wives protesting, and not the men?" asked Eanmund.

"Like I said, if you'd been listening, the males are largely apathetic (at best) to the plight of these unborn eels. The mothers within the otter community have much more empathy for these innocents. It is a natural maternal response."

Eanmund's muzzle showed red. The table occupants expected a lecture on the horrific nature of the coming ceremony, but in the end all Eanmund said was, "I'm glad the mothers are protesting. I don't know what to do... If the majority of husbands don't share my views, it's as though we've become seals, swaying with the seaweed of the ocean, every direction the tides flow. No one is responding to the recorded words of The One that created the seaweed and the tides."

The ceremony was to be held in a building near the docks where Nick had first come to Enbala. This would provide easy access to the arriving delegation from the depths.

As Nick, Eanmund, Murin and the children approached the docks, the night was again dark and the air cold with wet. A multitude of

Enbala residents were mulling towards the designated path of the arriving delegation. From the sounds of the conversations it was apparent some of the gawkers were supporters, and others protestors of the coming demonstration.

The pathway, from water to building, soon filled along its entire path with the island's residents and visitors. Otters, crabs, seals and others could be seen lining the way. Nick even spotted a seahorse among a group of crabs.

The mothers were out, and a number of them had flags made from woven santor hairs. Nick was unfamiliar with the characters, but he was relatively sure they said something like "No Ceremony Here" as there were just three characters on most.

The general murmur of the crowd suddenly gave way to a thrilled noise near the water. Several large dark shapes were emerging from the blackness where the island met the abyss. Two of the largest eels Nick had seen emerged from the water, looking every which way. They paused at the boundary of water and land.

It seemed they were guards. When they were sufficiently satisfied that there was no risk, the largest of the two slapped the water three times with his tail. Five seconds later several eels emerged wearing decorative flourishes indicative of a religious ceremony.

Following the religious eels, was a female eel. Nick remembered his friend in the enclosure, and his heart ached a little. There was a different look in this eel's eyes though; one of hardened resolve.

Nick asked Murin, "Why is she going along with this?"

Murin replied, "She is a royal princess, with an heir already. Another brood would complicate matters. Her husband, and their laws, require that she participates in the ceremony."

Slowly the delegation made their trip to the waiting location. The crowd's response was muted. An occasional dull clap, or hiss, was the extent of the noise, excepting the sound of shuffling as they struggled to see these alien creatures and historic enemies.

Eanmund whispered to Nick, "This the first official eel delegation during my lifetime".

As they passed Eanmund's family Murin hissed, but the eels had only eyes for Nick. They looked at him with the same deep contempt in their eyes that he remembered from the island.

As the nearest eel passed beyond the family, his tail swung and snapped on Nick's shin, dropping him to the ground in a frontward fall. The eel never looked back, but the passing female eel seemed to smile as Nick fell beside her.

Aelred, Vian, and a half dozen of Enbala's doctors and council members were coming down the path from the building to meet the delegation. There'd been smiles and greetings. Enbala's leaders made sure the crowd saw them with these important visitors.

And then they were within the building. The majority of the crowd dispersed quickly. The "protest", if it could be called that, had failed in eliciting any form of response.

The glow of the energy balls leaked out of the ceremony's building at several cracks, but mostly the building was sealed from prying eyes. A small crowd gathered around it, at first, but several hours later only several dozen islanders were still lingering in the cold.

Eanmund had sent the family home immediately after the delegation had entered the building, saying, "I want our family nowhere near this atrocity".

Then Eanmund had withdrawn from the crowd and Nick found him talking to himself quietly, on a fence nearby, mostly enshrouded in darkness.

Nick, unsure what to do with himself, approached Eanmund and asked, "What are you doing?".

"I'm talking to the Creator, telling him my concerns. Asking that he takes the innocent into his kingdom."

Nick knew that this was a private conversation, and decided he'd see if he could find his friend the Aenenya again; he was not ready to rejoin the family at the otter's home. The eels had brought back too many memories, and knowing the ceremony was happening left a strange feeling of sickness in his stomach whenever he considered it.

It was difficult to see the path along the waterfront in the dark mist. Nick stumbled often, and even fell several times, as he tried to venture back to the place he'd first met the Aenenya. He was dirty, with mud on his clothes, hands and knees. Nick also felt low considering the eels, his life, and how alien and alone he felt tonight, despite the hospitality of Eanmund's family.

Adding to his burden was an eerie feeling of being watched by unknown denizens of the deep. After seeing the eels rise from the depths, it was easy to imagine other heartless creatures watching him stumble down the coastline in his dejected state. This realization only served to bring him lower, the thought that something might be watching him struggle and enjoying it.

As he drew near the rock where he'd rested and met the Aenenya before, he thought he heard a familiar splash from the pulsing water.

And Nick began to realize she was talking. It wasn't words, but a feeling. A feeling that at first seemed to push him away, but as it grew, he realized she wasn't pushing him away in distaste, but she was issuing him a warning.

"Why?!" he asked, focusing his thoughts and feelings back on the water.

"Enemies! Danger! Violence!" was the black impression that flooded his thoughts.

Nick's mind jumped to eels, but it was a thought he put there. That was his context of danger tonight. But he also wondered if he had seen a shark-like image in his mind not of his own making.

"Flee, escape." his friend impressed upon him.

Like a man destined for the electric chair, he gave up in that moment, and replied back "No."

She was suddenly staring at him, right next to him. The splash she caused startled him, and she asked him "Why?!"

She was beautiful, in an alien way. But more human and feminine than anyone he'd seen since leaving reality... or Earth. He still wasn't sure which it was. But seeing her form he regained some composure, he was still male regardless of where he was, and his instinct was to impress. Perhaps those 19th century sailors and novelists were less imaginative than he'd previously thought.

He quickly considered his loneliness, and his foreignness. He wanted her to understand, but he didn't know how to make her understand him and these feelings that were plaguing him.

But she did, she heard those thoughts, and he felt it. He felt deep, deep, understanding. She was mostly alone too. And the ocean tonight was foreign to her; not as she expected or had ever hoped for. Whatever was going on out there was weighing down her thoughts as well.

And together they felt understanding. Briefly. It was odd, but almost happy. As though they'd both been searching for just that, understanding. He'd unconsciously drawn closer to her, and the water. She too had risen largely out of the water, and her arm drew around the back of his neck and pulled him in, kissing him.

It was fantastic. He'd missed "human" touch greatly, and he hadn't even known it. He was flushed with happiness and felt joy in her too, although it was reserved.

Suddenly he felt her grow in excitement, and the idea of escape seemed to come from her. She pulled slightly away and smiled at him, a wonderfully happy smile with a glint of an idea in her eyes.

And then she started pulling backwards into the water. Her arms were still around Nick. The night was dark and the bank was wet; Nick's balance had no ability to repulse her pull.

He was in the water. It was frigid and unexpected; a stark contrast to the warm excitement he'd just felt. She was still radiating with the thought of escaping with Nick, and Nick was still within her arms. He struggled to formulate his thoughts in a focused response as his body fought the cold and inability to breathe.

"No!... Can't... Breathe!... Help!... NO!....let me... go...".

She'd pulled him down about ten feet, which in the dark was absolute blackness to Nick. For some short period of time the blackness was what he saw, before the black transitioned to his thoughts. Nick wasn't aware anymore. But as he was fading he had felt that she'd realized something wasn't right.

It occurred to Nick that he was freezing. He started to reach for a covering, but came to the realization there was no covering.

And sore... he was very sore. He wasn't lying on a soft bed.

His eyes started to open. He struggled to identify where he was. The sky was a light blue, the light blue of pre-dawn twilight. A bird shot over his head.

He opened his eyes wider. He felt relief, but strangely it didn't seem to be his own thought.

A relieved sigh to his right focused his attention and he turned quickly to find the Aenenya laying beside him, a tear still in her eye as she stared at him, her chin resting upon her hand. It was apparent she'd been watching for some time.

She leaned forward and kissed his forehead. He reached for her, but she saw his arms and pulled away suddenly.

The emotion changed. She was apologizing, and slinking to the water's edge a short distance away.

He struggled to rise and chase her, but she was too quick and his body was much too beleaguered with cold, sore and tired.

There was a shared feeling of sorrow as she passed into the water and was gone. He watched the water where she disappeared in utter disbelief that her presence could be erased so quickly, cursing the water for its covering powers. Within seconds even the ripples left behind were extinguished, and the primordial pulsing of the lapping waves were all that remained.

Nick had stumbled to his feet, and was slowly beginning to traverse the path back to his residency at the otters'. The protest, the eel ceremony, the kiss, they all filled his thoughts as he stumbled on.

The sun was rising and the hills of Enbala were emblazoned with the brightest oranges and reds Nick could imagine, contrasting with the black and purple shadows cast by the majestic peak and forests. Dew sparkled everywhere, a surprising consequence of that dark and moody night time fog. If there was a creator, it was as though he was showing how easy he could wipe away the darkness of night with his colorful, bright and omniscient paintbrush.

Nick entered the village from a side path and again found himself struggling to recall where the otters' home was. If a society could invent floating energy balls, couldn't they invent house paint to help express their individuality?

He'd mentioned painting homes to Eanmund once. He'd only laughed and said, "What a vain culture you come from! We believe it is what is within the home that sets it apart."

Yeah, well, Nick couldn't see inside the homes when he was walking by them.

The oldest otter child appeared in the lane, likely on his way to take his position in the choir for the morning revelries.

"I'm glad to see you!" Nick shouted.

The young otter jumped, it was obvious he'd been engrossed in his own thoughts and Nick's outburst was not expected.

Nick followed up with, "I can't tell these homes apart still. Where am I?!"

The little otter shook his head and said, "We're three streets that way", pointing towards the mountain.

Nick chided, "What's such a little guy doing wandering around with such big thoughts?"

The otter was quick to respond, "You're one to talk man. Your thoughts and mouth always seem to be filled, but with what, my father is still not sure."

Nick was a little taken aback. "... Yeah, well... I'm just not sure I agree with your father on everything either."

"You say that so easily... but maybe that same thought weighs heavily on me. Then you suddenly yell at me and I jump."

"What do you mean?" asked Nick.

"Well, why should I care what the eels do, on our island or off? They won't listen to me. What influence will I have, so why should I let it weigh on my mind? Why does my father expect me to care about some eel ceremony?"

Nick thought, but not for long, and responded, "You'll have to figure that out. Sounds like you're beginning to think for yourself... it can be difficult to balance that with a respect of your father, when you disagree."

"But do I give my father's opinions the weight and bearing they deserve? My father is a good man, with convictions, and he deserves my careful weighting of his instruction."

Nick was surprised by this. Had he given his father's opinions "weight"? No, no he probably hadn't. It wasn't as though his own father's convictions had been unknown to him, he just hadn't respected them. The majority of his father's Christian views had gone against what his friends and school teachers were suggesting, and he'd been largely influenced by the latter. But now that he missed his father, he also realized that he should have listened to him more.

"I... I can't give you advice on this... Now get to revelries or you're going to miss it!"

Nick was thinking about his own father as he searched out the otter home three streets away.

As Nick entered the home, he practically collided with Eanmund.

"Good, you're alive." Eanmund said, without much passion.

"Yeah, I couldn't sleep after the eels showed up."

Eanmund replied, "I hope the confused man and the old record keeping otter weren't the only ones that had difficulty sleeping with the events of last night. Though I'm wondering who cared. The eels and their traditions are now on Enbala, not through war but through politics. I should have foreseen that. If only I'd been more active in that ridiculous island council"

Nick couldn't speak to that either.

"Yeah, I've got to get some sleep now."

"Not if you want to continue living in my home; it is day and we work. We are not seals, and I've had my fill of strange cultures invading this island. Come on, we are going to morning revelries and then the repository. Get your things."

Nick hadn't ever seen a large crowd at the repository but today there was one, gathered near the entrance.

Eanmund saw it too, and thought that his repository might be in danger so he burst into running. Nick decided to follow suit. For having short legs, Eanmund moved remarkably quick. As they ran past the last few towering trees before dropping into the valley the repository rested in, Nick found himself well back from his host. He wondered if the fierce running was an outlet for the anger Nick sensed burning in Eanmund this morning.

Catching up with Eanmund, at the edge of the circle of onlookers, he found a look of disgust on his visage.

On a patch of grass Vian was wriggling and writhing, like an earthworm drying on concrete.

"What the hell?!" Nick instinctually said. He knew Eanmund didn't know what that meant, but he also felt weird saying irreverent words near someone he thought of as religious.

"What is he doing?!" Eanmund kept yelling at an equally confused crowd.

Aelred, standing nearby, glared at the newcomers.

"Quiet! Do you have any respect?"

"Why should be quiet when this invader is behaving madly?" said Eanmund, stepping muzzle to muzzle with Aelred.

"He is mourning!"

"Perhaps there is pleasing news this morning! And why, may I ask?" said Eanmund.

"'Pleasing news?!' You would revel in another's pain? You are the friend of records and nothing else."

Eanmund paused, backing his nose a little away from Aelred's, "You're right, eel, otter, seal or man, tragedy I should hope for no individual. That is not my place. I am proudly a keeper of the repository, both in occupation and heart. Perhaps you should try the second part."

Aelred ignored the insult.

"He is mourning, in the way of the eels, for his queen. She is near death after last night's ceremony. It is physically trying for the female participant."

"Female participant to murder; yes, I imagine it would be" retorted Eanmund.

Nick had no need to imagine.

"Will she die?" asked Eanmund, out the corner of his mouth, loosely in the direction of Aelred, as they watched Vian begin a fresh round of flopping and crying in agony, throwing grass and mud into the air.

"It's unknown. She will stay on Enbala for some time, until she has strength to leave our doctors. She surely would have died if the ceremony had happened in the ocean."

"Hm." was Eanmund's response.

The crowd quietly watched the spectacle for some moments before gradually losing interest. Vian's labors seemed forced, and his endurance was lacking, making for long breaks between feigned periods of intense emotion.

Nick walked with Eanmund into the repository. Whether to Nick, or himself, Eanmund said, "She may still be on Enbala for The Restitution."

"That sounds formidable. What is 'The Restitution'?" asked Nick.

"Every 500th day we offer our finest santor to the Creator, as remediation for our falling short in his decrees. Do you not have something similar in your world?"

"Remember, I told you that our sacrifice system was abolished by the death of Jesus."

"Oh yes, the Creator's son. Truly a fascinating concept... the perfect sacrifice. But we still sacrifice. Although I dread this year's restitution. The Great Shark's ceremony is a stain on the island. I don't think we have a santor large enough, or perfect enough, to cover our shame."

"The santor is killed?"

"Yes, and a dab of his blood is placed on the forehead of anyone that wants reconciliation. Without such, we fear our supplications won't be heard because he can't associate with our unclean ways."

"Does the Great Shark require reconciliation too?" asked Nick.

Eanmund paused his perusal of the ancient records in front of him.

"Well, that's a fascinating concept. I've dug through the Great Shark scroll you've seen, looking for that information. While he certainly requires death, I can find no record that relates it to reconciliation. From what I can tell, the world has been mistakenly attributing our Creator's characteristic of forgiveness to the Shark, assuming they must be similar in deity. But when I read through their records, I find absolutely no opportunity for his followers to have reconciliation."

"When I was younger, and had longing in my chest, I collected my research into one scholarly record. Largely, it was direct quotes from known and accepted records, with only several editorial and explanatory notes. I thought I could prove to the world that The Great Shark offered no forgiveness; but only several reviewers within the repository ever saw the work. They said that the written word was not enough, the records were not enough. They claimed that a society could adopt a belief through verbal tradition combined with time. My record was then labelled as 'controversial', only to be seen by the extremely curious who come to the repository to review controversial works. It is not to be shared outside the repository. Last I checked, my work has been moved three times; whether that means it was opened, I do not know."

"But I still maintain that The Great Shark offers no forgiveness, he is simply bloodthirsty. A horrific God. Any attributes of forgiveness have been stolen from The Creator and mistakenly attributed to the Shark."

It occurred to Nick, as they sat cleaning dust from an ancient record, that Eanmund hadn't invented his beliefs, nor weighed a group of options and picked his favorites (as Nick had). No, Eanmund believed what the written records of the repository said. He trusted these documents more than he trusted his culture.

From what Nick had seen, not all Enbalans believed like Eanmund did. It seemed there were others, even on this religious island, that failed to believe the repository was a source of truth.

This was an "aha" moment, as Nick had never really understood why Eanmund was at odds with Aelred.

But who was right?

Nick thought that Eanmund was closest to the original sources. But could a religion adapt? Should it?

Nick decided that depended if the religion was originally truth, or made up. If a culture artfully produced the religion, then it was acceptable to adapt it. But if the religion was based on truth, then it couldn't be adapted, or it would no longer be truth.

So that was the question. Or rather the explanation of Eanmund's struggle. Eanmund believed that the records held the truths of the Creator. His progressive counterparts must think that the Creator's records are simply the invention of worldly writers, and subject to change at society's discretion.

Nick's head hurt at having thought so hard. He was left with the question, "Who was right?" and for that he had no answer. But he felt like he could respect Eanmund more, because he lived appropriately to his beliefs. He wasn't just stubborn, another thought that had occurred to Nick on occasion.

"We call on you to cancel this Restitution!" yelled the eel ambassador, to the Enbalan council.

The council chambers were packed, warm with body heat, and the tension was palpable.

In a cavernous room, surely built from the tallest and oldest Enabalan trees, the eel ambassador glared and up at the Enbalan council from the speaker's podium, which was made of a strange polished dark wood with hues of bright purple coursing through the grains. The walls behind the speaker had stairs and seats carved into their ledges, making the steepest stadium seating Nick had ever seen.

The floating energy balls of light seemed somehow richer in this room, and although the technology was still new to Nick, he could sense there was an air of antiquity to the large and beautiful examples shimmering above the crowds.

All eyes were on the ambassador as he called for the abolishment of The Restitution.

"Our Queen cannot be in the presence of such activities. It is completely and entirely unacceptable!" he reiterated.

A council member interjected, "Then take her back!"

Another council member corrected the outburst, "Eyalin, that can't be done. The doctors don't think she would survive attempts to move her until her condition improves."

The ambassador, red with anger, addressed the question.

"We would, of course, take our queen back, if only we could. But at this time she cannot be moved and we cannot allow her to be on the island during the heretical restitution you call The Restitution. Your feigned restitution is an abomination to The Great Shark, and puts the immunity we've allowed Enbala to act within at risk."

At this another otter jumped up.

"'The immunity' that you've 'allowed'?! What utterly putrid and disgusting words! I'll remind you that Enbala predates any known records of The Great Shark. You allow nothing; the Creator grants our right to be here!"

"And may I remind you," retorted the eel, "that our territories now surround Enbala. Whatever our disagreements regarding beliefs, you are no longer an isolated island floating in unclaimed territories. You rest among our territories."

"The waters surrounding Enbala are International territories!" shouted another otter from the council.

"And we surround and control access to those international territories."

"You are not the only denizens of the deep. What of our other neighbors; what do the whales, seals, turtles and Aenenyans say regarding your claims?"

In a shockingly dark manner, smiling oddly with his nasty teeth exposed, the eel replied, "The whales, seals and turtles avoid these waters. And I doubt that you shall see another Aenenya."

Nick thought of his dreamlike encounters and chills ran down his spine; it seemed that the eel was hinting at something. Had they attacked the Aenenyans?

Again, the eel sneered, saying loudly, "I call on Enabala, for the sake of peace and diplomacy, to cancel this Restitution."

"Peace? Is there a risk of non-peace?! Will we be attacked by the eels now?" asked the otter at the middle of the council. It was as though he'd just woken up to the threats of the eel. Years in council had made him apathetic, procedural and almost incapable of understanding words that didn't match his preconceived thoughts on a matter.

After some time the eel replied, slowly, reeking of deviousness.

"Of course the Deep State wouldn't officially attack... But, there are lawless and extreme gangs of Great Shark followers that do such things, and this Restitution will be an inviting scenario. I am here for your safety, to warn you. I am your friend."

At this Eanmund stood, "Nonsense! Complete and utter trash! Anyone with the slightest common sense knows your trained soldiers masquerade as these 'gangs'!"

The eel glared at him, feigned insult, then began gathering his belongings to exit the podium. After several seconds of this activity he looked up, and with a sense of drama hissed, "Let it be recorded that I warned you; the government of the Deep State recommends strongly against holding the Restitution while the eel

131

Queen is on Enbala. If you still hold the Restitution, you do so at an elevated threat of extremist attacks."

The room erupted in loud conversation.

"Quiet, quiet!" shouted the otter in the middle, as the eel and his brood slithered out the door.

"We must take a vote."

A weakly, old otter, near the end of the council, stood. He was shaking. The eel's threat had interrupted his comfortable old age with a threat to his existence. He was ready to do anything to regain the comfort he'd rested in moments before.

"I... I.... Well...Hear me please... I believe we should consider the eel's words. Would it hurt to miss one Restitution at the reward of ensuring continued peace?"

Eanmund was again on his feet, "What peace? Shall we forfeit our peace with the Creator for the reward of peace with the denizens of the Deep State?! Surely you can't be suggesting such a thing!"

The old otter looked at Eanmund and responded, "We do not all agree with your dogmatic regurgitations of the records, Record Keeper. A good creator would not turn on us for desiring peace."

"A good creator could not stand to be in the destructive hateful presence of the Deep State, and you are choosing to do their bidding. What is it that you do believe; folly of your own invention? Or perhaps we shall become the seals, without anchorage in any faith, tossed where-ever the waves may leave them; waves created by their own ever-swaying minds!"

At this the audience and council erupted. Almost everyone was yelling.

"Silence, silence!" was again called for by the middle otter in the council. After several minutes he was able, to a small degree, silence the room enough to be heard.

"There may be no need for this banter. Let us take a preliminary vote; shall the Restitution continue, despite the presence of an eel queen on Enbala? Raise your paws if you're in favor of performing the Santor rites, per our customs."

Giving Eanmund some respite from the furor he was in, the majority of the room raised their paws.

The middle otter said, "Thank you, let us discuss for a minute."

The council whispered among themselves. Several otters looked disgusted.

"Then there seems to be no need for further argument and division. Let the records show that the Restitution shall go forward, despite the dire warnings of the eel ambassador. Also, the council notes that we leaned towards absolving this Restitution, but the citizens have swayed us."

The room started buzzing again. One angry otter yelled, "Because you have lost touch with the citizens!"

"Quiet, quiet!"

As if to save face, the middle otter changed his tone and continued, "Further, let the records also note that the performing of the Restitution is as old as the records of our island, and that we continue performing the rites knowing that to discontinue them would be to lose a part of our island's identity This fact is irrespective of an individual's belief in the rites restorative power in regards to relationship with the Creator."

"What a fool." muttered Eanmund. "Without the Creator as the heart's focus, The Restitution would be as pointless as negotiating with the eels; an empty ceremony that would achieve nothing."

Restitution reminded Nick of the Christmas season. As it approached, the songs sung at the morning and evening gatherings changed, largely reflecting the upcoming ceremony. The island's citizens seemed in greater cheer as they were preparing, in the marketplace buying food, and around their homes, cleaning and tidying.

The cheeriness most surprised Nick. He even brought it up with Eanmund.

"Why is everyone so happy? It sounds like a brutal ceremony," he'd asked.

He hadn't expected the intense manner in which Eanmund was going to reply, but this was another subject Eanmund felt strongly about.

"Let's discuss that later, when we can sit and have a longer discussion."

Later that day they gathered around a table. Eanmund had also invited his oldest son to join them. Like Earth, there were fermented drinks, and this was one of the rare occasions where Eanmund was indulging, and offering the same to Nick, although not to his son.

Nick wasn't going to pass an opportunity to drink, but with the first taste he thought, "Whoa, that's weird!"

The drink tasted of the sea, but fermented and with an aftertaste of fish. He thought they must use seaweed as part of the production process.

He found himself pining for a strong bitter IPA beer. But then he remembered, maybe if he hadn't had a drink, he might not have had the accident which, presumably, left him stranded in this alternative world.

Months, maybe even a year, later (he hadn't counted days, and sometimes regretted that), Nick found that "alternative world" still didn't sit well with him.

Eanmund began today's teaching, slowly, contemplating his approach.

"Man, you said you thought the Restitution was brutal. Why?"

"Don't you slaughter a santor and place its blood on you?"

Eanmund's visage contorted into a weird grimace. Surprisingly, it seemed like his son had nodded in agreement with what Nick said. "Well, if that's how you think of the Restitution, brutal is the right word."

"But you're off Man. Way off."

"How? What don't I see?"

"You don't see that the brutality has already been committed, long before the santor is offered. The santor is the restitution, the payment."

"'Payment' for what? Your sins?"

"If that is what you call it, when you rebel against your Creator, then yes."

"But how do you know that you've rebelled? It's not like he tells you."

Eanmund paused before responding to the last comment.

"I sometimes can't believe you have been helping me in the Repository. You haven't taken in any of our writing's most fundamental concepts. Our Creator is unchanging; what he has illuminated as his standards, they remain. Many, if not all of the standards he has given us were written down and are accessible at the Repository. But... most know when they've transgressed."

"Ok, fair enough. But why the blood, and the santor?"

Eanmund again thought, and responded, "From knowing you, I fear you may not respond to my next question as I'd hope. But, let's try. As a youth, when you errored, were you punished?"

"Yeah, sometimes. But you're punishing the santor, not you. The santor didn't commit the deed."

Again Eanmund's son seemed to be nodding along to the words Nick spoke.

Eanmund looked to him and said, "Heed my words, son, not the foolish man. I asked you to sit in because I've noticed your recent leanings, and I thought you'd do well to hear this too."

Turning to Nick, he continued.

"And there is where you are wrong Man. The santor bears no punishment. They do not know they're alive. What difference is it to them if they die of sickness, old age, for food, or sacrifice? They simply are no more. Their mind no longer requires of them foraging or fleeing from danger. Oh... (smiling slightly) and we can't forget procreation. They never once considered their being."

Nick's modern American mind struggled with this. He haltingly asked, "How do you know?"... although something within him told him that Eanmund was correct.

"If you can't grasp that, and imagine the Santor is self-aware, then you will struggle with what I am yet to say. But, try to consider that I might be right. A santor does not know it exists."

"Now listen. The Santor is our most important animal; its meat gives us food, its skin provides for the records, it keeps the island's vegetation at bay, its refuse enriches our soil and we use its bones as tools. To lose a santor, and the rules require it to be our finest example, is a great cost to us, not the santor."

Nick thought, and said, "Ok, I can understand the loss, or price. But why a santor? When I was wrong, I was punished, not my pet."

"Can you believe, it's because the Creator is good?"

"That's just like a religion, when you're asked a hard question, redirect and respond with a question" Nick shot back.

"There was no redirect. He created you, so what can you give him? Will he take your flesh when you apologize for scarring his creation with your indiscretions?... No, he wouldn't be good if he hurt those that came to him in humility asking forgiveness."

Nick, again, responded in a sarcastic manner, "'Scarring his creation'? What, am I starting forest fires?"

"You might, but it needn't be that extreme. Because the Creator is good, his will is what's best for this world in all ways. When you transgress in any way, you hurt his perfect plan. Even in the small things. Can a good God appreciate those actions? Would he not, then, be a participant in harming his own goodness?"

"Ugh, this is making my brain hurt."

"I am trying to say that the santor is given with a repentant heart. It is a gift of something dear and important to us, and it is a thing that the creator gave us to use, so it's not outside of his plan that it be used as a sacrifice. It is a gesture that shows restitution is more important than the best things of Enbala."

Nick pondered this. "Ok… but shouldn't there be varying degrees of offering based on the severity of the screw-up?"

The otter's eyebrows raised. "I get the connotation of 'screw-up', but that is a new term for me."

This time Eanmund paused much longer.

"Now here's the conversations I enjoy. The deep. The contemplative. Those dealing with the most important concepts in the universe…"

"It does seem that the records point to the santor not ever being sufficient. That there's a greater restitution of some type at work, or going to happen. It's unclear in the records. It's partly why your Jesus stories fascinate and intrigue me. I mean, the sheer fact that you're not destroyed the moment you transgress points to some greater grace, preluding and extending beyond sacrifice, that hasn't been revealed to us."

Nick felt like he was on overload. He was grasping parts of this, but not all.

"Ok... but... why isn't the Great Shark just another name for the Creator? Why can't the Shark followers be associated with this Restitution ceremony? Why is there such a hoopla about the Queen being on the island during the Restitution."

"Their Shark requires that they work for him, enabling his dominance; he does not ever mention a desire for restitution. I've read the Great Shark records looking, and found no sign that he wants relationship. He wants duty. And he, and his followers, actively participate in the harming of the creation... but what Creator would work against himself? What creator would need to conquer his creation by harming it?"

"The Shark's followers recognize his aggressive, self-aggrandizing, unsatisfied character, and they emulate it. If they achieve, no matter the cost, they feel they've advanced the Shark's kingdom, and that they are in good stead with him. And they hate the idea that they can't stand before our Creator without making restitution. See, there is a humility necessary here. In their mind, they are already the sweet flavor in the mouth of the Great Shark, and it's an egregious insult to suggest that they need to restitute themselves before a Creator. To them, it diminishes their self-worth. And, especially for a Queen, this is unacceptable. It is only pride, but they hate The Restitution, and to have a Queen on island for the ceremony is the worst insult."

"The Great Shark asks that they conquer a dominion, not restitute themselves into relationship with a good Creator. And this, in itself, is silly. If the creator brought this world forth from darkness, he could conquer this world in the smallest whisper. This world is his, in the palm of his hand. A true creator can reclaim his creation with the slightest wave of his hand. But it's a testimony to love, and mercy that he engages the self-aware, and encourages them to restitute. And that's why we find such joy in the Restitution ceremony. It is a good God, allowing us to grow closer to him, in a forgiving and loving manner."

"Ok... I think I get it. And so, the Shark following eels are angry that you're insinuating that their Queen is unacceptable before the Creator? Just because the ceremony is on the same island as her?" asked Nick.

"Is pride not strong where you come from?" asked Eanmund.

"Pride? No, it is very strong," said Nick.

Then he had a large swig of his drink. What Eanmund was speaking made some sense, and this concerned Nick. He wasn't sure what to do with it.

Nick thought that he'd like to talk about these concepts with the mermaid-esque woman of the deep. Like the Arthurian Lady of the Lake, her mystery made Nick believe she must have wisdom; he wanted to run the words of Eanmund past her. He had no reason for this conclusion, but still he made it. He needed a second opinion, and she was the only third party he could think of. He was unable to understand these concepts on his own, or at least accept them. He didn't trust that he could make right and wrong judgements; it went against the post-modern American doctrine he'd embraced.

The morning of The Restitution started earlier than other mornings on Enbala. The oldest otter son dressed in a ceremonial robe for his choral performance, and left before the others to prepare his voice for the morning songs gathering, which also began substantially earlier than usual.

As The Restitution approached, Murin had produced a number of outfits for Nick that were simple and effective. But this morning she produced an outfit for him with additional garnishment, some gold borders and drawstrings produced something of a medieval effect. Eanmund, also, was bedecked in formal garb.

Walking to the gathering hall, searching, overcoming, reverberating basses and falsettos of a thousand singers of Enbala floated across the island in an ethereal way. The sun was still behind the mountain, and the light escaping around it was purple tinted, light stained with the black hue of the retreating darkness. Mist glimmered on any metallic object, and an overall aura of peace and beauty coated the island. The floating energy orbs were tinted a deep red in obvious homage to the day, but adding little light to the path, which seemed to (appropriately) slow the travelers. All felt different, all was painted in the richness of ceremony.

"This singing... it reminds me of the night I arrived." Nick whispered.

"Yes... that was our celebration of the Creation; also a holy day," was the hushed, but happy response.

Nick hadn't considered that not all otters attended daily services, but it was apparent they hadn't been by the unexpected and unusual large droves now entering the monstrous hall. It seemed that some were re-acquainting themselves, as they wandered around staring up at the woodwork and decorative flourishes.

Three rows of singers lined the entire inner-sanctum, serenading the entrants. The seats were filled to brimming, and Nick ended up sitting with the children, while Eanmund and Murin found seats closer to where their oldest son was stationed.

Roughly an hour of beautiful, harmonic, reverberating and airy canticles preceded the sermon. Then, a wizened old otter, with white in his fur, shared mostly the same Restitution points Eanmund had shared with Nick, though with less conviction in voice and body language. Nick wondered why Eanmund wasn't in front; he'd be more convincing.

Before being dismissed, the choir again rose, but now the music was celebratory, and loud. There were smiles, singing along loudly, and otters dancing in-place, which forced Nick to bite his cheek for fear of laughing. Otters dancing was both heartwarming, and hilarious.

There was no industry to rush off to, so after morning revelries the family, and others, lingered for a long time in the sanctum. The Restitution ceremonies would not begin until late afternoon.

Nick was relieved when they finally made their way to the house and brunch; he had no context for the familial inquiries made that morning, and had listened to the responses with little interest while his thoughts travelled prematurely to food. Now that food was on the horizon, his attentiveness (and mood) was improving.

After brunch Nick noted the family was changing their attire.

"Do I need to change?" asked Nick.

"No," Eanmund explained, "You're in fine garments for the spectator section. You'll enjoy The Restitution from the area where the tourists, ambassadors and others are permitted. It's removed from the ceremony, but within view. And the best news for you, there will be food. Do I know you now, Man?"

Nick laughed, "Yes, that sounds ideal. But why won't I participate?"

Eanmund stopped his gathering of items, and regarded Nick with gravity.

"Why?... Have you grown faith in our Creator? Do you want to restitute yourself before him?"

Nick quickly said, "No, I just thought it was a thing everyone did."

Eanmund sighed, a deep belly sigh.

"While I fear others may share your thought (more than I'd prefer to know), this requires faith and belief. It is not a 'thing' for 'everyone'. A real work is being done here, and unless you want to take action with the Creator, why in the world would you want to partake? Without the restitution, the santor death is the brutality you feared it was. Now you want to wear the blood of that brutality?"

Nick felt himself flush with embarrassment, and he responded, in a surprisingly loud way, "Why does everything have to go to the worst-case scenario with you?! Why couldn't you have just left it at 'this isn't for everyone'. Nope; now I'm brutally killing the santor myself!"

He turned and stormed out of the house. The children and Murin looked into his passing wake with open mouths.

He was headed for the ocean, and the spot where he'd previously met the mysterious mer-lady. He needed a break. Something different. Someone not Eanmund. He needed someone that talked less, and listened more.

There it was, that old pain in his heart. He missed his mother. It didn't matter which world he was on now, she wasn't there. She had listened to him, even when he was wrong.

She, also, had believed in restitution through blood. The blood of Jesus. It was bizarre how both worlds had come to similar conclusions.

She'd always been so empathetic and warm to him. He missed that dearly. He wanted the best for her; he wished his mother to be in Heaven, as he headed towards the ocean, hoping to find another understanding soul.

Thinking of his mom, he also came to memories of his father. Nick's soul was troubled. Loneliness sat on his chest like a heavy black rock, making it hard to breathe or look forward in the world before him.

Nick stood at the water's edge, staring out at dark clouds meeting with a darker sea. The weather had changed dramatically since the beautiful morning, with black clouds rolling in; the dark tones they brought reminded Nick of his time in the eel enclosure. A chill in the air added to the feeling.

It was quite at the water's edge. The rest of the island was congregating near the pasture lands, around the traditional sacrifice area. Haunting, brooding, floating vocal solos floated down to Nick from the looming grass hills, as various musicians added their skills to the day's festivities, serenading the gathering crowds with suitably somber, pensive and celebratory carols.

Nick scanned the black and grey, searching for any break in the unsure mist. He received no reward. Strangely the water appeared as-if in a doldrum, not even stirring to foam the break where it kissed the island, despite the chilly winds above it.

Yet, Nick felt that perhaps he heard "... danger...", but it was faint, and very far off, if he hadn't imagined it.

After a half hour the cold and loneliness were realized in sufficient portions, and Nick decided to join the crowds at the island's visitor Restitution viewing area. Eanmund has previously mentioned the location of the spot where visitors viewed the Restitution. Nick realized that was where he belonged today, if anywhere. He was only a visitor, at best.

As he approached the visitor viewing area, at the bottom edge of the hills and pasture land, he was shocked to find it filled with outsiders, including eels. Nick paused on the trail. A crab was approaching from behind him and he asked it, with some strain of fear in his voice, "Excuse me, but do you know why there are eels gathering?"

The crab was taken aback for a brief second, scampering backwards as he took-in the strange man form that had suddenly materialized before him and questioned him.

Clicking his pinchers together with instinctual warning, he slowly replied, "You're the man they've talked about... I thought you'd be bigger. Why are you asking me why the eels are visiting the ceremony? Don't they have as much right as anyone else?"

Nick swallowed, unsure quite how to respond.

"Well, yes, I suppose. But the otters told me the eels hate The Restitution. And I know they asked the island's council to cancel the ceremony because their Queen is recuperating in one of the village's buildings."

More clicking of pinchers.

"I don't know of that", the crab replied, "but I did hear that the eel delegation was going to present an award to one of the otters for his hospitality hosting one of the eel's youthful representatives. Perhaps they'll issue the award, and leave before the ceremony begins."

Nick turned and regarded the eels gathered at the viewing point. The crab must have seen his fear because he said, "Do you fear the eels man? Well, looking at you I can see why; it seems nature has given you little natural defense. Stay near me man, I am adept at fending off errant eels and you'll suffer no such issues by my side".

Together, the crab and man made their way up the trail and into the gathered crowd of non-believers.

When they reached the crowd, Nick noted that these particular eels looked like those that attacked the ship. Militant. They too took note of Nick, with squinted eyes and a few low hisses. Nick questioned ever coming up the trail, but decided his best recourse now was to stay very near this crab that had offered him security.

Higher up the hill were permanent and beautiful gathering areas, with ancient seating carved out of an almost black wood, fronted by a platform where most of Enabla's leadership gathered. The seats were arched, with intertwining vines carved throughout and wrapping them together, looking almost gothic in nature, the obvious work of master craftsmen who'd spent immeasurable hours carving.

On the stage, interspersed among Enabala's leadership, were several ceremonially draped eels, and Vian, the eel Aelred had been custodian of in the Repository.

From afar, Nick realized that Aelred must be the one receiving the reward, and soon his thoughts were confirmed. A pre-ceremony to the Restitution began, with Aelred and his eel companions standing on the stage before the mostly Enbalan crowds and leadership (although there were crabs and other ocean dwelling believers in the participant area).

An eel stood and spoke on the stage, and his words were clear and loud, heard even in the distant viewing area of the heathens.

"We thank Aelred for his hospitality, and openness, in sharing the cultural treasures the Repository holds with Vian, our eel representative. May this reward we bestow upon Aelred serve as a reminder to all cultures that we, the eels, are working towards a peaceful future for all."

The participant crowds cheered in enthusiasm up on the hill.

At Nick's viewing area, the enthusiasm was lacking. The eels surrounding Nick responded to this speech by hissing quietly and glaring towards the stage.

After Aelred received his reward, the eel delegates, and Vian, slithered off the stage. It seemed likely that Nick's crab friend was correct, and they were leaving the area before The Restitution began.

The eels in the visiting area made no motions to indicate leaving. They were at attention, and without humor. Glaring up at the island's gathering, watching in anticipation of the coming ceremony. Nick wondered why they remained; if they'd come to see Aelred receive his award, it was finished. And he couldn't imagine they wanted to be a part of The Restitution ceremony.

A number of singers, musicians bearing instruments, and choirs passed through the hilltop stage platform, each providing their heartfelt prelude to the ceremony as the eel delegation left the island. The rhythms were strong, with heavy use of minor keys and lilting melodies floating placidly over the deep chasms built by the heavy recurring notes.

Finally, one of the otters that frequently spoke at the morning gatherings, took the platform. He spoke another restitution message very similar to the one given that morning, although it was difficult to hear everything he said from the location of the visitor viewing area. Nick was sure the Enbalans were hearing every word from their nearby perches though.

Nick had stopped thinking about the eels, but a hiss brought his attention back to his fellow visitors. Several eels were writhing together, working themselves into a strange hysteria. He thought they were fighting, but it was strangely controlled, as though they were warming up for a battle.

Finding this odd, Nick decided he'd better find Eanmund and tell him. As he started towards the upper field an eel slid in front of him, placing his eyes directly before Nick's in an intense gaze, with a quiet but deeply threatening hiss, his smiling lips exposing his vicious teeth.

149

Nick suddenly saw a flash of orange and the eel's head flew away from Nick's face at a high rate of speed. Nick's companion, the crab, had delivered a strong pincher blow to the side of Nick's opponent's head.

"I don't know where you're going man, but it wasn't smart to leave me. I can't follow you any higher up this hill; The Restitution is no place for a soldier crab like me and I won't go up there."

It didn't matter anyway. Several fresh eels had taken the place of Nick's first assailant, and Nick and the crab soon found themselves fending off the slithering bodies right where they were. The eels weren't biting, but it was apparent that they were not going to allow Nick to travel any further up the hill.

Above them, the ceremony was progressing. A thunderous symphonic rhythm began, adding intensity to all that had preceded it. The speaking was done. A huge, young, deep grey santor strode forward at the beckoning of its keeper. It walked upon a trail of the leaves from the trees that surrounded the repository's hallowed halls.

The santor had caught the eels' attention, and they no longer busied themselves with harassing Nick and his friend, allowing Nick also to look up the hill.

The grey of the santor shimmered in a brief sunspot beaming through the clouds, and Nick thought that they must have poured oil upon its beautiful skin, which highlighted the shadows of muscular bulges across its wide body. It was the finest santor Nick had seen.

The otter that had given the earlier restitution message, now approached the santor with a large sword, unlike any Nick had seen on Earth. It was apparent it wasn't a weapon of war, but one of ceremony. Rare metals and jewels glimmered across it, and the blade had a serrated curve that was likely necessary for the strong skin of the santor. The otter had donned a robe of deepest red, which seemed almost to glow as several nearby energy orbs reflected off it.

Nick had earlier wondered why there were orbs in the middle of the day, and had thought the cloudy day warranted their inclusion. Now he saw that the orbs were positioned to highlight the ceremony, and he wondered if the same effect would be seen when the blood was shed.

The santor and the otter both strode towards a structure off the hillward side of the platform, between the visitor's area and the islander's seating area. Upon it, there was a gated enclosure, obviously used to hold the Santor in place (it reminded Nick of an oversized cattle chute). The santor walked forward into the cell, and a board was placed behind his rear legs, holding him in place. Jammed into the stall, his long and graceful neck dangled forward, over the front bars of the chute. At this time the otter placed his paw on the snout of the beast, which seemed to comfort it.

Suddenly, with his other paw, the otter thrust the sword through the neck of the santor. He must have placed the blade through the spinal cord because the santor's legs went slack instantly, the board behind the beast propping it forward, and up, so its head remained over the front of the chute. A hole in the blade of the sword allowed the otter to pull the sword down from both ends. As the blade edge fell through the bottom of the neck, blood began pouring out. At the knees of the otter, below the neck of the santor, a large wooden basin, stained a deep dark red from centuries of restitutions, gathered the blood.

As the blood flowed, the eels around Nick commenced screaming and hissing in a deafening and horrendous turmoil. But they were not content to only vocalize their disdain, violence was clearly their intent as they surged up the hill, towards the ceremony and its participants.

Their mannerisms, in attack mode, led Nick to instantly believe these were either the eels from the ocean raid, or similarly trained compatriots.

Nick also saw eels coming from low-lying areas around the restitution hill, and he realized this was a full-fledged attack.

The first eels were reaching the seating areas and mayhem was ensuing. Otters were trying to escape their seats, and below them the upward flow of the eels looked rather like a wave breaking over rocks, as their attack gathered. Some otters were being thrown wildly over the edges of the seating area into the grass below, either by eels, or by their own escape maneuvers.

Eels were grabbing, biting and throwing otters indiscriminately and with startling fervor. Grass, blood, ceremonial clothing and bodies were flying everywhere.

In the corner of his eye, Nick saw a lagging eel passing by him and, with shock to both him and the eel, he grabbed its tail with all his might and gave it the hardest pull he could muster, planting both legs and yanking back with his entire body.

Much like a lizard, the tail end gave way into Nick's hands and the eel screamed in pain as it whipped around and tried to bite Nick. He would have been successful, but again a flash of orange batted the eel's snout down and into the muddy ground.

Enraged the eel enveloped the crab and their fight became a crashing, careening mix of eel flesh and crab shell, slamming and rolling down the hill.

Nick, feeling indebted to the crab, dropped the tail and grabbed the nearest stick he could find. As the eel and crab ping-ponged down the slope, Nick chased them, offering his best baseball swings to any exposed flesh of the eel during brief interludes when the crab and eel seemed to be wrestling, rather than rolling. This went on for several minutes and Nick realized they were several hundred yards down from the visitor viewing area, approaching the edges of the village. An occasional building began looming up in their path of mayhem.

Finally, the rolling came to a stop against a large structure, tall, and similar to Eanmund's home. The crab and eel were still battling, with Nick offering his best swings with the stick when the eel was turned towards him.

The crab fought valiantly, dicing the eel's soft sides with his claws, but the sharp teeth of the eel were digging into the crab at every soft spot. Finally, they seemed to be wrapped in an embrace, with the eel biting the crab's head and both pinchers of the crab dug into the sides of the eel. Nick was smacking the eel with his stick for all he was worth.

But it was the crab claws that dropped from the embrace first, falling limpidly to the ground. Nick continued to beat on the eel, but it seemed to be regaining its strength without the crab's pincher's digging into its underbelly. It slowly uncoiled from the crab, and turned its head towards the incessant slapping of the man.

Nick saw the head revolving towards him, and his instincts told him it was time to run. He dropped the stick and darted away. Glancing over his shoulder, he saw the eel following him, not quite as fast but with sure intention.

Nick regretted dropping the stick. Without a weapon, Nick thought his best option might be to evade the eel among the buildings in the village. He ducked, dodged, zigged, zagged, and sprinted until the eel was not to be seen behind him. It had obviously lost much of its endurance in its efforts with the crab.

Where the steep pitch of one home's roof met the Enbalan soil, Nick saw a gap he could slide into, too small for the body of an eel. He rushed into this space. The inner wall of the residence met with the pitch several feet back, providing a triangular shelter of only several feet.

Nick struggled to control his breathing. He did not want his pursuer to hear him.

He turned his back to the wall, peering back through the logs making the roof slope a shelter, finding large cracks and fearing that his aggressor would catch sight of him.

From this vantage point, he found he was also looking back up the hill towards where the attack began. He saw two flare like fires launch from the ceremony area, flying impossibly high and fast into the sky for balls of fire, and then the whole island shook when a green dome seemed to materialize over it, flickering much like the windows in the repository, changing the grey gloom of the day to a frightening omniscient green hue, as all light now had to travel through the dome to reach the island.

Nick's gaze reverted back to the present, as the eel had found its way to Nick's roofline. He must have smelled Nick, because he stared at the roof as if he knew his prey was hiding behind its protection. He slid forward, dropping to the ground and looking through the small space between the roof edge and the ground. Seeing Nick's legs he began to bite the roof, tearing away chunks.

Nick thought furiously. How could he live through this ordeal?

The idea that came to Nick was to reach Eanmund's home. Maybe Eanmund had escaped the melee on the hill, and would have a weapon that could repeal the attack of the eel. Or, maybe Nick could find a weapon even if Eanmund wasn't there. Anything, even a kitchen utensil would be better than nothing.

Nick burst through a crack on the far side of the roof, opposite from where the eel was ripping the roof edge away from the home. Unfortunately, the eel saw Nick exit, and the chase began anew.

It was the same as before. Nick running, weaving, dodging and hiding, with the eel ever-present in pursuit. Finally, Nick saw Eanmund's home and rushed to it, bursting through the entryway.

The oldest son of Eanmund dove behind the seats in the family's gathering area.

"What are you doing?!", yelled Nick.

"What am I doing? I'm here to change clothes after my performance. Then I'm heading to the ceremony. What are you doing, crashing in?!"

There wasn't time to explain as the eel began slamming into the doorway.

"The eels are attacking!" shouted Nick. "How do we fight back?!"

"How would I know?!" asked the otter. "We are an island of peace, not war!"

The loud banging continued, shaking the home, and openings began to appear in the door where the eels biting and ripping teeth were piercing through the portal.

"Is there a place to hide? Why not under the structure, where the food is stored?" asked Nick.

"Yeah, good idea! Let's go."

Nick opened the hatch and the youthful otter crawled in. At that moment the eel crashed into Eanmund's home.

Nick dropped the hatch door with only the otter inside.

Nick turned and ran. The eel's nose pounded him squarely in the back and he flew forward about ten feet, landing next to the closet doors built into a hollow on the central pillar of the residence.

Nick rolled into the hollow, narrowly avoiding the snapping teeth of the eel. He pulled the doors closed behind him.

Again the eel took to ripping and slashing at the wood. The whole house began shaking as each tearing bite of the eel reduced the structural strength of the central pillar. Eventually the eel tore an opening large enough to place his head into. He slithered his head into the hole and said, "Prepare to die, Man."

A crack, like that of nearby lightning, punched their eardrums as the central pillar snapped.

Giant structural roof beams began raining down as the central support collapsed. As each hit the floor it shot dust into the air, and within several seconds nothing could be seen but a haze. Continued crashing, thudding and cracking sounds of the structure collapsing overloaded Nick's auditory sense.

As the noises quieted, and the dust retreated, Nick found himself in the fetal position, still tucked away in what remained of the central beam's hollow core, now open to the air above him. Nick slowly stood. A beam laid on either side of his hollow, and one dangled from overhead nearby, threatening to fall from what little remained of the structure. After some little time had passed, and it seemed certain there would be no more falling, Nick ventured out of his hollow.

Nearby, the eel lay dazed and wounded. A large timber had fallen across his back, trapping him and greenish fluid oozed out from under his body.

"Help me Man", it croaked.

Nick, seeing a sharp sturdy broken wood beam, picked it up and walked to the eel.

"Help me" the eel again begged.

Nick looked in its eyes. Even in this moment of need, the eel's eyes spoke only of evil and treachery.

Nick was done. Nick didn't want to worry that the eel might free itself. Nick didn't want to fear the eel again. And Nick was angry. He brought the sharpened beam up with both hands and drove it down into the eye of the eel, presuming its brain lay somewhere behind that hideous yellow orifice.

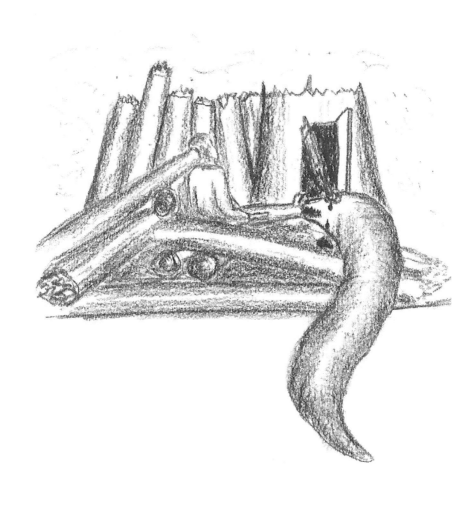

The eel's head began writing with such intensity that the stick, now sticking up and flaying back-and-forth, struck Nick with a force that toppled him backwards. When Nick fell, the back of his head struck the corner of a broken roof beam and Nick lost consciousness.

On the hill, mayhem ensued. When the eels attacked it took everyone by surprise. After all, the eel delegation had just presented Aelred with reward for his diplomatic efforts. An eel attack was, possibly, farther from the thoughts of the citizens than it had ever been.

Within the seating area, a stampede of otters had pressed towards the small ancient exits. Before the eels ever reached them, otters were being bumped over the edges of the stands and trampled underfoot. It was difficult to tell if the red blanketing the stands was discarded robes or the blood of fallen, but it was surely a mix of both.

When the eels reached the otters, their modus operandi was to bite them, then, with their sharp teeth embedded, snap their strong necks suddenly backward while releasing their jaw; this would throw the otters into the air and largely leave them stunned and out-of-breath when they landed, ripe for carnage, if there weren't others immediately available for the eels to turn their terroristic actions towards.

Eventually an otter remembered the island's shield system and ran to activate it. Instantly several distress mortars fired into the air and the island's shield deployed, enveloping most of the lower lands in the green hue Nick had seen. At the same time, an energy pulse distress signal was sent to the mainland; the gathering energy of this pulse is what Nick had seen rising in the air.

The responding mainland seals were on the island quickly. Their military had airborne vehicles that used energy, rather than Bernoulli's Principle, to stay aloft. By using energy for lift and fuel, the machines could be streamlined and the seals could fly faster than Earth's planes (which are encumbered by onboard fuel, and subject to air's dragging effect on wings).

The eel's must have known the seals could be there quickly and had plans to address it. The energy blanketing over The Restitution served like a spoken command. When the eels saw the balls fire upwards, they immediately turned and headed for the sea, leaving in their wake the punctured and broken bodies of numerous otters.

It all had happened relatively quickly; but the eels had caused mass destruction, directly and indirectly. Several of the viewing areas had collapsed, and everywhere otters were writhing in the pain of their bites as the air re-entered their lungs and they recovered their wind after their flights, falls and fights.

Because the seal pilots could see the crowds at the ceremony from the sky, most landed there initially, leaving the eels to disappear into the water's edge. While the protective dome should have kept them in, there were numerous inland tributaries for the eels to disappear into along their path to the sea. Only two were captured by pilots who had spotted them heading for the sea as they approached the island.

Medically trained animals began providing triage up on the grasslands, as the seriously injured were moved back to town and, in several cases, flown to the mainland.

There was a surreal aura in the pasture lands. The dome was still in place, and the new, green-tinted, calm, which followed so shortly after calamity, was too much for some of the emotional to take-in and they sobbed uncontrollably.

The seals set guards at watch points around the entire island. An eel invasion had long been a possibility, and most on Enbala didn't know the seal military trained for responding to this scenario.

Only a day before the Enbalan citizens would have passionately protested the presence of seal military guards on the island, but with the events of the Restitution there was little, if any, pushback. In fact, it seemed most otters were happy to welcome the seal's military protection to the island.

Mark received the hospital's call at work. Nick was moving in his bed, and the machines were recording more brain activity than had previously been seen.

This was big news, worthy of celebration, but it also complicated things. Mark had been working with a lawyer, the hospital, a private nursing company, and the local hospice to bring Nick into his own home although he was still in the coma and reliant on feeding tubes to survive.

"Mark, this is Dr. Rosenwald, Lead Physician. Everyone here at San Gabriel's knows how devoted you've been to your son, so I personally wanted to call and give you the news", she'd said.

Now Mark was preparing for yet another weekend trip into the desert.

Could it be? Would his son come out of the coma?

What would he remember?

Would he be the same as he was before, mentally?

Nick's body had lost much of its muscle, but that could be restored.

Mark could think of little else as the work week progressed.

He found himself praying often, and only for Nick. Sure, there were other things happening in his life, but they all seemed to pale in comparison to Nick's plight.

During one break, Mark found a back storage-room and shed a tear or two.

Unexpectedly a youthful coworker barged in looking for supplies.

The youth saw Mark, and his eyes fell to the floor.

Mark, being a "Man's Man", realized he felt embarrassed at his tears.

"Sorry."

"Sorry."

They both apologized at the same time.

Mark said, "No, this is no place for personal issues. I'll be getting back to work. Get what you need."

But the youth replied, "We all know what you're going through... I hope that if anything ever happens to me, I can handle it with the same strength you have."

And he closed the door and was gone, without taking anything.

Mark wanted to yell after him, "What strength, you moron?! I'm sitting here crying! What the hell are you talking about?! Come back here, get your crap, and ignore this silly old man!"

But he just took a deep breath, stood, folded the metal chair up, and leaned it against the wall. It was time to go back to work.

Nick couldn't abide waking in this familiar place again. His eyes opened to a scene reminiscent of the cell he first stayed in when he came to this world. He was wrapped up, and the omniscient green light from the walls was bathing everything; Nick knew he must be in another medical treatment center.

Nick started yelling and thrashing.

"Hey! Hey! Where am I! Someone! Get in here! Talk to me!"

As he yelled, he remembered running from the eel.

"Let me go! What happened?!"

Then he realized he wasn't permanently bound.

He wriggled his upper body out of the cloths, and lifted himself into a sitting position.

An older otter, with a kind disposition, rushed into the room.

"Are you ok?! I'm so sorry, we're quite busy and we weren't sure when you'd wake up."

Nick asked, "Am I ok? Don't you know?"

"Well", she replied, "we scanned you and you seemed ok. There's a large bruise at the back of your neck, and we assumed that's what caused you to lose consciousness, but we don't see any muscular, nerve, or bone damage. I'm asking if you're ok in case there are symptoms you feel that we couldn't see while you slept."

Nick felt a little embarrassed.

"I'm sorry... I was being chased by an eel... I think he's dead, but that's the last thing I remember."

"I was told there was only one eel that lost its life today. Plenty of otters did though. We are very busy with those that were injured. And... on that note, when you feel well-enough you are free to leave. You'll see the exit when you pass through the room's portal. I'm afraid I must get back to those in need. The teeth of those vile eel creatures do so much damage; they puncture and infect everything. The infections are like a timed-delayed second attack."

And she was gone.

That was it?

Nick didn't need to sign a bill, a waiver, or something?

Several of his outer garments were laying nearby, and he began putting them on. They were very dirty and torn. This only added to his alien feelings. Dressed, he paused a moment before heading for the portal out. He didn't know exactly where he'd find himself, or if he would draw attention in his ragged clothes.

In the hall numerous medical personnel were rushing down the hall with purpose, taking in little to nothing of those things that were outside their missions. The torn and soiled clothes of otters lay everywhere in the hall, as well as a few sobbing otters. Some otters had minor injuries, and others were presumably mourning a loved one within a nearby room. No one noticed Nick. It was the first time in this world that he'd felt as though he wasn't of interest.

Once outside, Nick wound his way towards Eanmund's home. Or, at least, what remained of it.

Seals with military-like uniforms were everywhere. One rushed straight up to Nick and said, "At your earliest convenience our commander wants to talk to you. He's stationed down at the town's docks. It is imperative you go there immediately. I will escort you. Be prepared, you will be leaving the island."

"What... Why?!"

"I wasn't told. My orders are to bring you to the command center, and provide you the details I did."

"Well, can I at least tell my host family? They need an explanation. I fought with an eel and destroyed their home."

The seal seemed to snort, "You... 'fought with an eel'?"

"Well, mostly I ran from it and got lucky, but in the end, yes... I killed that eel... I remember now... I stabbed it right in the eye with a sharp board."

Nick's body gave an involuntary shudder as he thought about that moment.

The seal's eyes grew large.

"That was you?... I already know the house. Yes, I can escort you there first... I think you've earned it."

They picked their way through the crowds. Everyone was outside: Enbalans, tourists, delegates, and seals. And absolutely everyone was discussing the day's events, and what was to be done.

As they approached Eanmund's, Nick saw the family standing next to the destroyed home, surrounded by a large gathering of seals. When they came to the edge of the crowd, Nick shouted "Eanmund! It's Nick!"

He saw Eanmund look towards him with a ferocity that startled him.

Eanmund began pushing through the crowd, making a path to Nick.

When the final otter gave way, Eanmund exploded out the side of the crowd, running to Nick, and slamming him squarely with both paws in the middle of Nick's chest.

"What have you done Man?!" he yelled.

Nick was going to fall backwards, again, but the seal extended a flipper and saved him from toppling over.

This only allowed Eanmund to continue pounding Nick in the chest.

"Why?! Why did you come here?! What possibly possessed you?!"

"What...?" Nick began to ask, but couldn't get any other words out because the otters flying paws had begun striking him wildly everywhere, including his face.

Otters grabbed Eanmund, pulling him back, and the seal came between them.

"I think it's time to see the commander, Man", said the seal.

Nick was beyond confused.

An otter slipped away from the crowd and approached them.

"Do him no harm otter, he's under the protection of our commandant" said the seal.

"Does he know?" asked the otter.

"What?" Nick asked.

"Eanmund's son was killed when the home fell."

Not one of Eanmund's paws could come near the power with which those words hit Nick. His soul broke realizing that he was responsible for the death of Eanmund's son.

And Nick couldn't escape his omniscient self-pity either; his soul also broke knowing that Eanmund would no longer be there for Nick. In that moment he realized that Eanmund had been something of a father figure, and he'd just ruined the relationship.

The news-bearing otter studied Nick's dumbfounded face.

Nick couldn't think how to reply.

"I... I... I'm... sorry?"

The seal, seeing how pathetic Nick was, barged in.

"Come on man, we need to get to the Commander."

They walked down the hill, towards the docks where Nick had arrived. Now, it seemed, this was also to be where he departed from the island.

The Commander was under orders to bring Nick to the mainland. Nick was to be questioned by the seal's Council on Oceanic Affairs.

Nick spent several days at the seal's base camp next to the docks, before he left for the mainland. They said he wasn't a prisoner, but he was certainly detained. All the while, he wondered if Eanmund might come down to talk about The Restitution day's events, but he received no visitors. It was as though the island had quickly and willingly forgotten him.

When the day arrived to leave for the mainland, Nick was partially relieved. Boredom had set in at the seal camp. He was given some menial tasks, like helping prepare the meals and gathering the waste, but mostly he'd been very bored. The seals had little interest in Nick, and some seemed to disdain him as the cause of all the trouble. Few spoke to him, and those that did only offered commands to aid him in his camp duties.

Nick left the camp, and Enbala, on another floating ship. This one was governmental in nature, lacking some of the amenities of the ship that had brought Nick to Enbala, and transporting only seal personnel except two other passengers.

Nick was shocked to see Aelred, and the eel, Vian.

"What is that eel doing here?!" he yelled, running to step in front of Aelred and Vian, as they entered the ship.

"Arrest this eel! This traitor!" Nick yelled.

Aelred stopped patiently and glared at Nick, as did Vian.

Several seals approached Nick and began pushing him away from the new arrivals.

"Quiet Man, they also will speak before the council."

"What?!", Nick yelled confused, as he resisted their physical and painful chest bumping and prodding flippers.

"Vian should be arrested, or whatever it is you seals do to enemies."

"You need to be careful, Man," one of the seals barked, "You're lumping Vian in with the terror that befell the Restitution only because he is an eel; he did not contribute to the actions of the eels that you witnessed. There were witnesses that maintained that Vian remained with Aelred throughout the incident."

"He was part of the planning! He must have known!"

"You can't make biased statements like that. Perhaps on Enbala, but when we reach the mainland such disparagement can get you sent back to the enclosure at the edge of the world. Vian is an ambassador of the eel government, who passionately deny any fore-knowledge of the attack. They say it was perpetrated by simple, common eels, who were enraged at their queen being on island during The Restitution."

"What about the eels that you captured? Is that what they say as well?"

"Well... only one captured eel remains. And he's presently being escorted onto the ship as well. Strangely, he killed the other captured eel in their enclosure while we waited for passage off the island. But he maintains that he acted of his own accord, he was not sanctioned."

"But…" the seal pushing Nick whispered.

"But nothing" barked back the seal that had been talking to Nick.

"But what?", said Nick.

The second seal continued, "… but I can tell he's military. He undoubtedly has a military bearing, although he denies ever taking part in eel military campaigns. It's hard for a soldier to act as a civilian, and this one does it particularly poorly."

They were now at a distance from Aelred and Vian, and the seals had stopped pushing Nick.

Several guard crabs were now escorting an eel through the door, much as Nick had been escorted at the compound, pincher drawn back and ready to strike.

The first seal, with Nick, had begun barking at the second seal, "You are an eel bigot! I will report you to the Ministry of Bigotry!"

The second seal replied, "Stating a truth doesn't make me a bigot. You haven't seen a pattern yet?! Isn't it convenient that these vigilante eel attacks always seem to happen where their leaders might find an attack advantageous?"

In rage the first seal started barking "Bigot, bigot, bigot!" and as he snapped his jaws at the second, he started barking, stuck his chest out, and repeatedly bumped him.

The second seal threw his head back and barked, "Fool, fool, fool!" Then the second seal began bumping too. They were chest bumping and yelling loudly, their noses pointed to the ceiling. Everyone in the ship looked towards them.

Their Commander, a large seal, rushed in, bouncing both seals back several feet as he chest-slammed into them. He also knocked Nick to the ground in his hurry.

"Quiet, both of you! You are soldiers, not politicians. It is not up to you to decide what is right. Show that you are seals! Remember, the multitudes are welcome on our beaches."

The second seal muttered, "But we have to fight the eels, and clean up after them, not the politicians."

The Commander bit the second seal with such force that he barked excruciatingly at the pain and shrank quickly away.

The Commander spun on Nick.

"Not another word about the eels until you stand before the Council and answer their questions!"

There was an empty seat for Nick along the wall, far from Aelred, Vian, and the eel prisoner. In acquiescence, Nick quickly and silently took his seat. And there he planned to remain for the entirety of the trip, wanting nothing to do with his fellow travelers, be them eel, seal, crab or Aelred.

The Mainland

Nick had seen nothing of the mainland, despite being there for almost an entire day.

They had disembarked the ship at night, directly into a dreary governmental building of the seal's. There had been rooms made up with makeshift beds but Nick had slept little, and he was nervous about this inquest the seals were hosting. Without windows in his pod, he was again a prisoner, and had spent many tortuous hours staring at the ceiling, wishing for a small ball to throw against the wall.

Nick's seal guards had no desire to talk with him, nor need, as they were commonly switched-out in some form of a rotating duty post. The turn-overs were funny, generally consisting of barking, and chest bumping, noses turned to the ceiling with bare teeth glistening. Each shift turn-over there was an air of competition, and a note of winner and loser at the conclusion. Nick couldn't see how they could go about the turn-over bump dance day-after-day with continued ambition.

Finally, late in the evening, a seal barked out that it was time for Nick to get ready, the inquest was nearing. Despite his fears, he was glad to finally be on-the-move.

The hallways of the seal governmental building were just as dull as his pod had been. Grey benches, met grey floors, with grey ceilings above. All the grey had a rough, hard and glossy finish, seeming to imitate the rocky shorelines where seals are often found.

While the buildings at Enbala had seemed spartan, this building made Enbalan assembly halls seem as though they were decorated for the Mad Hatter's tea party. Grey on black on grey.

Nick chuckled to himself, thinking that the grey seemed to match his captor's; differing shades of grey fighting for dominance.

They accessed the Council's room through a large portal which swiveled open as they approached. Nick and his three seal captors passed through comfortably despite being abreast. The room they found themselves in was commensurately as expansive.

Similar to a Roman amphitheater, staired platforms rose from the central landing. The room was filled; eels, seals, crabs and otters peppered the platforms, along with some less populous creatures like seahorses, and frog-like beings (these were new to Nick because he'd been entirely near salt-water, and these were fresh water beings).

An ooze of water emanated from the upper parts of the room and cascaded down the steps, leaving each platform drenched. Nick noticed the otters were sitting on small carved pedestals, allowing them to avoid the water.

The seals kept Nick moving towards a closed-off section along the far wall. As Nick passed beside the crowd, he realized Eanmund was sitting on a platform just off his left, and he was in a heated debate with the three otters that accompanied him.

"Eanmund! Eanmund!", Nick yelled, stopping for a second, as a guard seal bopped him in the back with its wet cold nose, forcing Nick to regain his pace.

Eanmund looked a little surprised as his eyes flashed to Nick, but then his brows furrowed in anger and he turned not-only his head, but his entire body away from Nick and towards those he was engaged in dialogue with.

Depression washed into Nick's emotions. A cold, blue emotion, which paired well with this grey environment.

He was ushered into an enclosed seating area, to an awaiting carved pedestal. He sat, dreading the coming proceedings.

An eel was brought in with seal guard escorts, and also led to the holding area. The eel's guards positioned him several platforms down from Nick. It turned, and glared at him.

"What?", Nick growled, looking down at him, regarding him with some attitude of hatred.

The seal guards, noting the interaction, responded to Nick, "Do you recognize this murderous traitor from Enbala?"

"Traitor?" Nick responded, confused. The eel could be called a lot of things, but he wasn't sure how traitor fit.

"Yeah, this friendly slimer, one of the two eels we captured, turned on his cellmate and ate a large portion of him."

It dawned on Nick that he might recognize this eel from the crowds that were watching The Restitution near him.

Suddenly the eel lunged for Nick, its sharp teeth snagging Nick's garments near his feet. Nick yelled out, kicking furiously at the eel, but he couldn't get it to release. With small nipping motions it was creeping closer to his leg.

Nick winced as pain suddenly reached his brain, and he saw his pants soaking to red as the blood drenched into the Enbalan cloth.

The seals were on the eel now, chest bumping, flipper slapping, nipping, barking loudly, and pointing their snouts to the sky in an effort to feign dominance.

Eventually a crab scrambled up and latched onto the tail of the eel with its claw, which won Nick's release.

Nick glanced towards Eanmund, only to find Eanmund was the only one in the room not watching the drama unfold; Eanmund's back was still squared away from Nick, despite the commotion.

While the crabs and seals tumbled onto the thrashing eel, Nick pulled his leg away and inspected the damage.

There were several teeth marks oozing a deep red. Another seal had scrambled to Nick and began applying a dressing.

While the drama had enfolded several very rotund seals had gathered on the central floor; their silky complexions and frilly costumes indicated that they were of status. They were watching Nick and the eel with unamused looks, and one of them could be heard saying, "Positive! Positive! The room will have positive energy! Positive!"

For several minutes after the incident the seal in front kept repeating the "positive" appeals.

The eel was still thrashing, now netted and held down by four seals.

Nick noticed there were eels in the crowd around the room, and they were glaring angrily at the eel causing the ruckus. The eels in the crowd looked suspiciously similar to some of the same delegates that had gifted Aelred at The Restitution, thought Nick.

The flushed and flustered seal yelling "positive" finally concluded, "If the eel cannot recover his positive energy he shall be removed from the room. He shall not influence our review of the incidents on Enbala negatively."

Nick wasn't sure, but he thought that sounded stupid. Couldn't the eel's disposition speak to his actions on Enbala?

The eel's guards dragged him from the room, while he writhed and snapped.

"Positive! Positive!" the seal resumed.

It became apparent they were calling the inquiry to order. Nick looked around; there was little positivity in the room. The seals, eels, otters, crabs and others present all looked agitated.

A small seal came forward to introduce the proceedings, "We shall discuss the incidents on Enbala, and how to avoid a similar incident in the future. Today is not a criminal processing, but a truth seeking, with legal ramifications. The Seal Council's Enbalan sub-committee is here to issue rulings, if needed."

An otter yelled out, "Of course they're needed, we were attacked by the eels, you dry noses!"

One of the rotund seals at the front barked "Positive! Throw that otter out! We shall have positive energy! The eels did no such attack, individuals did. 'Each is responsible to themselves', as our laws state. I hope you all understand that."

Seal and crab guards mobbed the outspoken otter, and dragged him out, just as physically as they'd done with the eel, although he was not resisting.

One of the rotund seals wriggled forward from the on-stage pack. In a ludicrously high-pitched voice he began, "For the records, at the 2,217th Restitution, on the island of Enbala, on the first day of the festival, a small group of eels attacked the proceedings causing mayhem, destruction and even death. The involved parties shall speak regarding this attack."

"The victims shall be allowed to share their memories. But, (and I remind that I speak for the Seal Council) as we have previously stated, the otters choose to bring undue attention upon themselves by practicing ancient and unlearned religions. These random occurrences are likely to happen until the otters accept the seal practices of harnessing positive energy in the atmosphere, rather than relying on a hope in a 'creator'."

"Now, it is negative energy that points to wrong in others, yet the otter religion continues to claim that beings can error based on application of outdated teachings of ancient mystics. The Seal Council is beyond this error and knows that there are only those that can exist within society, and those that can't; there isn't a need to lower ourselves into negative energy in dealing with these matters. You shall all respect each other with positive energy while within this venerable seal gathering place."

"And now, otters, please be precise and to-the-point. Why should the seals do anything further in this matter? Bring forward those that speak for you."

Eanmund approached the center of the room but when he reached it, he stood in a way that allowed him to keep Nick behind his back.

"Seals, why am I here?!... I am a keeper of The Repository, I store and treasure the mystic teachings you profane. And now, in my hour of tragedy, you require my presence and have the gall to request that I dismiss my beliefs also?"

"Positive Energy!", barked a rotund seal, his head thrown back, nose to the air. "We will have none of your ancient beliefs."

The squeaky voiced one echoed this interjection, comically.

The smallest seal, that introduced the inquiry, said, "Please, Keeper of the Repository, tell us only what happened and how we can assist."

Eanmund was exasperated, and he finally looked towards Nick, "It seems you are back among your faith now, Man".

Another seal barked, "The events!"

Eanmund was quiet for a long minute, drew a breath, and said, "We were attacked by the eels, and they killed my son. If you care for the plight of others, you should impose punitive actions against the eels and their deep, dark kingdom."

He said it loud and fast, so that all in the room could hear it.

The room burst out with conversation, yelling and interjection.

The fat seals of the council kept barking about "positive energy", although it was clear these words had no effect on the crowd.

The eels were hissing, and shouting "Negative energy, negative energy."

Otters and crabs throughout the crowd were shouting their support of Eanmund. Others were talking loudly among themselves.

Another one of the Seal Council's delegates began speaking, his chubby jowls jiggling, "Who has the veracity to make this statement?! Did all the eels attack your son? No! One eel attacked your home. And several others attacked the island. These are the criminals. Do not disparage our neighbors of the deep! You have one more chance, Keeper. Can you add value to today's efforts?"

Eanmund now glared at the seals he addressed.

"How long until they turn their attention on invading the mainland, seals?" Eanmund asked.

All of the seals began shouting at Eanmund to stop talking. But he didn't.

"You sit here, saying 'All that matters is positive energy', while your weaker neighbors are destroyed by the eels. You say it is simply cultural growth and mixing, while the eels overrun community after community by terror and violence. But one day, while you bark 'Positive! Positive!', the eels shall be ripping your throats out by the daggers that are their teeth, and the last thing you will see is the hate that is in their eyes."

The room erupted into mayhem.

Several seals were forcibly bouncing Eanmund out of the room, almost before he'd finished his speech.

The eels were yelling that they wanted their chance to speak.

The jiggly-jowled seal spoke, while Eanmund was removed out of the chamber, "I sentence that otter to one hundred days of service to the Conglomeration of Seals. Hopefully, in serving the seals, he shall learn the truth of 'positive energy' from their magnanimous example. I now invite the eels down, to share their thoughts on the matter."

A long eel, with prideful eyes slithered to the center of the room.

"Citizens of our world, the Great Shark kingdom wishes you positive energy forevermore. We are saddened by the actions of a few swamp-dwelling eels, who had absolutely no affiliation with our government or leadership. I, personally, had just rewarded an outstanding Enbalan for his diplomatic efforts when this horrific attack occurred."

"We hope for only peace with Enbala. In fact, we'd like to live among them. We are hoping the Seal Council might consider granting some Enbalan territory, among the waterways, for eel habitations, so we can move forward together on Enbala."

An otter yelled, "You attack us and then ask for our land?! Only seals would be stupid enough to entertain that!"

The seal guards quickly removed another otter amidst the now familiar barked chant of "Positive!"

The jowly seal called forward the Enbala Ambassador.

A handsome Otter, who Nick couldn't recall meeting, took the floor.

"Wise seals, I greet you with good and positive energy. May you, the eels, and all our neighbors, bask in the warmth of your knowledge."

Nick didn't know who this was, but he did recognize a politician as soon as the words flowed out. No one on Enbala spoke in that manner. This was their representative? How did he represent anything Enbalan?

The slick otter continued, "I represent a new Enbala, one willing to embrace the outside world, rather than constantly filtering it through the teaching of our fore-fathers and their records."

Nick was shocked to hear an otter so unlike Eanmund. He looked to the other otters to see how they were taking it in. Several looked angry, but the majority seemed at peace as the oily words of this Ambassador oozed through the room.

The Ambassador continued, "For too long we have fought the eels. We recognize that it is a wonderful opportunity that has come out of our tragedy. Paw-in-paw... well, paw-on-scales, we could approach the future united, rather than at odds. Let us consider the proposal of the eels; we should form a sub-sub-committee for establishing Enbalan Eel settlements."

Nick couldn't believe his ears. After his experiences Nick had lost the ability to consider eels peaceful. In the enclosure, at sea, or on the island, eel violence had found him everywhere he went. And now the otters were inviting them to join Enbala as residents?

The squeaky seal spoke, "Thank you, what an encouraging message from the otters. We shall establish a team to found the sub-sub-committee for Enbalan eel settlements. May the future be filled with positive energy!"

"Now, we also wanted to hear from the man, as he was a first-hand witness to much of the events of the day."

A seal was pulling Nick from his pedestal and pushing him to the front.

The air was cold and clammy at the base of the steps. Nick could hear the fat seals breathing loudly as he looked up at the crowded room. The room quieted.

"I… I'm not sure what I'm expected to say."

A seal behind him barked, "Tell us what happened at The Restitution".

Another added, "With positive energy".

Nick felt flustered. Everyone was staring at him. In a fight or flight situation his mind chose fight and he found himself saying, "What the hell does that mean, 'positive energy'?! Are lightning bolts worthy of pleasing your emotions supposed to jump from my mouth?! We were attacked by eels, just as Eanmund said. At the enclosure, on the open ocean, and on Enbala I've learned that the eels are horrific, and I think inviting them to live on Enbala is a terrible idea! There is nothing 'positive' that I can say."

Nick saw mouths opening everywhere as he spoke these strong words that surprised even him; as the growing roar of the assembly room engulfed him, he realized that he did feel strongly that the Great Shark religion was terrible. He had decided. And he'd stood up for Eanmund, even if Eanmund might never know, and that felt good. Eanmund deserved it.

Seals were pulling him out the room now. The fat seals were sentencing Nick to 100 days of service too. Probably better that way; where else would he have gone?

Despite sharing a small cell, Eanmund still wasn't talking to Nick. In fact, when Nick had entered the cell, Eanmund had growled ferally for several moments. Now he sat, with his back to Nick, probably praying to his Creator.

Nick tried to respect Eanmund's feelings. He'd thought about the inquiry, wondering what the findings would be. He'd tried pacing at the opposite end of the cell, away from Eanmund. It was all fruitless. Eanmund was the only point-of-interest in the cell and Nick didn't have the wherewithal to sustain his own meandering mind.

"… Eanmund… I know it probably doesn't mean much, but I wish I hadn't run back to your house…. If I could do it all over again, I would go somewhere else. I'm not sure where, but it wouldn't be your home."

Eanmund turned coldly, facing Nick, but still sitting on the cold grey floor of the cell.

"… Eanmund… please… I want to be your friend still."

Eanmund's eyes narrowed.

"Friend? Friend?! You don't get it do you? While it was easy to blame my son's death on you, I know that day's situations were out of your control. But that's the thing man. I know that there's more at work here, but you don't. You're a fool. I want nothing to do with you because I can't see gaining any profit from it, and I've given up on you profiting from me. I believe you are a fool."

The room went silent… and cold. Nick thought he could see traces of his breath. Nick's arms folded across his chest to fight the chill, and ward off shaking.

"Why? What makes me a fool? I'm new to this world, why shouldn't I be confused by it?"

"But you're not, man. You've been here a long time. You've experienced enough to form opinions and beliefs. Even learn skills. Do you realize that while I was teaching you in The Repository, you never once proactively asked me a question? What did you think, I needed someone to go with me to fetch records from the towers? I was trying to adapt you, and prepare you. But now I realize I wasted my time. You don't learn. You don't recognize the situations around you, nor do you have the impetus to work. You are a lump. Your brain inputs anything, filters it through a desire to exist without accountability, and then outputs the most benign path forward. You labor to offend none, but in doing so you are a blatant offense!"

Nick struggled for a response, "You're wrong... I'm in this cell because I agreed with you and stood up for you."

"How many times have the eels tried to kill you? Of course you'd be against them now. But, if you'd read any of the records in The Repository, you could have come to the conclusion that they've been doing similar since the doctrines of the Great Shark were unleashed. Even if you'd never been attacked! But you don't have the intelligence to intake experiences that are not your own and come to rational conclusions. Everything, for you, must be through your experiences. You have no established rights and wrongs, and so you make decisions as each situation affects you, never in preparation. But you don't establish right and wrong, you are not the Creator, you are nothing but the frost on a wave in a huge ocean. You decide nothing. The entire world is established already, and your feelings and experiences mean nothing. You could be gone tomorrow and no one would miss you."

Nick was madder than he expected.

"You don't think I realize that! Sometimes, when I'm in these damn cells that I always seem to find my way into, I break down, sit on the floor, and cry."

There was an odd pause from them both at this omission; Eanmund was not a crier and did not think highly of males doing such things.

"I'm not even in my world. I know I am nothing, and I wonder if I will ever be someone again. At least, when I was in your home, I felt as though I had an identity and others gave me some value."

Eanmund grew even redder, yelling, "So we validated you, did we? Perhaps that's the greatest disservice we could have done! Stop complaining about these cells you find yourself in. They aren't your prison, they are your protection. You can't exist outside these walls. I tried to teach you how, but you thought I was working for you, to enable your existence. No, you fool, I was trying to teach you how to join, and be a productive member of the world that exists with or without you. It exists by the rules The Creator established for it."

"How many dying Enbalans must you personally witness, or foolish seal councils, before you realize the conclusions others already believed based on the records? What makes you important enough to need to re-try the world? Are you the Great Judge? No! You are certainly not more than anyone else!"

"I hope dark lonely cold nights in cells teach you that you aren't the world's judge, for you must learn it. You are a created being, just like the rest of us. And the world shouldn't be brought to you and filtered through you. So how will you join us, align with our culture's learning, and be a part of the world we live in? Or will you forever be relearning the past, as you make mistake after mistake in judging the world, acting as though you're a judge?! Realize you are not as important as you think you are!"

Nick was shaking now. He wasn't entirely sure why, but tears were streaming from his eyes.

"Screw you Eanmund!" he shouted.

Eanmund scoffed, "What does that even mean?"

But the burning in Nick's chest wasn't directed at Eanmund... no, Nick burned because his world has just been hit with a sledgehammer. Nick felt the truth in Eanmund's words as they bombarded him. Nick had been living for himself, without regard to history, culture or religion.

But what Eanmund was revealing fought his programming. Nick accepted all religions and peoples with an open mind, didn't this make him tolerant?! But wasn't he just imposing his own judgements then? Was he God, to make the decision that all actions and cultures are "right". Don't some ideas fundamentally disagree with others; how could both be true. Coexist?

The lands the Great Shark followers were over-running certainly weren't coexisting, they were being destroyed. Were Nick, and the seals, enabling this by giving all beliefs equal favor, regardless of the lessons of history?

Nick sat, letting this heavy mental weight descend on him. He realized he wasn't a wonderful person because he'd been accepting of those ideas that ran contrary to history's lessons. His acceptance of all wasn't free of consequences, or the peaceful path. And it was destroying him to realize that tolerance might have victims, and wasn't an effective solution for wrongdoing.

It was Nick's turn to sit in the corner of the cell and think.

Eanmund, again, stationed himself at the opposite end of the cell. And there they sat. Each with their back to the other. Each angry with the other. But, each was also angry with themselves. For Eanmund, he felt as though he'd failed in teaching Nick. Eanmund had felt a burden for Nick's future, and at this time, he didn't have any hope for Nick.

A large, muscular and confident seal entered through the cell's portal. His muscles rippled as he passed in. A guard crab was following him, but the seal turned around and nipped at it, giving the crab a throaty bark for measure. His nose didn't go to the ceiling, his eyes rested on the crab considering how to handle him. The crab reversed course immediately, and left the seal alone in the cell with Nick and Eanmund.

"Get up. Gather your stuff. It's time for you to serve your sentences."

It was a command, and he had the bearing to issue it. He stood at attention, watching them with his large black eyes, as Nick and Eanmund scrambled to gather themselves.

"Let's go," he said, the instant Nick and Eanmund had placed their last shoe on.

Two (much) smaller seals tried to block the portal as he strode out.

"Sir… you don't have final approval… we're not sure you can do this!" they blurted.

Instead of raising his head and barking, as most seals would do, he lowered his nose, and slammed the side of his head against both of them, in a single swinging motion, knocking them backwards and well clear of his path. Cowed, they both lay where they fell onto the grey hallway.

"Let's go!" he barked to Nick and Eanmund, who were exiting the room with much trepidation.

"Who is this guy?" Nick asked Eanmund.

"Very obviously a soldier," Eanmund replied, "... a real soldier," he added when he looked at the guards lying in the hallway, who were slowly beginning to right themselves.

A crab guard, waiting in the hallway, began following Nick and Eanmund, his pincher drawn and ready to strike. But this time it was different. This time his back was to Nick and Eanmund and he was scrambling backwards, protecting them from any who might approach from the rear.

Down numerous halls, and through several open spaces they travelled, eventually bursting out of the seal's governmental buildings into a large cityscape. The buildings were tall, as Enbala's were, but mainly made out of grey and green stone, unlike Enbala's large timber structures. These buildings rose in wavy designs, mimicking the rise of seaweed in dark seas. The window portals were dark grey, the stone had no color, and any embellishment or trim was white and green, reminiscent of the foam and plants found decorating rocks in cold oceans. Between the buildings snaked both dry pathways and waterways.

The seal and crab launched themselves onto a floating vessel, spartan, but resembling others moving in the paths between the buildings. Like the boats Nick was familiar with, energy seemed to be holding these carts aloft, and they were zooming all around the arteries of the city in various guises; obviously some of them were for personal use, others commercial. And floating everywhere, similar to Enbala, were bulbs of floating energy, but here they were colder, a sanitary blue.

Nick was aware of the coolness of the seaside city too. This place had little in common with Enbala, which Nick had become accustomed to.

The vessel they were climbing into bore the unmistakable aura of a military vehicle. It was painted in various hues of grey, obviously for camouflage, and it was more utilitarian than the other examples in the nearby area.

Another muscular seal was already at the controls, waiting to go.

"Get on" said their commander. Nick and Eanmund exchanged a concerned look. The crab followed Nick and Eanmund onto the platform, slightly bumping them with his shell, pushing their slightly reluctant forms farther onto the platform.

The shuttle shot up, higher than the traffic, and quickly wound through the urban aquapolitan cityscape. Tall grey and green buildings started to blur past as the platform sashayed through them.

Both Nick and Eanmund quickly fell to their hands and knees, struggling to balance with the swaying deck and fearing being thrown off. The two seals and the crab remained at alert, even possibly tactical; the crab was still watching their rear, the driver focused only forward, and their liberator was scanning the skies to either side of the platform.

They were quickly out of the urban scene, and flying over lakes, rivers, pathways, domiciles, and other buildings, some obviously for agricultural use. The land began to divide itself into the unmistakable quilt of farm land. Only, instead of squares, here the land breaks were curving, following the elevation changes in established terraced boundaries, without a straight line in site.

Now, with open air, their flight path steadied. They seemed headed towards distant hill-lands that rose next to the unmistakable dark grey expanse of a large body of water.

Their liberator stopped his searching and turned to them. He lifted a latch on the floor of the platform.

"Listen to me. I don't have time to explain. Climb into this hole and don't say a word. Things will go much smoother if you remain quiet."

The hills were approaching and Nick realized he could see another compound, appearing similar to his first home in this nautical world.

"I don't want to go back to a compound!" Nick yelled. He was yelling with emotion, but he also had to yell due to the sound of the air whipping past their ears.

The driver snorted a small laugh, and started smiling.

"Yes, it looks like the eel compound, doesn't it?! But it's not! Now get in the hole, trust me!" said the large seal.

Nick wanted to object; trust a seal? Surely Eanmund wouldn't go for this.

He glanced at Eanmund, but Eanmund was crawling into the hole.

Slightly exasperated, Nick followed him.

Inside, the quarters were quite close. They could only lay, the ceiling being about 10 inches above their heads, consisting of the deck of the platform. This had to be the storage compartment for the vessel. Eanmund and Nick's shoulders were jammed together in the tight space.

"Why did you come down here?!" Nick yelled.

"Pbbbt" Eanmund said, sticking his tongue out and making a raspberry noise, "it's obvious we're not supposed to be noticed".

The absurdity of this made Nick smile. He knew the Enbalan gesture for silence was what was known as a "raspberry" on Earth, but its use in this tense situation seemed particularly funny to Nick.

Nick continued, "Yeah, a seal told us to be quiet. But I thought you didn't trust seals?"

Eanmund said, "I don't, but this one isn't acting as a seal. He has conviction. You probably didn't recognize it. But, the seals haven't always been guileless. This one reminds me of the seals I've read about. Brave strong seals. Now quiet."

The platform was slowing. They heard the clicking of crab feet moving on the deck.

The air became quiet as the platform came to a stop.

"Sir." came a voice.

"Returning to base," said the driver.

More clicking, a whirring noise, and then they were whisked along again. Only now it sounded like low and slow flight, with a deep guttural sound coming from the energy bays under the vehicle and very little wind sound rushing over the platform.

The wind noise died entirely. The guttural noise rose and tremors shook the platform, as though it was struggling to remain aloft. Then the noise of heavy solid metal latching together was heard.

And then the guttural motor noise was killed. A deep, creepy silence rushed into their hollow.

Then the hatch they'd climbed through slammed open, causing both of them to jump.

The seal in the hatchway saw them jump and he laughed.

"Sorry," he said, "but you can get out now."

They both scrambled out of the hole. Nick, in the second of quiet when the motor died, had imagined himself in a casket and the memento mori gave him the creeps. He wanted out of the hole, yesterday. Eanmund seemed no-less pleased to get out.

The seal kept talking, "You're at our base now. But the guards at the gates aren't actually ours, they're contract help, contracted by those clueless bureaucrats you've been visiting. They do it purposefully, using the guard's reports to spy on our comings and goings."

"Why does it seem like we're not supposed to be with you? And who are you?" Nick asked.

Both he and Eanmund were brushing themselves off, their hiding place had been quite dusty.

The seal laughed, "And where are you supposed to be? No one knows. But I thought the two of you might offer our team some service. And, because the bureaucrats can't do anything quickly, I thought I'd just take you before your sentences ran out and you were headed back to Enbala… or something."

He glanced towards Nick as he made the last comment.

Eanmund spoke up, "You're talking like a bureaucrat now, talking a lot but not answering our questions. Who are you? And where are we?"

The seal glanced at Eanmund, then back to Nick. They'd begun moving. They were entering deeper into the facility. The movements of the large seal, the apparent leader, and the movements of his compatriots, were ever-purposeful. The spartan, clean and utilitarian surroundings hinted at their purpose.

"We've crossed paths on two occasions man. You don't recognize me?"

Nick was surprised by this. It had never occurred to him that he knew this seal, or that the seal knew him.

"No… no… I don't remember you".

Nick was looking around now. The seal had called it a base, and that seemed an apt description. Matching vehicles had filled where they parked at the platform. Now they were deeper within a protected area, with storage containers lining the walls, the lighting was minimal, and there was no attempt at decoration.

The seal said, "I'm addressed as Lead Caelin. I was at the enclosure, they called me down, asking my opinion when you arrived. And we were the first team on Enbala the day of The Restitution."

While Nick tried to process what that meant, Eanmund was first to respond, "Why weren't you in Enbala faster?"

"I had recommended we be stationed on the island when we learned that the eels were coming to the ceremony. This enraged the seal's Enbalan sub-committee. They threatened to disband my teams. They claimed my distrust of the eels wasn't grounded and promoted negative energy."

"And I lost my son because you weren't there fast enough".

There was a short awkward silence as they continued moving into the base. Nick broke the silence, "Your name is 'Lead'?"

The seal chuckled, as did the crab.

"Lead is my role, my name is Caelin."

He paused, then said, "Eanmund, the attack on Enbala still frustrates me. I've long trusted my intuition, but I didn't act on it that day and it cost you. I was hampered by bureaucracy but I've overcome that before. And I'm sorry for not trying harder that day. But, in part, that's why you're here today. I was watching the Enbalan hearing and witnessed your removals. As you were dragged out, I realized that you might be able to help us, so I withdrew you before a bureaucrat could stop me. I'm going with my gut on this one."

"What do you want with us?" Nick asked.

"I thought your penalties, for disrupting the Enbalan sub-committee, should be to aid my teams as advisors. Man, you've spent a lot of time with the eels and are more aware of their true ways than most seals brought up in our brain-washed culture."

"Eanmund, you know their violent history and could act as a spiritual advisor; we still have a number of seals on the team that trust the Creator, despite the 'learned' opinions of the seal cities."

They had entered the center of a large living area. There were additional seals mulling about in this place. Some were gathered in an eating area, food spread before them, with window-like openings revealing an ocean view. Some were lounging about the central area, talking, cleaning tools of war, and a few even napped. From openings along the outside of the central area seals were entering and leaving. It was a busy space.

"This is where we live," said Caelin, "and so will you for a period of time. We've prepared a cell for your stay."

Nick grimaced at the word, "cell".

Suddenly a seal burst from a hallway, barreling at Nick. Nick yelped and dove desperately behind a nearby piece of furniture. The seal initially slid past Nick, but had soon recovered its trajectory and was on top of him, pinning his legs with its huge chest. The seal threw its head back and began barking loudly.

Nick, screamed. Not a manly yell, but the scream of a man who thought he was going to die. He could only sustain one such burst before his voice box was over-extended, and after that he began yipping as he desperately tried to slide away from his aggressor, pounding the seal's thick chest with his fists.

He turned to Lead Caelin as it occurred to him that he might provide help.

Surprise washed over Nick. And confusion, mixed with shame. Caelin was laughing, hard. As were many of the seals in the room. Eanmund stood with an amused but lightly-concerned look also.

The seal above him stopped barking, swung his whiskered muzzle down to meet Nick's gaze, and laughed, saying in a deep growl, "Don't ever forget this man. You must know your role here, which is under us."

Then he complacently moved towards the kitchen area, chuckling in a way only a seal can.

Nick lay on the floor, breathing in large breaths of air, trying to recover from this experience.

Lead Caelin came over and helped Nick up.

"Forgive Byono, he is a warrior and his humor is... different."

Nick couldn't even think of a reply. He was surprised to find his legs still worked after having a large seal on them.

He looked at Eanmund, and it was only then that Eanmund actually laughed aloud.

"Not funny," was all Nick could come up with.

Lead Caelin continued the tour of the living quarters, and introduced Eanmund and Nick to their shared cell. There wasn't much to note. Everything was utilitarian, devoid of decoration, save for several well-used war implements hung on the wall presumably as ornamentation. Their cell was square, grey, contained two boxes for personal effects, and two long shelves for beds.

A New Vocation

In the following weeks Eanmund and Nick began to assume roles. Eanmund more so than Nick. He was esteemed as a teacher, and gave a series of interesting evening training sessions on the history of the Creator, Enbala, the eels and the Great Shark religion.

Nick learned that the Great Shark was originally a minor god, one of numerous from the deep sea's polytheistic ancient history, and as time passed the Great Shark's religion had amassed from an amalgamation of those small gods, adapted into one Shark form, to fit the deity desires of the denizens of the deep, and to compete with the Creator (for the small and multiple gods never retained much following).

The religion of the Creator, worshiped on Enbala, was as old as recorded days, and largely unchanged, save for revelations further illuminating known character traits.

The Creator had mercy, shown by valuing relationship, humility, justice and love. In contrast, the denizens of the deep valued strength, power and discipline. The modus operandi of the deep ocean's religions had been at odds with the Creator since Enbala's earliest documents. The Creator and the harshness of the deep's religions were not able to coexist fundamentally.

Nick felt sure the Seal Council would object at these characterizations, but not these warriors. Once, at meal, Nick asked one of the seals if he believed Eanmund's lectures. He answered Nick, "Yes, it explains much. It aligns with what I witness. This team is often first on the scene after atrocities committed by followers of the Great Shark. We know what their power-thirsty endeavors bring: strife, violence and destruction. But, by the time the shore-bound population learns of any offensive eel actions, the details have been white-washed in an effort to keep an uneasy political peace with the deep."

Nick's role in the team was unclear. Lead Caelin wanted Nick in the water with them on missions, but their first training exercises together had been hugely unsuccessful. To breathe underwater, Nick was given a rebreather device, that worked similar to gills, withdrawing the oxygen from the water and providing air to Nick for breathing.

Once in the water, Nick was a remarkably slow swimmer. Even after their support team produced fin-like attachments for Nick's limbs, he was still slow.

The communication translation work done in the energy rich atmosphere did not work well in the water. Nick struggled to hear Lead Caelin's commands.

And Nick couldn't see. The seal's large black eyes provided them a thousand times more sight ability when moving underwater.

The warriors began calling Nick "Buoy".

At meal times, Nick tried to sit near Eanmund, but as Eanmund's classes progressed he became more popular with the warriors.

Nick wasn't able to converse with warriors; those without purpose often struggle for words to say when confronted with those that live their entire life with purpose. The warrior's talk was of war, strength and tactical advantage. Nick didn't know how to carry a conversation on these topics, nor did he have the passion necessary.

Eanmund and Nick were largely quiet when together. The loss of Eanmund's son had affected their relationship greatly, and now, with Lead Caelin taking responsibility for Nick, Eanmund felt released of any obligations to teach or instruct Nick. This left little for Eanmund to say to Nick, and Nick had little to report back from the training exercises, as he was often far from any action, swimming to find or catch the team.

The sound of cracking lightning woke Nick. Bright light was splashing over his eyelids. Peering up at the ceiling he saw waves of energy washing through it, increasing in brightness until the energy cracked like static in a ruffled sheet. Then it would start over, with light waves of energy. This was the alarm system for the base.

Lead Caelin burst through the cell's opening, "Nick! You aren't up yet?! Did you notice the alarm? Buoy, you can't swim or hear. Let's go! There's been an attack on a crab community in the South Seas."

Eanmund was also struggling to rise.

"Yes, get up Eanmund", said Caelin, "and pray for us. That the Creator may protect us, and the crab community that's come under attack by the invaders."

Caelin was pulling Nick out of the room as Nick struggled to get his clothes on. They, and the other reporting team members, swept quickly to the vehicles and blasted into the air, heading south. Surrounding Nick, seals and crabs were cleaning and double-checking weapon mechanisms, tucking away loose ends of combat uniforms and preparing mentally for the fight ahead. One seal had his eyes closed and was bobbing his head to music only he could hear.

Nick, next to Caelin yelled, "What is happening?"

"We received an urgent message that a crab colony in the South Seas, near the eel compound you were stationed at, has come under attack by eels. These outlying colonies are frequent targets for the eels, and sometimes the Seal Councils won't even allow us to respond. But, in this case, the close proximity to the compound makes this colony strategically important to us. Some of the crabs that live there work at the compound as guards."

Nick remembered his crab guards. Strange to think those strong and ever-poised guards might be at the disadvantage tonight.

The seal's natural shape, designed for swimming quickly through water, was also remarkably aerodynamic. Travelling in the open-air flying vehicles didn't bother the seals. But the air blew past Nick's face at such a rate-of-speed that his features began to deform, pulling his cheeks back into unsightly jowls and, if he left his eyes open, pulling at the edges of his eye sockets exposing the pink flesh under his eyelids. The seals laughed, one asking him, "Buoy, how does your species survive?"

Nick's eyes quickly dried out in the wind, and he felt cold with the wind-chill over his skin. He found himself closing his eyes for large portions of the flight to wherever they were going. HIs core temperature dropping, Nick began shaking. Finally, after what felt like an eternity of disorienting blind and cold flight, the ship began slowing. As Nick opened his eyes, his shipmates appeared and their countenances indicated they were having a leisurely trip.

The sun was dawning. When the ship slowed Nick felt the sun's rays warming his frigid skin. Ahead of them, those same rays were glancing off and illuminating the dome of an energy field barrier, massive in size, and extending down into the depths of the sea they were now over, just off the gray coastline of the South.

The ship was nosing towards the dome. Nick's fellow passengers all stood, facing the barrier; there was a look of expectation, and for some, even a glimmer of excitement in their steely eyes. The dome was so close Nick could hear the cackling of the energy; he expected the ship to stop but instead it accelerated, jamming the dome and cutting into the barrier.

At that second all the trained passengers jumped forward. Nick, not expecting this sudden slam into the dome, sprawled headfirst into the energy barrier. His adrenaline surged and was fueled further by the warrior cries suddenly emitted by the others as they flew, literally, into the barrier.

The collision with the barrier wasn't as harsh as Nick expected, the dome giving way to allow partial entry into the energy field. When Nick's face contacted the energy dome it still hurt smartly, like being struck by a lighter slap, but his nose wasn't broken. Unfortunately, Nick couldn't find any air once his face was in the energy barrier, and he was stuck.

Nick was like a fly on tar paper. He could barely move any appendage, and certainly couldn't escape the field. He thrashed with his strongest efforts, fueled by the adrenaline and panic. The panicked motions and lack of oxygen quickly sapped him of his strength.

Nick might have thought, "Is this odd situation how I die?", or considered how to conserve his energy, but in his panic Nick could

only think a primal "escape, escape, escape" subconsciously, his body attempting pre-programmed actions. Nick had lost all rational thought.

Suddenly a nose slammed into his body, teeth sunk into his clothing, and a seal yanked him through the field, into the interior of the dome.

As soon as he was through, he was falling. They'd struck the dome meters above the water. Air flew by him, the water rising up to meet him at a rate of speed which didn't allow him to adjust his body in time for impact. He hit sideways, in a painful belly-flopping style. His ear concussed, and stung sharply on impact although he'd probably fallen only about 20 feet. Already worn-out, it took Nick several seconds, laying in the water, to remember that he should try and swim.

A shadow suddenly appeared above him. Again, a nose and teeth pulled him, this time into a raft.

Nick wheezed in large breaths of air. His eyes were tearing at the trauma of what his body had just went through. What was previously a wind chill had elevated to the death shakes following his especially traumatic experiences. As the adrenaline left his veins he collapsed into the raft floor, face down.

Only to hear laughing. And the elevated camaraderie of those involved in sport.

He opened one eye and saw the seals having a grand time. Lead Caelin had his head cocked curiously nearby, and after several seconds prodded Nick with a flipper.

"Hey, you all right Buoy?"

Nick, coughed, spluttered, and replied in a whisper, "...what happened?"

More hearty laughs erupted around the raft.

Lead Caelin looked a little embarrassed.

"Honestly, I forgot about you.... We have a fun tradition, with energy domes, and I forgot to pay attention to you".

"Fun?" was all Nick could muster.

"Yeah, the eels have been using that tired old energy field for as long as we can remember. It's become sport to see which of us can hack through it first. Last through gets kitchen duties."

"You!" laughed a crab.

Nick looked very confused.

Lead Caelin continued, "You find joy anywhere it can be found as a warrior. I don't expect you to understand. But I did forget that you wouldn't be participating. Well, it'll be better for you to learn the kitchen duties anyways."

More laughs. Nick realized that it was hilarious to the seals that he'd almost died while they were having great fun. He rolled over on his back as energy returned to him. He seemed to be intact, no broken bones or water in the lungs (a small miracle, he thought).

Around him the warriors began final preparations, withdrawing implements of war from their uniforms and tucking away the last loose edges and tightening straps.

Lead Caelin turned to Nick with his breather device.

"Here, you're going to need this."

"You expect me to go down there?!"

More laughter.

"It's not like you think," said Lead Caelin, "there's a 95% chance the eels are gone. It's a game the eels play. They attack a lightly defended area, and quickly set up the weakest of defenses. Then they wait. If they see their energy barrier fluctuating, as we cut through it, they quickly disappear back into the bowels they come from. But if the stupid politics of the seals blocks our deployment, which it does more than I care to admit, than they begin dominating the area and its residents, forcing complete servanthood to the Great Shark, or death. We're here, they'll have left. We just need to verify it."

The warrior team was ready.

"Let's go Buoy," one of them barked, and they all disappeared into the water.

For a second Nick thought of remaining on the raft, but then he thought of encountering an eel on his own. He put the breathing apparatus in his mouth and dove into the cold water.

It was darker in the water, but bubbles traced the trails of the quickly disappearing team. Nick struggled to swim down. He noticed the water wasn't very deep, and several crab domiciles quickly appeared through the murky water, only about fifteen feet down.

The seals were bursting into, and through residences, as they scoured down a central way with structures accumulated on either side of it.

As Nick's eyes adjusted, he saw a dead and mangled crab lying beside the way. It had several large bite marks out of its shell, fleshy meat hung out and swayed in the water.

Nick shuddered and struggled to swim faster towards the warriors who had been clearing each residence quickly.

Nick lost sight of anyone on the team. He swam towards an entry where he thought he saw a seal silhouette enter.

Inside was dark, eerily quiet and completely foreign to a land-living animal. An underwater crab home had different needs from a land home. Passages between living areas could be along any of the dimensions. There was no need for air treatment and lighting was minimal. As a whole, Nick thought it felt somewhat tomb like. He was thankful to come quickly to the rear exit, although a strange noise was emanating from the far side.

As he passed through the rear passageway, he came upon a scene that caused him to stop short. One of the seals had found an eel. The eel was now pinned to the ground by the heavy seal, who was relentlessly body slamming, head butting, and tail pounding the eel with a fevered hatred.

The seal caught sight of Nick in the corner of his eye and barked ferociously, "Get out of here!"

There was a palpable passion and physical threat purveyed by the seal that scared Nick.

Lead Caelin swam up.

"Get off him Aldick."

Aldick snarled at Lead Caelin.

Lead Caelin instantly transformed into a beast barely recognizable. He shot at Aldick with ferocious speed. He delivered a powerful broadside that sent Aldick squealing and crashing across the ocean bottom.

The eel tried to shoot out in escape. With the same speed and power with which he addressed Aldick, Lead Caelin crashed into the eel, sending them both rolling in a swirling cloud of mud and ocean vegetation. Seal fur and eel flesh flashed through the mud and seaweed as they rolled violently in their struggle.

When the mud began to recede from the water, and a semblance of calm returned, Nick saw that Lead Caelin had subdued the eel to such a degree that the eel appeared lifeless. Lead Caelin was tucking a weapon into his uniform.

Lead Caelin looked at Nick with dark and intense eyes. "Let's go", he said.

He grabbed an edge of the eel with his mouth, blood pouring from the puncture wounds, and he began to swim up, dragging the eel with him. A haunting howl went out from Aldick. Through his clenched mouth Lead Caelin made the same sound, but muted. And then, in the distance, additional responses were heard. Aldick was following Lead Caelin, and Nick decided to do the same. As he rose above the roof of the structure they'd been next to, Nick saw all the team members were also heading upwards towards the raft.

Suddenly a large, dark, and ominous shadow zoomed past above at a high rate of speed. The shadow passed directly in front of Lead Caelin, providing a contrasting background to the red blood flowing out of the eel's wounds and down Lead Caelin's muzzle and bulging, flexing neck.

It seemed that Lead Caelin didn't take notice of this close encounter with the shadow; Nick had looked to him for a response and had seen none, not even a turning of the head.

The team members were not blind to the shadow's intrusion. As the shadow approached Nick and Aldick, a shark became visible in the black. Nick felt his bowels loosen. But Aldick simply snapped at the side of the shark as it passed, the shark doing the same in return. Neither put much effort into biting the other, reminiscent of two dogs nipping at each other when first meeting.

As the shark slid past Aldick the tail batted Nick. The power and force of this hit was shocking to Nick's human body; it felt like being punched by a heavyweight boxer. The rebreathing device floated out of his mouth, and his body was pushed several feet backwards into the water holding him. The stun was such that Nick's dizzy mind didn't recognize that the breathing device wasn't in place, and he began to breathe normally, causing water to enter his mouth. The unexpectedness of the water caused panic. Nick started to thrash and flail again. Later Nick would claim that he was searching for the rebreather, but the seals would maintain that he'd "lost his mind" at that point.

Aldick's canine teeth tore into Nick's arm as Aldick dragged him hurriedly to the surface. They were not far from the surface, and had Nick retained presence of mind he likely would have swam there himself.

And again, he was lying on the raft gasping for breaths.

Nick wanted to know about the shark but was tired of asking what was happening. He wanted to be back at the base. He wanted to be in his dull cell, staring at the ceiling. He'd had enough excitement. There'd been a shark. So what? How was this different from nasty eels? Or talking seals? What the hell was the point of any of this? Did his life have a point?

The raft was filled with the discussion of a team that had won the battle and finished the fight. Aldick was the center of attention, as he was the only one that had come upon an eel.

When Nick's breath returned, he lay there, devoid of the energy to move. Devoid of the desire to continue.

Similarly, the eel also lay motionless on the platform next to Nick. Nick wondered if he and the eel were the same, both aliens and prisoners to the seals.

Lead Caelin, sensing that Nick had no idea what had just happened, spoke, "The sharks often remind us of their presence. The eels will do their dirty work, as required by The Great Shark, and the sharks disavow knowledge of it. But they can't keep from flexing their muscles when they know we'll be near. We've learned, after a few mangled flippers and scars, it's best to simply ignore them. In their own way, they are fools, the enemy's version of our own politicians, pulling strings, grasping for power, prolonging a dishonest peace, while leading us into ever larger problems."

Nick's father, Mark, had tears running down his face. Seated in a cold and impersonal corner of this hated hospital, Mark struggled to read Form 72.

Form 72?! That's all it came down to?! Form 72... how could this be the end of his boy?

Hours earlier he'd sat in the doctor's office, in a small plastic chair, staring across a wide mahogany table at an immense leather chair, haloed by framed degrees from expensive colleges, while an immensely annoying little man-in-the-chair told Mark that Nick was statistically beyond hope.

The little twig of a man had not only recommended that Nick be euthanized, but he put the decision on Mark, telling him that it was the moral thing to do.

Form 72. The form to euthanize one's son. The Loved One's Euthanization Form would be a more realistic name.

Can't have that. Then they'd have to call the abortion consent form "The Baby Killing Form".

Mark had learned doctors, nurses, and the hospital in general, never called things what they actually were. Mark had deep mistrust for the hospital after his experiences during Nick's long stay. Now he was expected to believe them when they told him the right thing to do was to order his son's execution?

He cried, and held the pen to the form, suppressing an urge to throw up. His hand trembled.

He threw the clipboard for the 3rd time.

He heard footsteps come running.

A perky nurse came around the corner.

"Is everything all right, sir?"

"No!" Mark yelled, "Everything is not all right."

"Please don't yell at me, sir; did you throw this?", she asked, picking up the clipboard.

"Yes! Yes, I did! Is that a problem for you, Ms. Perky?"

"I'm getting security," she said softly as she retreated back into the hallway she appeared from.

Mark felt embarrassment. And shame.

A month ago his angry, stress-filled outbursts had led to a breakup with the nurse he'd been dating. He'd really liked her. His heart hurt more at this thought. Nick's life... his relationships... everything he loved was slipping through his fingers.

"Why God?!... Please... Please help me," he prayed.

The short prayer enabled Mark to temporarily recover his emotions. Mark quickly escaped down a corridor in the opposite direction of the perky nurse searching for security. He needed fresh air, and had no desire to talk to a young overly-eager hospital security guard practicing their policing skills before a law enforcement career.

As Nick prepared for sleep, he regaled Eanmund with the day's adventure. Eanmund, as had become typical, simply let Nick talk.

Truth be told, Eanmund was barely listening; he'd spent the day in the seal's small repository preparing, and reminding himself, of some fundamental truths about The Creator for his next class. Now that he had an interested audience, Eanmund felt driven to thoroughly prepare his presentations. He felt purpose that he'd lacked on Enbala.

Nick blabbered on, and on, about how he'd almost been hurt, almost lost his life, felt belittled, etc., etc., etc..

"Victim, always a victim", thought Eanmund.

Finally, Nick came to the part where he'd laid on the raft and contemplated if he was any different than the eel lying next to him. At the mention of an eel, a member of that group that killed his son, Eanmund became enraged; especially since Nick seemed to be implying that he was like them.

"Shut up! Shut up you stupid stupid creature! The seals don't treat you like an eel; you act like an eel and then whine when we respond accordingly!"

He continued, "Even now you're clueless to the utter mess you leave behind you. I don't enjoy your presence. I don't want to hear you talk. To me, you represent my son's death. That may not be rational, but not everything is!"

"But your mouth flies on, completely ignorant to all the signs that I exhibit that say 'leave me alone'."

"Do you realize, when my son died, the pain in my heart was so great that the thought of eating didn't occur as a need for almost two weeks, and even to this day I have the scarcest of appetite?"

"When I see you, hear you talk, that pain of my son's death, that stabbing feeling, inflicts my heart again."

"And then you drone on and on about the issues you cause, blaming them on others. Shut up!"

Nick defensively sputtered, "How is this my fault? Any of it?"

Eanmund strode quickly and ferociously to Nick, placing his muzzle inches in front of Nick's nose.

"You cause your problems by your utter patheticness. What are you?! We know you are 'man', but what, in any world, are you? You're not a warrior, a religious man, a businessman, or a laborer. I find you to be completely and utterly useless. You require the constant looking after of a child, and show no will, or effort, to become anything self-sufficient. Then, as you pathetically flounder through situation after situation, often requiring rescue, you whine about your situation. You cause these things man! You are pathetic! Be something. Become something. Learn something! Strive to become free by being a 'man' of some worth. Because, right now, you are nothing, and yes, you seem to have as much value to our society as the Great Shark slaves. Which is none. You offer nothing of value; it is no wonder you relate to them. And at this point, I despise you for it, because I see it too. Now shut up and let me rest in peace!"

Nick laid awake for hours, at times burning mad, but at other times completely and utterly convicted. But he had doubts and fears. What could he become? A warrior? He didn't think so… but for some reason Lead Caelin was bringing him on these missions. Lead Caelin certainly knew what qualities made a warrior. Eanmund was right. Nick had to learn to find his own way in this world. He would talk to Lead Caelin in the morning.

Earlier, as they prepared for the day, Eanmund and Nick had been silent. Nick was embarrassed. Eanmund felt relieved by the silence; he had worried, when he woke, that the 'man' would want to talk about how he'd been victimized by Eanmund; the man was constantly babbling about how he "deserved" to be treated.

It was breakfast now. Nick sat at the table watching the others while the seals, crabs and Eanmund merrily ate their first meal of the day.

Aldick had been given a special food treat for his capture of the eel, and it was served to him in the shape of an eel.

Nick had decided to talk to Lead Caelin about his newfound desire to become... well, something. He'd chose the seat next to Lead Caelin at the table. Now, as he watched Lead Caelin interact with his men, he felt nervous and every time he came close to breaching the subject with Lead Caelin, the seals would gain Lead Caelin's attention before Nick could muster the courage to address him.

Finally, during a lull in conversation, with the warriors happily engaged eating, in a whisper, Nick asked Lead Caelin if they might talk quietly.

In his usual voice Lead Caelin said, "What's on your mind man?"

Several warrior's eyes darted to Nick.

Nick, pathetically, tried to find the words he'd been batting around for hours.

Nick whispered, "Lead Caelin... I need to become something. I need to find my own way. A way that can sustain me... I mean, I need to learn to be self-sufficient. Can you train me?"

Lead Caelin looked at him with large black eyes. "Train you to do what?"

"I think… I want to become a warrior."

Lead Caelin stared without blinking for a long moment. Then, from the depths of his belly, a huge laugh rose up, shaking Lead Caelin's entire body as it broke out and filled the room.

Eventually he said, "A warrior? Ha ha ha! Team, the man wants to be a warrior! Ha ha ha!"

The table erupted. There was laughter from all corners of the room. A few of the warriors were laughing riotously.

Nick's head hung. His self-worth was at an all-time low.

There was one seal that wasn't laughing. One of the grizzled veterans. Nick glanced his direction, looking for a sign of empathy.

When Nick's eye met the eye of the seal, it charged him, roaring. The table flew. Food bits strewed across the room. Several crabs were knocked to the floor.

The seal banged into Nick, hard. Nick flew backwards, out of his seat. The breath burst from Nick's lung. It felt as though ribs broke on impact. The seal's teeth tore into his shoulder.

Almost as suddenly as it began, it was over. At least the attack on Nick. The commotion still reigned in the room.

Nick looked over to see Lead Caelin and the veteran battling furiously. Crashing around the commissary, seals rushed to their side, trying to rein them in.

Finally, Lead Caelin subdued the veteran.

"By the name of Enbala, what were you thinking?!" Lead Caelin shouted at the offending seal.

"I'm sick of him! I couldn't take anymore! Why is he even here?! He's worthless! And then this baby eel, this 'Buoy', compares himself to us? "A warrior"?! I can't stand it Caelin. I had to teach him a lesson; I'll wager he doesn't open his mouth saying stupid things again."

The veteran was being restrained by several seals and a crab. He seemed to relax after his short speech, and they began to loosen their holds on him.

Nick expected Lead Caelin to come to Nick's defense, or even retaliate. Nick looked expectantly to Lead Caelin.

Lead Caelin snorted, and looked at the veteran. He said nothing. Then he looked around his now destroyed eating area. Then at Nick.

Nick didn't appreciate it. Lead Caelin was looking at him not like an equal, a peer, or even a friend. No, Lead Caelin looked at him as someone looks at a dog that's committed its last atrocity before going to the pound.

Lead Caelin looked back to the veteran. "We'll talk later; when you calm down. I somewhat agree with you... but I fear this may be my fault. I haven't been clear with the man. I will talk to him, outline my expectations, and then address everyone. You all deserve to know what he is doing here. Or, at least, what I was hoping for."

Then Lead Caelin breathed out deeply, paused, and started chuckling again, muttering "A warrior... heh, heh."

He turned to Nick. "Come on man, we need to talk. Let's get out of here."

Nick and Lead Caelin moved through the hallways and storage rooms of the base. The cold, dark and moist passageways chilled Nick to his soul.

At first their movements were quiet. Nick had no idea what to say. If he was forced to leave, he was clueless what he would do.

Lead Caelin started, "I'm sorry man. I had the impression that you had the self-awareness to consider your predicament... I guess I was wrong."

Nick felt convicted; without Eanmund bringing it to his attention, would Nick have realized he must develop skills to exist here?

Nick's shoulder throbbed from bites; it did not improve his downcast mood.

"You are not, and will not be a warrior. Banish the thought from your mind."

Nick's exasperation broke through, "I need to become something. I'm not a dog."

"What's a dog?"

"I just mean, I need to have a skill, a purpose. How will I survive in this land, without living off charity? Should I follow Eanmund, become a scholar?" Nick asked.

Another chuckle from Lead Caelin.

"You're full of jokes today man. No. No, you can't just set your mind to become something you don't have the passion, capabilities, or discipline for. You must develop those first."

Lead Caelin continued, "I haven't talked with you about your future because I didn't think it was my responsibility. But it's occurred to me, who else would talk to you? But who, other than The Creator, can tell you what you'll be? I can offer you my thoughts though, if you want to hear them."

Nick said, "Yeah... yeah, that'd be nice. I'm really struggling here."

"Yeah, that's true."

"I want you to provide value to my team, with what you know about the eels. It's hard to verbalize my thoughts but I'll try."

"When we go into a situation, I want you to consider what you've seen, combine it with what Eanmund has taught you, and advise us with any information that occurs to you that might be relevant to our situation. After all, you did live with the eels for a period of time; few can make that claim."

"And when we collect an eel, like the one we're holding now, I want you to take a strong lead in understanding why they were encroaching outside their territory."

Lead Caelin paused. He was blocking the hall's light, and towering over Nick. Being in his silhouette was intimidating.

"Man... I fear the eels, well, likely their shark overlords, are preparing something. Something new and big. It's been too quiet lately, and the few attacks seem distractions at best. It's very important that I figure out what they're really doing. I need you to help me figure out what they're planning."

Lead Caelin's serious demeanor sobered Nick; the self-loathing he'd been enjoying was suddenly gone. Nick realized Lead Caelin was worried about something bigger than Nick's future. Nick's thoughts flashed back to the attack on Enbala.

He couldn't think of anything to say that would match the severity of the moment. The topic was severe, and Lead Caelin had entrusted it to Nick. Nick felt inadequate in a different way. At least now he felt incapable, rather than useless; a small conciliation he thought.

Nick responded, "I understand. I'll do my best."

Lead Caelin and Nick entered the cell where the eel was skulking, extending almost the entirety of the rear wall, pressed under his shelf in a recess that remained darkened from the eerie glow of the energy illuminated walls.

"You, eel. Get out here. Now.", said Lead Caelin, in a manner that was familiar and confident.

"Eat seaweed seal," the gloomy shape responded.

A laugh came from the guard seal stationed in the open doorway, and he pressed a device he was holding in his flippers.

The eel writhed in pain.

Then there was silence as the eel continued to lay on the floor, motionless under the shelf.

Lead Caelin still seemed unfazed.

"Turn to me eel, or are you a coward?"

At that challenge, the eel slithered out, keeping its head low. Its eyes were filled with the hate Nick had come to know and would always remember.

Lead Caelin asked, "What were you doing in that crab colony?"

"Colony?", spit the eel, "Is that what you call your trespassing on the Great Shark's territory?"

Lead Caelin responded, "It's been a crab colony for hundreds of years. You have no claim to it."

The eel hissed back, "The Great Shark has a claim to any colony in his dominion."

The eel began racking in pain again.

Lead Caelin turned to the guard, barking "Stop, now!"

As the eel panted before him, Lead Caelin bent forward and said softly, "What did your over-Lord promise? Your own home? Freedom? Promotion?"

The eel's eyes turned to slits, suspicious of this line of discussion. Lead Caelin was aware of more than the eel assumed.

"We were promised nothing that isn't rightfully ours. The crabs are non-believers and deserve nothing but conquest and servitude."

Lead Caelin put his muzzle right in front of the eels.

"The crabs are free, and citizens of our nation. They have every bit as much value as you. More... many of them contribute positively to our society."

The eel spit at Lead Caelin and yanked his head back.

"Your seal society is beyond worthless."

Lead Caelin turned to the door.

"Hit him."

In seconds the eel was lying snout-to-the-floor, again.

Lead Caelin laid his chest on the eel's neck and spoke directly into the side of his snout, "What are the sharks planning? I know they're up to something."

"Your future slavery," hissed the eel.

"Hit him."

And again, the eel was struck with energy that caused convulsing pain.

"What are the sharks planning?!"

The eel was silent. It only glared at Lead Caelin in the flickering low light of the cell.

Lead Caelin rose up.

"Fine, I'll go get the bigger energy unit. The 'truth teller', as it's known around here."

As Lead Caelin passed Nick he gave Nick a small nod. Then he was gone. And it was just Nick and the eel in the room.

Several seconds passed and the eel raised his head. There was an odd look in his eyes.

His sudden change in mood was notable. His head was up and staring at Nick with all the haughtiness of the eels from the compound.

Nick glanced nervously to the guard who was still in the doorway, holding the trigger.

The eel began to glide past Nick, but then turned. And turned. And turned again.

Nick realized he was being circled.

Then the eel began to taunt him.

"So, you are the man? Will you serve us, as you serve them, when we destroy them?"

Nick's first instinct was to cry out to the guard. Surely he could, and should, shock him again? He was threatening Nick.

But as Nick turned his head to look at the guard, his injured shoulder burned. It reminded Nick of the day's events.

Nick resolved that he would try and get information out of this eel. But what? They all said the same thing? What would be new?

"'Destroy them'? You've had hundreds of years. Why are you going to win now?"

Now it was the eels turn to be surprised. He hadn't expected the man to do or say anything, just tremble.

The eel's body, coiled around Nick, suddenly tightening in upon him. He was beginning to squeeze Nick!

His tongue level with Nick's nose, the eel looked down into Nick's eyes, probing; was there more in Nick than the eel had surmised?

Nick could barely breathe, the fishy smell from the eel's mouth was overpowering, but he was determined to listen, if the eel would speak.

Then the eel spoke, slowly. And in a whisper.

"The time has come. The skies will darken for the arid world... its energy will fail it."

Lead Caelin came back through the door. Seeing Nick being squeezed by the eel, he instinctively took the trigger from the guard and pressed it.

The energy pulsed through both the eel and Nick. Nick's arms recoiled into a frozen "v" shape as the energy tightened and held his arm muscles taught. For a brief second the eel's embrace threatened to collapse Nick's rib cage.

But then it was over. The eel slumped away from Nick, as Nick's legs also buckled and he fell over, on top of the eel's body.

Lead Caelin grabbed Nick and pulled him to the door. As soon as Nick could regain his breath he said, "He spoke to me. I don't know what it meant, but he spoke to me."

And for the first time Nick was useful to Lead Caelin, telling him what he'd heard.

The eel refused to talk again.

Lead Caelin, Nick and the team retired back to the living areas for some rest and recuperation. Just as they were settling down, after a hearty meal of spicy clam soup and a bread-like substance, the door flew open and in strode a group of older, frail, pale and grumpy seals.

"Lead Caelin, we need to talk. Now." said the seal at the front of the group.

A fierce look was on Lead Caelin's visage. "About what?" he practically growled.

The seal that addressed Lead Caelin looked around at the room full of warriors, all glaring at him. Most the seals and crabs were either lounging or involved in games when the new arrivals barged in. A palpable clash in ambitions was occurring; the warriors were trying to relax and the officials were there to ruin that. Everyone in the room sensed the tension, and the speaking official responded with a tone of contempt.

"I won't speak in front of the laborers, Caelin."

"'Lead' Caelin to you," in another growl. "What is this about?"

"The prisoner."

"I thought so, what lies have you believed now?"

The seal addressing Lead Caelin became flustered and began yelling.

"I told you, not here! As representatives of the Council we are still in charge here! Now get up, and meet us in the discussion room!"

With that the delegation streamed out, avoiding eye contact with the warriors that they claimed to be in charge of.

Lead Caelin looked towards Nick, "You're coming with me, eel expert."

Then Lead Caelin looked to his men, "What is the poor eel's plight this time? Was he visiting his crab family? Religious pilgrimage, en route to Enbala, just passing through?... Perhaps he has too many little eels and travelled to a crab village for snipping of his manhood?"

All the warriors started laughing.

Lead Caelin slowly collected himself and made his way through the doors after the politicians. Nick followed.

The room was small and smelled of wet fish. Nick felt his stomach begin to turn. The walls gleaned with the ethereal green energy light so common to utilitarian rooms in this world. There was a table in the middle of the room, made of black stone, and the seals sat on the floor around it. There was nothing else notable about the room. There weren't even windows, and the portal through had been admirably thick; Nick realized that what was said in the room could not be heard from outside.

The seal committee had been briskly discussing something, but as Lead Caelin moved in, with Nick, they stopped buzzing and turned towards them quietly.

The same seal that had ordered Lead Caelin to the room spoke first.

"What is the man doing here?"

Lead Caelin was slow to respond, and brusque in his reply, "He is my eel expert."

One of the seals in the group snapped back, "That is my office's role."

Lead Caelin turned to him and said, "The man has lived with the eels and faced several of their attacks, and lived. Can you say the same?"

Nick thought Lead Caelin's statement might win the argument but the seal replied, "His perspective does not replace years of seal schooling on the theology of eels!"

Now it was Lead Caelin's turn to yell. "And I think it does! You gave me the power to select and employ the members of this team and he is my on-team eel expert. I prefer his life-based perspective to your biased schooled opinion; that is my right, given that you chose me to lead this team."

"Did your 'expert' inform you that you've captured the son of the eel's top religious advisor to the seals?"

"I'm not surprised. Whenever we capture a seal they are always something similar," said Lead Caelin.

"Why do you always assume they are lying?! Your bigoted views put your ability to lead this team in extreme jeopardy," said the seal that had called them to the room.

"You need to study the eel's beliefs. We have been using the Enbalan Record Keeper to refresh us on the beliefs of the Great Shark. He tells us their ancient texts brag of the Great Shark tricking his enemies by lying, and the eels now consider it an honor if they can successfully get their enemies to believe lies."

"We are not the eel's enemy!" shouted one of the delegates.

"Then why are we in this shadowy room?! Why do I risk my life almost daily?!" shouted Caelin.

He added, "If this eel was the son of a delegate, you would think he would have told me already."

Then, with rich sarcasm, he added, "Maybe he doesn't know he's the delegate's son yet."

Although they were of differing opinions, several of the seals couldn't resist smiling at the implications of what Lead Caelin said. Nick had learned, from his time with the teams, that seals greatly enjoyed jokes that were suggestive of others behaving badly, especially in regards to promiscuity. The absence of joking of that kind while he was in Enbala made this humor stand out all-the-more now.

"Did he have any weapons when you found him? Did you see him in any act of aggression? Just finding him at the crab encampment is not sufficient evidence to warrant detaining him." said another seal, in a feeble old voice.

"Why else would he be there? And who are you, committee member? I don't recognize you." said Lead Caelin.

The leader of the seals responded, "He is not a member of the committee, he is our law expert."

"Ah, that explains much," said Lead Caelin.

Then Lead Caelin's body language became forceful, and Nick saw him assume the command authority he used with his men. He said, "I can't stop you. We are wasting our time here. We do not see eye-to-eye, but we both know that your government has already decided how to address this. Take him, and be gone. Come on Man."

Lead Caelin got up and moved out of the room. One of the committee members shouted after him, "It is your government too."

From the hallway Lead Caelin snarled, "Don't remind me."

Mark and his lawyer stood in the waiting area of the Court House. They'd pleaded their case before the judge and now the judge was considering the merits of the parties.

The hospital and the insurance company presented that Nick was statistically dead. Only a handful of cases had ever awoken after being in a coma for this amount of time. The hospital, or at least their legal representation, and the insurance company argued that Nick should be taken off life support.

At times, during the hearing, Mark had been both in tears, and blistering mad. At one point the judge called for a five-minute break and took Mark aside and told him that he must get himself together or he might be held in contempt.

How could he gather himself together? This was Nick's son they were talking about; although the hospital and the lawyer talked as though he was already gone, careful to only use past-tense when referring to Nick. Now Nick was "the body" to them.

Mark offered another prayer to the Lord. Mark needed the judge to rule in his favor by 2 PM, when Nick was scheduled to be taken off of life support. Mark wasn't sick, but he couldn't remember having a worse feeling in his stomach and chest. It was amazing how the clock on the wall could move so fast, and yet so slow, at the same time.

At the hospital the Doctor reviewed the notes, and prepared for turning Nick's life support systems off. He was aware that the father was seeking an injunction against the hospital, but unless it was received by 2 PM it was within the hospital's rights to take Nick off of life support. In the doctor's consideration, the body was only taking up space now; statistics dictated the doctor's thoughts, romanticism long having been left by his wayside, replaced by the cold factual writings of textbooks and medical journals.

As the doctor re-familiarized himself with the systems helping Nick breathe, feeding him, and stimulating his pulse, he heard a faint static noise from his radio but no transmission came through. The radios seldom worked well. He'd get the message when he moved to an area with coverage.

The doctor turned off Nick's feeding system. That would no longer be necessary. As he moved towards the breathing system a nurse rushed in, breathless from running.

"Stop!" she wheezed.

"Why?" the doctor asked frigidly. He was frustrated. He felt he knew the answer, but he also questioned it, his mind asking "Why draw this out?"

"We (large breath) tried your radio. (Large breath) They have an injunction (another breath). He was given six additional months by the court," said the nurse.

The doctor sighed, then looked up the process to turn Nick's feeding tubes back on. Failing to find it, he called a nurse who would know.

Nick woke up to commotion. He could hear the warriors talking, laughing, and moving through the halls, but there was no alarm for a mission; this was different, the sounds didn't match the sounds of fight preparation. Fight preparation is a hard sound, tense, with a clanging of metallic noises as equipment is prepared. No, the warriors were mulling, but it surely wasn't for another mission.

Eanmund was sitting up in his bunk as well.

"What's going on?", Nick asked.

Eanmund replied, "It is a day of worship for the warriors."

Nick sensed sarcasm in Eanmund's voice and wondered why.

Nick rose and put on his garments.

Venturing into the hall he was greeted with a surprising sight: one of the grumpiest warrior seals trundling towards the commons area, wearing bright and happy colors.

Following the seal, Nick was again surprised to see a variety of colors and costumes decorating the commons area as he entered. The seals and crabs were buzzing; there was a genial atmosphere in the room Nick hadn't sensed before. As Nick took it in, Eanmund cleared his throat behind him.

"Mmrrmmm" sounded Eanmund.

Nick looked at Eanmund and noticed a striking contrast to the others in the room. Eanmund looked grumpy, angry even.

"If it's their worship day, I don't understand why you're unhappy," said Nick.

A nearby seal looked at Nick quizzically.

Eanmund said, "It is not a religious day.... well, I should rephrase... today has nothing to do with The Creator."

Another nearby seal said, "Lighten up Record Keeper, it's just a game! We're not studying your old books today!"

"Yes", Eanmund snipped back, "and you give it more effort and care than any of my discussions."

"And why would I not? It's actually interesting!" said the seal.

Eanmund was standing his ground this morning, "Yes, you'll put your athletes above your Creator. But is that wise? Will your athletes do anything for you?"

The seal turned, bumped Eanmund with his chest, put his muzzle to Eanmund's, and said, "I was raised with one of the athletes in today's games. Are you saying he's less important than your sleep-inducing discussions? He is a great seal, and you'll have respect to remember it Record Keeper!"

The seal pointed his nose at the ceiling and gave several loud barks, while his chest continued to bump Eanmund's. The whole room had now turned to see what the unexpected unfriendly commotion was.

This enraged Eanmund. Nick had to restrain a laugh when Eanmund tried to chest bump the seal back, to no effect.

Eanmund was yelling, "'A great seal'?! Why?! Because he can play a game well?! That doesn't make him great, it makes him gifted. How do you know he's not a terrible seal?! But yet you all blindly worship them whenever the games begin!"

The seal facing Eanmund was done with conversation. He ferociously bit into Eanmund's shoulder, lifted him by it, and threw him through the closed portal and out of the room. As the portal retracted under the force of Eanmund crashing through it Nick heard splintering and snapping.

Nick saw Lead Caelin rush to the rescue, but this time he didn't say a word to the seal that attacked. He went straight for Eanmund, who was still prostrate, grabbed him by his garments, and dragged him down the hall, away from the portal, the commons, and out of sight.

There was laughter throughout the room. The seal that had bit Eanmund turned to Nick.

"You, the other one that doesn't belong. Do you want to open your mouth too?"

Nick replied quickly, "Nope. I'm good."

The seal's eyes narrowed. "'No Sir.' Learn some respect or I'll throw you through the portal too…. now get out of here. Find your teammate."

Nick was confused. Did the seal think Eanmund and Nick were a team? But Eanmund disdained Nick. As Nick's brain processed the seal growled, loud and sharp, "Get out of here!"

Nick scrambled for the door. The laughing increased exponentially.

Down the hall and around a bend Nick came to Lead Caelin and Eanmund in a heated debate.

"My sentence ends tomorrow. I'm leaving, returning to my job, home and family!" said Eanmund.

"Can't you serve willingly?! We need you!"

"No chance!" Eanmund yelled. "I thought I was making headway but today showed me that I've made none. They entertain me as a necessity to their duties, not because they have an inkling of interest."

"Why do they have to have personal interest? You're still achieving my goals. I wanted you to teach them the context of this war, not convert them to The Creator's church."

Eanmund looked at Lead Caelin and said, "That may have been your intention, but it was not mine. The words of The Great Creator are empty, dead, and entirely devoid of meaning without a healthy respect of The Creator. I'm wasting my time if the slightest display of sports trumps their interest in their maker."

Lead Caelin was getting mad now, "And why should they take interest in you Eanmund? Is that your pride speaking? They work hard and should have an opportunity to have some great times indulging in the unimportant occasionally."

"But it's not just indulgences!" said Eanmund, still yelling. "Their athletes have taken the place of their God. They know where their favorite athletes live, who the athlete's partner is, the athlete's thoughts on pedantic subjects, and a complete rundown on the athlete's physical characteristics. Yet it pains and bores them to hear a few minutes discussion about the Creator of Worlds."

"And you're going to solve this by yelling at them?" asked Lead Caelin.

Eanmund looked a little taken aback at this statement. "Lead Caelin, this was no plan of mine. I had no intentions when I entered that room. I spoke in anger, and quickly; both things The Creator's teachings say are wrong."

"So, is your wrong 'better' than their wrong?" asked Lead Caelin.

"It's not a comparison; there are no rankings!" snarled Eanmund.

The walls began to pulsate, and the call-to-duty alarm rose.

"Oh no!" said Lead Caelin, with a noted sense of alarm in his voice. Almost to himself, he said, "Not today... I have to do something."

Lead Caelin suddenly left Eanmund and Nick, running towards the bunk areas.

Warriors began hustling past Nick and Eanmund, both of whom were still standing in the hallway unsure of what exactly to do with themselves.

Now the commotion sounded like an upcoming mission. And the warriors looked angry. Their day of games was not going as desired. Several bumped into Nick and Eanmund as they passed them by.

Lead Caelin hurried back towards them with a box.

"Eanmund," he said, "You're coming with us today. I want you to see why your contributions are important."

Together Forward

Nick looked around the cruiser as they sped over land towards the newest incident; never before had he seen the warriors look so angry and contemptuous. They were snarling and snapping at each other over the smallest of infringements: one sat too close to another and was bit, another's uniform was touching his neighbor's and he was bit.

The timing of this mission was odd, even to Nick. Normally the eels took advantage of small hours for their attacks. This was the prime of the day. Maybe the eels were counting on the distraction of the athletic games.

The location was odd also. Never before had they flown over land towards the densely populated coastal areas. Previously, the eels had seemed content nipping at the outskirts of mainland society.

There were also a plethora of mainland inhabitants, in their cruisers, heading in the same direction. Lead Caelin eventually had to slow significantly, almost to a stop, to avoid hitting others.

"What's going on?" Nick asked.

"They are travelling to the games," replied Lead Caelin. "We can bypass them though, there is an elevation reserved for emergency official use."

They started to rise and soon they were travelling at great speed again, above the throngs.

Suddenly another cruiser veered in front of them, coming from below and crossing to above them, and then correcting to dodge back below them. Lead Caelin reacted quickly, but the heads of those in Caelin's cruiser passed within inches of the hull of the wild vessel. All of their necks and backs felt whiplash from the cruiser's evasive movements. The G forces had been immense.

Lead Caelin yelled something which surely must have been a curse word. Then he yelled back at his team, "They've obviously taken in too much of the fermentation!"

Looking back, Nick watched the cruiser bumble downwards towards the traffic jam. Only it didn't stop when it reached the queue and slammed into another cruiser. It was a glancing blow, which sent both vessels spinning into a cloud of dust in the green field below them. Lead Caelin's cruiser was blasting along at such a pace that by the time the dust clouds erupted from the grass, they were spots on the receding horizon. The cruisers, fields, towns and cities were rapidly passing by below them.

Nick thought about the drunken pilot. That had once been him, and now here he was.

What was "here"? Did it matter?

Things had changed, and he'd had no control. Nick tried to think; in any way, did he cause his fate?

Eanmund and Lead Caelin challenging him to find purpose found their way into his thoughts. Could he rise above any of this, or was it his fate to be pathetic in this world? And if he did find purpose, what could he achieve? What was success in this alien world?

Nick smiled a little when the thought occurred to him that, perhaps, if he became rich here he'd attract another mer-creature.

A few warriors glanced at him with strange looks. But he wasn't the only one to smile to himself when travelling to a mission; the warriors often had complex inner conversations during their travels to engagements.

On the coming horizon a glint of gold caught his attention. Soon he was staring, in wonderment, at the source of the light. Huge statues of strong golden seals, in action poses, rose from the flat land of the mainland and parted the sea of cruiser traffic below. The cruisers were gathering at the statues. There must have been forty statues, hundreds of feet in height. And they surrounded what could only be a stadium, in any world.

Lead Caelin yelled back to the men. "Do you see that box near the rear of the cruiser? It contains civilian garments. If we complete this mission quickly, I will find a way for us to get into the games."

It was true; there was a box that Nick hadn't noticed on the cruiser before. It was the box Lead Caelin had carried in the hall. Nick found himself frustrated, he wanted to be aware of his surroundings, and it continued to be a discipline that eluded him.

Beyond the statues, and the arena, the crowds of cruisers disappeared. And the sea came back into view.

Lead Caelin pointed to the sea, and said, "There is where we've been sent team!"

Eanmund, who'd been silent and also pensive for the flight, looked uninterested at this announcement.

The warriors made their final uniform preparations and braced for the pending impact with an energy shield. Instead, no energy dome appeared.

And as they came nearer to the water Nick realized that several shapes at the surface were eels nonchalantly watching the skies. At the sight of Lead Caelin's vessel an eel dived, likely to warn its compatriots. With an eerie air, the others remained bobbing in the sea, simply watching the coming warriors.

The cruiser slammed down onto the water, with about a foot of energy padding between the hull bottom and the surface.

Eanmund looked disgruntled at the force of impact, as he struggled to maintain his balance.

"Let's go men!" shouted Lead Caelin, and the others rose and approached the edges of the cruiser (which was bobbing on waves it created by landing heavily).

One or two of Lead Caelin's seals and crabs were already in the water when several more seals, wearing the uniforms associated with the Seal Council chambers, suddenly burst out of the water and came barking into the middle of the boat. They were immediately challenged by several of the largest members of

Lead Caelin's team, and heated battles of chest bumping and barking ensued before Lead Caelin's repeated yells of "Shut up! Enough! Enough!" could be heard and obeyed.

The seals from the water were growling ferociously. So were Lead Caelin's warriors.

One of the new seals said to Lead Caelin, "Caelin, what are you doing here?!"

"We heard concerns of a large amount of eel activity near the games. So, we came."

"Did you bother to consult the Council?! They could have told you that this is a joint technology effort. There is nothing to worry about here."

Now Lead Caelin was noticeably nearly growling. "What do you mean?"

"This is an energy harvesting project," said the council seal.

"Everything harvests energy. The walls. Our buildings. Ships. This cruiser. What do the eels have to do with it?", asked Lead Caelin.

"The energy isn't for us, it's for the eels," said the council seal.

He continued, "The Council believes that with more energy in the depths, they'll have more constructive interests. Now we're partnering, installing energy harvesting lines, that the eels themselves developed, to funnel light energy into the depths. The shallows here, near the arena, have the best light qualities. ... Put on your gear, I'll take you down to see the efforts."

Lead Caelin looked to his team, all of whom were staring at him, and said, "This we need to see; now our Council is empowering the eels, literally. Gear up."

Everyone put their gear on and followed the council seal and Lead Caelin into the water.

Nothing could have prepared Nick for what he saw as his eyes passed through the wave barrier. Golden statues rose from the sandy bottom, their tops just below the surface; most were half buried, with a variety of sea life clinging to them.

Only these statues were different from those Nick had seen at the arena. They were not strong seals in athletic poses; Nick saw crabs, otters, one eel, and some seals, but all lacking athletic stature.

The warriors had been working on improving their underwater communications equipment, and it seemed to be working. When Eanmund saw the statues everyone heard him say, "In times past the plains nearby were not used for sporting purposes, but all manners of gathering. Great creatures that loved and followed The Creator, preached on those plains. There was a time when they were celebrated, but now their effigies have been flung into the water, to make way for the new arena and the athlete statues you saw as we flew in."

The team continued to paddle down. Near the feet of the statues (most buried in sand), snaking their way through the giant forms, were teams of seals and eels, placing energy gathering devices and conduit. Although the technology was certainly different, Nick noted the system being installed looked similar to Earth's solar panels and electrical cables.

The seal that was introducing them to the project, looked back at the group.

"Here you see the future! Eels and seals coming together for the betterment of both. We are building for tomorrow, and a brighter tomorrow the eels of the deep shall have! With the peace this is sure to generate, both eels and seals will richly benefit from this project," said the very proud council seal. Not only was he proud of this project, but he was also proud to give the speech he'd memorized from a Seal Council memo.

Nick watched the work. As did Lead Caelin. Quickly Lead Caelin's team became restless and seemed ready to return to the boat and, without doubt, the games.

One of the hopeful seals spoke up, "Let's go Lead Caelin. There's nothing for us here."

But Lead Caelin's eyes were squinting at the work.

"Prepare yourselves, we are going to throw the stone," he said. "Two of you will not be going to the games."

"Why?" said one particularly antsy seal.

"Yeah, why?!" said the council seal.

"Because these eels are not construction workers. They are soldiers."

"Foolish," poo-pooed the official.

Lead Caelin looked sharply at the council seal, saying, "I know military. These eels are too organized, they watch their leaders with too much fear, and they move with the purpose and confidence militant. I know military when I see it. Something is suspicious and we are going to provide security for your project until I feel comfortable with what's going on here."

The council seal became flustered, his veins flushing with anger. "No, you will not stay! I don't want or need you here. Caelin, I will take this to the Council!"

"Do it. They've never responded to anything in a timely manner, so even if they disagree with me, I still have days until I'm forced off your project."

"You know what your problem is Caelin?! You can't respect any eel. To you they are all plotting."

Lead Caelin sounded back, "This has nothing to do with prejudices. Look, I have the man who lived among the eels in the

244

enclosure. He is right there, on my team. Man, come here. Do these eels look like common eels, or are they militant?"

Nick came forward. Surprisingly, the council seal seemed to also value Nick's opinion, asking, "So what is your take, man?"

Nick looked out at the workers. He thought of his friend, the mother, within the enclosure. Did these eels share any of her demeanor?

Sensing Nick's probing eyes, one of the workers looked up at him. The eel's eyes were cold and the disdain for Nick was blatant. There was no hint of his old friend's eyes in this worker.

As Nick looked from eel to eel, he also began to see what Lead Caelin saw. There was no comradery. There was no light in their eyes or small talk. These were cold and strong eels, laboring to a cold and purposeful task. The work was too on task, there wasn't any joking, and these eels were all strong with training and young in age. Their movements were purposeful wherever they went.

Nick felt confident in his judgement. He didn't see his friend from the enclosure anywhere below him. He saw the others in the enclosure: the unfriendly, the proud, and the violent. This wasn't about disliking eels, or prejudice, Nick was using his experiences to make an informed judgement. Still, he struggled, his education had taught him to dismiss his experiences and to believe that there was no wrong in the hearts of others.

Nick's eyes drifted up and he saw Eanmund swimming. Nick thought of Eanmund's dead son.

Nick said to the official, "These aren't your common eels. I also see militant within your eel workers here. They remind me of those that attacked at Enbala."

The council seal stared at Nick for a moment, deciding whether Nick could be trusted. Then he turned to Lead Caelin and said, "Fine. Until I can address the Council, station your team as guards. But they must not block the work and corridors on the ground. They shall either swim, or view the work positioned above, on the old worthless statues."

As the council seal swam off, Lead Caelin turned to Nick, saying, "I didn't like him in our training years either."

The receding seal responded, "The feeling was mutual," obviously hearing him.

The seal team gathered into a huddle at Lead Caelin's command. He withdrew a stone ball from his uniform, the word "DUTY" painted onto it. He threw the ball up in the center of the huddle. The huddle erupted into a teaming mass of bubbles, muscle, barking, growling, swimming, flipping and bumping. Finally, a seal popped out the side of the mass holding the ball. He rushed to Lead Caelin, gave him the ball, turned to the others and said, "I'll see you at the games! Well, some of you, ha ha."

And then the seal was off to the games in a swirl of bubbles.

The same scene was repeated until only two warriors remained. One of them looked at Lead Caelin and said, "You'll tell us how the games went?"

Lead Caelin laughed, "I'd be an eel warrior if I did that to you. I might bite you for thinking that I would."

Eanmund and Nick were swimming nearby. Lead Caelin turned to them, "Well Record Keeper, I have the rest of this day from you. Come with me. Help me inspect this site. You too man. I want to understand this energy harvesting system better."

Then turning to the two guards he told them, "Take posts at the far ends of this flat. If you see additional eels approaching, in any significant numbers, find me immediately."

"What about watching the workers?"

"There is no need. They will reveal themselves when it is time for them to do so. Until then, we can only suspect. As of now, they have their task and I don't expect trouble. If there is to be trouble, we will see reinforcements coming. Until we see an influx of eels, I'm not concerned by those laboring."

Eanmund said, "I agree with a seal; that is concerning."

Lead Caelin was already on his way to the nearest branch of the energy harvesting network. As they approached the two eels working on the section, the eels stopped and glared at Lead Caelin, Nick and Eanmund. They offered no salutation, nor excuses. They simply stared, silently. It seemed they'd had orders to not engage, at all, until the time was right.

"Record Keeper, what do you know of this system?" asked Lead Caelin.

"I know nothing of it from my time as Record Keeper, I did not pay much attention to technology records, but it is fairly similar to the systems powering every home on Enbala."

They moved to the closest network entirely connected. They could see the energy building on the surface of the panels, bubbling lightly in the water. When the panel reached significant capacity it would be withdrawn, in a flourish of bubbles, the energy drawn into the conduits snaking through the project and shimmering off towards the depths in translucent conduit. Unlike earth's wires, these conduits lit and pulsed when energy flowed through them. The blue light of the energy was astonishingly bright in these gloomy depths, among the shadows of the statues.

Several eels swam by overhead, glaring at the newest visitors to the project.

Eanmund stared at the energy gathering device contemplatively.

"You've been surprisingly quiet all day Eanmund; what's going on?" asked Lead Caelin.

"Why should I talk? I've come to realize my opinions aren't respected."

"Stop the pity party! My team are soldiers, not scholars. No matter how great a teacher you are, your teaching will lack the thrill of clearing a crab settlement of deadly eels. But I have told you before, and I'll say it again: I respect you. And I want your opinion! Is that not enough?"

Eanmund wasn't quick to answer, and first he sighed, but when he did answer his voice lacked some of the heaviness it had dripped with before.

"It surprises me how little energy is being harvested. These are quality components, and this system should have the ability to withdraw much higher levels…. It's as if this entire system is a ruse. Something isn't right."

Lead Caelin leaned his nose close to a panel and peered at the energy forming on the edges.

Eanmund laughed. "You're not a specialist in dwelling repairs, are you?"

Lead Caelin said quietly, "Life-long soldier, I've never had my own dwelling."

They started to move down the row again when a large explosion rocked them, sucking them up and down in the water, and then a passing concussion wave of energy pushed them all violently to the muddy ocean bottom.

Nick couldn't breathe. His breather had went scattering across the bottom. He scrambled to find it, but the burst and flurry of energetic swimming took heavily from the small reserve of air he had in his lungs.

Nick's lungs began to scream. He had to breathe, and now. He opened his mouth, as if to taste the water he was going to be forced to inhale. Then he saw a glint of black metal. He grabbed the rebreather and put it in his mouth just at the moment when his body was forcing him to inhale regardless of the substance to enter. He erupted into a fit of coughing as some water reached his airway, but with the breather in place he recovered quickly.

Eanmund and Lead Caelin were staring at a section of the network about fifty feet to their south. Water vapors, bubbles, mud and debris clouded the water and slowly dissolved into the surrounding water. Soon, all three could see a gap in the conduit, with jagged and shredded edges at either end of the gap, a testament to the force with which the conduit had exploded.

An eel practically flew to them shouting, "What did you do?!"

It was best that he was shouting because a loud ringing filled the ears of all three. Lead Caelin yelled back, "We did nothing, your conduit exploded on its own."

Again, a strange silence from the eel. He stared at them for several seconds, and then moved towards the broken conduit. More eels swam in. They gathered near the broken ends of the conduit, murmuring softly, assumedly so that Lead Caelin, Nick and Eanmund couldn't hear them. Their eyes kept flitting to the three though.

Eanmund said, "Something is very odd. Those conduits are normally made of inert, non-explosive materials, primarily melted sand."

After a little time, it became apparent the eels weren't going to have any dealings with Lead Caelin. He approached them, with the intention of asking what happened, but scores of eel workers quickly moved between him and the eels that were talking. The talking eels saw him approach and purposefully moved to the far side of the throng as the space between eel workers closed, allowing no passage through.

Eventually Lead Caelin, Nick and Eanmund moved on to exploring the rest of the conduit. It was the same everywhere. Conduit and network ran between the underwater hills, valleys, and statues, joining together on the central plain of the site, which was about 10 feet closer to the surface than the rest of the underwater plain. There were barriers in place around the center, as the main connection had not been made and the energy now being generated, was going into a variety of machines for construction (movers, diggers, etc.), or dissipating into the water.

The inspectors found evidence of several other explosions, with charred impressions left on a nearby statue base and craters from the resulting impacts still evident in the seabed. Lead Caelin and

Eanmund could offer no explanation for the exploding veins of the network.

The three eventually joined the guard posts on statues, watching the depths for an invasion. On occasion additional eels would flit in, and others leave, but there was no coming army this evening.

Lead Caelin said, "It's obvious that this is connected to an effort elsewhere; there is far too much coming and going for a construction project."

Well into the evening, the games attending teammates swam leisurely back into the area, most having partaken in the fermented pleasures offered at the games.

"Are we returning to base?" they asked Lead Caelin.

"No, we are camping on the shore here for a while. At least two guards will be on this construction site at all times."

As the depths grew dark with night (at least for Nick's small eyes, the seals large eyes serving them well in the twilight), the main body of the team moved towards the cruiser with the purpose to make camp on the nearby beach. Two very tired, post-games celebrations seals began their watch shifts on the statues.

Several days went by and the security posts began to feel routine. Lead Caelin had not assigned Nick to security, likely due to his poor underwater eyesight, so he had become something of a tagalong to Lead Caelin.

Each morning at the beach camp Nick and Lead Caelin would rise and start breakfast heating over the campfires; breakfast was a mushy concoction made from grains, similar to oatmeal. Some of the seals would dive into the ocean and bring back small fish to add to breakfast, which they'd eat raw. Invariably, if Nick smelled the raw fish he'd lose his appetite.

After breakfast Lead Caelin and Nick would venture down to the security posts and survey the construction site. Lead Caelin would typically spend several hours swimming around the site and reminding the eels of his presence.

Over the course of those several days Lead Caelin was required to return to shore and meet with Seal Council representatives with a variety of complaints and recommendations. The eel leadership did not appreciate the added oversight, and their leaders were complaining to Seal Council. While Lead Caelin seemed to enjoy great autonomy it became apparent the recent capture of the eel dignitary's son had affected Lead Caelin's ability to operate free of oversight. He was being told how many security posts he could have, where his team must be posted to, etc..

Lead Caelin told several Seal Council representatives to go "wag their flippers" (it took Nick awhile to realize this was akin to telling them "get lost"). This angered the self-important Seal Council reps.

On the third day, a larger seal delegation arrived. To this meeting Lead Caelin brought several of his team members, along with Nick and Eanmund, in an effort to match their numbers.

The seals adamantly attempted to persuade Lead Caelin to leave the construction site. They claimed that the oversight of the construction site was causing diplomatic issues.

But Lead Caelin would not back down. He was adamant that after the attack at Enbala he could not, in good conscience, walk away

from this site until he was sure there was no danger in the technology or the construction workers.

This enraged the seals. One of the seals began attacking Lead Caelin's patriotism, claiming that he was attempting a coup.

Lead Caelin finally broke, his anger rising. He chest bumped the seal that questioned his patriotism.

"Listen to me, you little office squeaker! I keep you, and your little Dreamer Council safe from the realities out here. I do that by risking my life and those of the warriors assigned to me. And to have a little piece of council flubber question whether I am patriotic... I'm about to feed you to the eels, piece by piece. Then you can ask them if they're peaceful, while they eat you with joy in their eyes."

Lead Caelin was towering over the seal, who had fallen onto his back and had one flipper up protecting his muzzle, in a picture of pathetic submission.

The other seals began talking loudly among themselves; words such as "crazy" and "unsafe" could be heard.

Lead Caelin yelled at them to go back to their council chambers, but in the safety of their herd they felt brave enough to resist him.

Eanmund was the one to address the seal group next.

"I lost my son during the attack at Enbala. Why, if your security expert tells you he feels something is off, do you not listen to him?! This is how honest citizens are lost. For the sake of your 'diplomacy'? Other than hurt feelings, it is hurting no one to have the security on site."

He continued, "You're the kings of untruth, so change the narrative. Tell the eels that Lead Caelin is working for eels, providing security against a threat of seal extremists. They'll believe you if you flatter them."

There was murmuring among the group, but it was much quieter after Eanmund's interjection. He'd obviously had some affect. At the least they were probably surprised to hear an otter from Enbala address them in such a way.

Eventually the seals moved off, but one of them accusingly told Lead Caelin that it was he that needed the oversight, not the eels.

The evenings at camp were pleasant. The weather was nearly perfect. The majority of the warriors would leave for the nearby stadium and different sporting events, but those that remained talked and joked in a relaxed manner that Nick hadn't seen at the base. Given purpose, these warriors were much easier to deal with; when they were waiting for something to do, they were a conflict prone group.

Each night there was a relaxing mix of food, conversation, humor, stories, fellowship and then sleep. All by the pleasing smoky smell of campfire. They'd fall asleep to the sound of tiny waves nudging the sand back and forth at the edge of the sea.

The council member's threat of oversight for Lead Caelin became reality the next day. Early in the morning, before the sun or warriors had risen, loud transport carriers landed in the field next to them. Military seals wearing the council's badge began de-embarking and setting up a camp.

Lead Caelin was yelling, "What do you think you're doing?!"

A seal with an official bearing approached Lead Caelin.

"Sir, it is a pleasure to meet the legend! We are here to provide site oversight, by command of the Seal Head Council."

"What do you think we're doing?!" yelled Lead Caelin.

"Then we should be able to work together well Sir. I've been told to stay here and work closely with you until you leave the site."

"Until I leave... not the eels?! The stupidity of our leadership doesn't cease to amaze me. Fine. Do what you have to, but I want nothing to do with you. We are not working together."

The seal seemed disappointed, but responded, "I understand Sir", and he moved off to set up his camp.

After breakfast Lead Caelin and Nick swam down to the security posts again. As Lead Caelin discussed the night's security with the post, Nick saw waves of slithering shadows approaching from out of the depths.

"Hey... Hey! Look!" Nick yelled.

Lead Caelin turned around and saw the eels instantly. He told the seal he'd just been talking to, "Get the whole team down here, now."

Then, very unexpectedly, Lead Caelin swam straight towards the incoming eels alone.

Nick didn't know what to do. He was starting to panic. The seal guard was headed quickly towards camp, and Lead Caelin was hurtling towards the eels. This left Nick alone on the statue they'd been guarding from, and he felt very alone.

Nick glanced down and saw several of the construction eels staring at him. They were also wondering what Nick would do. It was then he decided to stick with Lead Caelin. He swam desperately after him, although much slower.

When Lead Caelin reached the eels he yelled "Stop!"

He was surprised to find that he had no authority. He hadn't even made the eels pause. Eels blew past him, opening rank just enough to give Lead Caelin a gap to pass through. An occasional batted at him as it passed.

Lead Caelin was furious. He was an authority here, they were not free to ignore him.

He chomped into the passing tale of an eel, swinging the eel around to hit three other eels in the formation. The five plunged into fighting. The larger group of eels slowed and stopped, turning to watch the melee.

Finally, Lead Caelin had their attention.

The nearest two rows of eels circled around, in formation, to provide support to their beleaguered comrades.

Nick stopped swimming when he saw the melee begin. The power of the large eels and Lead Caelin were at another level; even if he wanted to, he could offer no support. Nick was as dangerous as a sea cucumber.

He looked down, trying to find a weapon. A crane-like structure, that had moved one of the statues several days ago, was close to the fight. Nick swam down, trying to find the controls of the crane.

Glancing up, he saw that Lead Caelin was holding his own better than Nick would have bet on. He was not subdued by the eel numbers, and was using one eel to pummel several of the others that were closing in on him. Still, the hordes were upon him and soon, just through the sheer weight of the slimy crowd, he would be overpowered.

Nick found the crane controls. It took him a minute to figure out how they worked, but soon the crane was moving in response to Nick's inputs and he swung its boom towards the fight. As the crane's mechanism reached the melee, eels began flying out of the mess, resembling bowling pins being struck.

Still, they were tough creatures, and upon regaining their senses they'd close back in on Lead Caelin. Nick continued to swing the mechanism through the crowd wildly; once he hit Lead Caelin, who popped out of the pack but was quickly beset upon again.

Then more dark shadows swarmed past Nick's crane, darkness flashing by him like the shadows of a passing skein of geese. Lead Caelin's team had arrived. Now it was true chaos above him. Still, Lead Caelin's team deployed no weapons because the eels had not done so. Seeing Lead Caelin in unrestrained physical combat was all the encouragement the team needed to follow suit. Soon eels, crabs and seals were crashing, slamming, biting, flipping, hitting and careening everywhere. Seaweed, bubbles, mud, patches of uniform and blood stirred wildly through the water, darkening the area of the fight.

Then the first casualty struck. An eel, fighting close to the bottom, had been thrown into the conduit of the solar gathering's arrays.

It exploded, in a rush of bubbles, mud, seaweed, vegetation and blood. From the hazy waters, where seconds before an eel had been, several large chunks of flesh floated out.

This gave a momentary pause to the fighting. All heard and felt the concussion and turned to see what occurred. At the sight of eel parts floating in the sea the tone of the battle changed.

Nick's flailing about with the crane was making no positive effect, although it had delayed the eels besetting on Lead Caelin long enough to get his team down to his aid.

Then Nick glanced away from the fight and saw Eanmund swimming with the seal that had landed in the field in the morning; behind them the new seal's team followed.

In the same fashion, and set to converge before reaching the tussle, a fresh squadron of eels were coming along near the ocean floor, all wearing military uniforms.

The eel leader hailed the seal with Eanmund, "Seal, what is going on here?!" he shouted.

"I don't know, I'm just arriving myself. Extract your eels and I will work to extract my responsibilities."

The eel snarled at him, but seemed to acquiesce to the plan.

The seal with Eanmund looked back at his team and said, "Extract our warriors!"

It seemed to Nick that some of the fresh group of seals were smiling as they went into the fray.

The leader of the uniformed eels again approached the seal he'd previously addressed.

"Captain Grey, I demand answers! Why is your team here?"

So, Nick thought, Captain Grey was this new seal commander's name. How aptly ambiguous for a seal.

But Captain Grey surprised Nick with his fiery return.

"You have no cause to be here, this is still seal territory and my jurisdiction! Don't ask me the question you should be answering!"

"We've been asked, by our leaders, to help oversee the completion of the work and guarantee the safe completion of the job and the return of our workers. It seems there's been a threat to the construction efforts by seal extremists; this is what the Seal Council told our leaders last night."

Nick remembered Eanmund's suggestion to the Seal Council representatives the day before; it sounded as though the Seal Council had done as Eanmund suggested, but with unexpected results. Now the eel military had been called in.

The fighting was over, the offenders having been pulled apart by the new arrivals, who benefitted from being fresher. The respective teams were regrouping.

Captain Grey addressed the eel military leader, "Then we shall be seeing much of each other until the conclusion of this project. I hope our teams can get along better in the future."

Then Captain Grey swam off to join his team. Lead Caelin, with his team, was already swimming back to the shore.

Nick was close to the eel commander, and he saw the eel's eyes smoldering with hatred as he lingered, watching Captain Grey disappear among his team.

At Lead Caelin's camp the evening was loud with jokes and laughter, especially from those that participated in the day's melee. An occasional loud heckle would be directed at the" fun killers" in the field neighboring theirs. But the air of comedy quickly receded from the ranks as their emotional barometers felt and witnessed the dark cloud Lead Caelin was under.

Lead Caelin wasn't laughing, or even talking. He was glaring. Glaring at the ocean. Glaring at the nearby field. His teeth were noticeably grinding as his thoughts weighted his soul.

Like the fading light, the noise of the camp also slowly reduced to almost nothing.

The realization was coming upon the team that something might be amiss, at a grand scale. Others were simply quiet because a lifetime of experience had taught them that it was the right response for an angry authority.

After darkness settled, a younger seal, whispering with a friend, started barking quietly in a humorous way. A seasoned veteran snarled viciously at him, quickly extinguishing the youth's noise and bringing the camp back to silence.

From the nearby field came only the professional sounds of Captain Grey's team; there was the buzz of camp and food preparation, but Lead Caelin's team would only occasionally hear commands and the faint discussions of duties, nothing more.

Captain Grey's team was procedurally accurate, taking great care to follow the rules without questioning who wrote them or why.

They'd obeyed seal commands since they were pups, and had no reason to stray from structures' safe comfort now that they were in the field. If anything, they found solace in their structure and rigidity, especially in this unfamiliar real-world scenario. They did not joke or engage in lighthearted banter.

In the quiet of Caelin's camp Nick stared into the fire. Swirling tongues flashed from the face of the fire, ebbing and flowing with calming assuredness. Fire was the same here on this world as it was on Earth, and that gave Nick some comfort.

Did the same creator make fire on both worlds, Nick wondered. If so, how did he conceive fire? Why did it burn red?

And why did Nick hear it calling him?!

He'd ignored the faint noise for some time, dismissing it as one of those odd coincidental noises that are never quite what you think they are…. but, it had become louder, and now he was sure.

Something was calling, "Man…. Man…. MAN!"

It wasn't the fire. He wasn't Moses. And the voice was feminine.

Nick had thought the noise was coming from the fire, but the sea was beyond the fire.

The sea! The noise was coming from the sea.

Nick knew what the voice reminded him of, his mercreature encounter on Enbala! He jumped up, only to be met with a growl from several seals, and a glare from Lead Caelin.

Nick slowed his gait. Trying, with great effort to appear nonchalant, he mosied past the fire, towards the sea beyond.

When he reached the sea edge, he wondered, "Now what?"

Then he heard, "Follow", the noise directing him further down the shore.

Soon he was beyond a small dune, out of sight of the encampments, both Lead Caelin's and Captain Grey's.

A shape appeared in the water. A telltale "v" approached, the foam contrasting in the moonlight, with a uniquely female figure at its front.

Nick's heart jumped, for a brief second he thought it was his friend from Enbala. But something in him knew this wasn't the same mermaid-like creature.

Nick took a step back with a little fear. Who was this figure in the dark?

"Who are you," he thought, with his best effort to form his thoughts loud and clear.

He seemed to hear "Oliphant", as she reached the sand just in front of him.

This mermaid was similar to the other, but wizened in the face and body, lacking the playfully strong and possibly flirtatious poise he'd so enjoyed previously.

As he thought about Enbala, and the kiss, it dawned on him that his audience knew what he was thinking about.

Nick's eyes sheepishly met hers.

"... my sister..." she said. There was a sadness in her words.

"... eels... death".

Nick took this in. At first, he felt very sad. Then angry.

Nick tried to cast his empathy to her.

She seemed annoyed.

"What do you want from me?", was the best thought Nick could come up with. He felt strangely intimidated.

He suddenly felt shamed; he wasn't sure if she was saying it, but he felt as if he'd been told, "This isn't about you!"

"Yes?" he questioned.

"The Eels…. plotting."

"We think so too," Nick replied.

"I know."

Nick didn't know how to respond to that. If he hadn't felt so odd, perhaps he would have asked "Why?", but instead he stood there remembering his Enbalan friend, and considering whether this mermaid meant him any harm.

Finally he heard her say several times, "A weapon… a weapon!"

Nick tried to think of what she was saying. Did she want a weapon? Did she think he had one?

He felt her exasperation, and finally she glared at him much the same way Eanmund sometimes did, and then she slid back into the water, thrashing her tail a little roughly in Nick's direction as she left.

Nick returned to camp slowly. Still, Lead Caelin noticed him as he approached.

"Take in some games, Man?"

Nick came over to Lead Caelin and sat beside him. He was quiet for a long time. In truth, the mermaid interactions seemed embarrassing to talk about. There was an intense feminine aspect to their visits that Nick feared he wasn't responding well to, and the seals might belittle him if they knew about it.

Eventually Nick spoke. He told Lead Caelin about the mermaids. Nick tried to edit out as much emotion as possible, but in the end he still felt embarrassed.

Nick wasn't sure if he expected heckling, but the response he received surprised him. It was almost awe.

"... what do they see in you?" wondered Lead Caelin quietly, as if he had suddenly gained some modicum of respect for Nick.

"Me? I don't know. But what do you think about 'the weapon'?" Nick redirected.

"Ah, now you're finally starting to think man. I'll try and find the mermaids in the morning. Perhaps, if there's one, there's more nearby watching what is going on. For now, all we can do is sleep."

As Nick turned towards his cot, he noticed Lead Caelin did not retire. When Lead Caelin thought all of his team was asleep, he moved quickly out to the sea and dove in.

"Wake up Man... now!"

A breathing apparatus was being thrust into his mouth as Nick's groggy eyes opened.

"We need to go! Something is happening."

Nick was pulled out of his bunk by Lead Caelin's teeth. He began scrambling groggily for his garments.

That moment, the eel that had talked with Captain Grey appeared out of the water with several others. He slithered quickly towards Lead Caelin.

"Why are your eels flooding, er, I mean… overrunning the construction site?!" Lead Caelin asked.

"It's your fault. We were told you would be protecting us from extremists, but then you attacked us. We don't know who the extremists are. We're concerned the 'extremist' is you, Lead Caelin. We've decided to bring in reinforcements, to protect us from the threat of your team."

"That's a lie. Why are they really here?", returned Lead Caelin.

"I have business with Captain Grey, and I've said enough to you. We will prevent you from launching any future crazed attacks on innocent construction eels."

"Innocent… I know they're building a weapon. I haven't figured out how it works yet. But I will."

The eel slithered to within inches of Lead Caelin's muzzle, its fishy smell overwhelming the clear morning air. "Hear me Lead Caelin, you know nothing, nor will you ever. Your type are all fools. Thankfully, this project will help us regain proper respect."

And with that he slithered past Lead Caelin, heading towards Captain Grey's camp.

Nick was dressed now, and he struggled to catch up with Lead Caelin as the team headed for the water and the day's duties.

"Where did you go last night?" Nick asked.

"I tried to find your mermaid friends, I wanted to know what they were trying to tell you."

"Any luck?"

"No, I thought I might have seen them a few times, but it was always fleeting and I could never know for sure. At the outskirts of eyesight, in the dark night ocean, the mind sees what may or may not be real."

"So, no success?"

"No, but I had a thought that gave me some comfort. If the mermaids were there, and active at night, I realized they were providing an added layer of nighttime oversight to the site."

Eanmund stumbled down to the water's edge. Lead Caelin and Nick both looked up at him. He looked tired and surly. He grunted something as a hello. Nick and Lead Caelin grunted back.

With a careful effort to add no tone or intonation, Lead Caelin said to Eanmund, "I thought you were leaving."

Eanmund turned a steady and sure gaze towards Nick and Lead Caelin. He replied, "I've been living only for myself since my son died. I've been looking only for my fulfillment. And I've been deeply unhappy. The creator instructed us to serve others, I need to return to that. Teaching allows me to do that."

There was a slight pause.

Lead Caelin simply said, "We'll be happy to have you with us."

267

Then Lead Caelin turned and continued towards the water.

Nick was about to follow when Eanmund said, "Man, I need to talk to you."

Nick, curious, turned back to Eanmund.

"I'm sorry, in my selfishness I've been atrocious to you. To satiate my grieving heart I've been inflicting punishment on you. Punishment you didn't earn or deserve. It wasn't your fault my son died."

Nick felt as though a strong weight had lifted off his chest.

"Thank you Eanmund, it means a lot."

Eanmund replied, "Strangely, I've been thinking a lot about your Jesus stories the last several days."

But, just then, Lead Caelin was disappearing into the water, shouting "Let's go!" as his head submerged. His team was just behind him.

Nick and Eanmund hurried to the water.

Nick quickly realized what the hurry was. Eels were everywhere. The ocean and sea floor teemed with them; like air-darkening flocks of birds in the air, eels were swimming and gathering in groups all around. The eels were everywhere.

"This isn't good," Lead Caelin communicated.

A squadron of eels breezed quickly past them, swimming in such a way to make Lead Caelin's team stop to avoid crashing into them. Lead Caelin's team was no longer threatening, they paled by numbers alone now. The eels could swarm the entire team in seconds.

Nick was glad when he saw Captain Grey's team entering the water.

Captain Grey swam to Lead Caelin and tried to start with small talk.

"Busy down here today."

"What do you want, Captain?"

"I just want you to know that I respect your opinions. Because I'm starting to see your concerns myself, I've called in a division of crabs to provide ground support. They'll be entering the water soon, from my camp."

"That's the first sensible thing you've said to me." responded Lead Caelin.

They both paused and stared out at the chaos of the construction site. Eels rushed to and fro, those on the sea bed connecting the remaining conduits between newly installed panels. The squadrons of swimming eels seemed to be providing a dome of overhead security to the site.

"Well, I'm off…. Let's hope there is no fighting today." said Captain Grey.

Lead Caelin's eyes narrowed, but he said nothing.

Captain Grey swam away to rejoin his team. They would provide support to the North of the project, and Lead Caelin's team was heading South. The crabs would come into the water between the eels and the beach. The only side of the construction project without protection bordered the deep dark depths; but Lead Caelin had suggested they leave that path open, to encourage an easy retreat back to the depths if the eels felt drawn to do so. It would be best for all, if that's where the eels went in a time of turmoil. By sheer numbers they might overrun the allied forces in any other direction.

And, shortly, a large division of crabs were scampering into the water, some scrambling one-upon-another, such was their numbers and frenetic energy. They changed the entire shoreward side of the project into a red-orange bubbling and bobbing hue.

Adding to the masses now gathered at the site, Nick could occasionally sense, and perhaps see, traces of mermaids in the hazy water beyond the site's perimeter. They too were interested and patrolling the day's happenings.

Far too many were gathered for nothing to happen. Most expected instigation to come from the eels, although some believed Lead Caelin was the bigger threat.

For several hours the construction continued with great oversight but little action to note. There was one conduit explosion, but such a thing had become somewhat commonplace and the eels seemed to have little regard to the injury or loss of life of an eel laborer.

With the passing of hours the guards began to relax. Perhaps this was only a construction site for energy harvesting.

Suddenly a river of eels began pouring into the site from the direction of the depths. They became visible at the depth where light began illuminated their body, and Nick thought they resembled hornets leaving a nest after an insult. It might have been fascinating that there could be such vast numbers of eels in a coordinated effort, if there weren't such dark implications.

Lead Caelin yelled to an eel official, "What is going on?!"

"They are bringing the central assembly for the array; it is very heavy. It requires many eels to move it."

And sure enough, a huge metal monolith began to loom out of the darkness. The swarming mass of eels seemed to be surfing it along, all laying before it, bowing to it as it trundled on; it was like a ball had been placed upon thousands of snakes, thought Nick.

What concerned Nick was that the monolith was shaped as an Earthen bomb.

"It looks like a bomb," Nick yelled to Lead Caelin.

"What's a 'bomb?'" returned Lead Caelin.

"A huge explosive device," returned Nick.

"Ah, a big weapon. I agree," said Lead Caelin.

The monolith continued towards its cradle at the center of the construction site. The eels bore it along similar to pagan's carrying their sacrifices to an altar, all bowing before it as it passed by and over them. It listed wildly this way and that, but never fell. It couldn't. There were simply too many eels holding it aloft; it could not fall. The monolith was crowd surfing its way into place.

As the monolith neared the center of the construction site, the sea around it became filled as if the water was a stadium. Eels, seals, crabs and mermaids all gathered around, on the seafloor and swimming in the water, jockeying to catch a view. The monolith was surrounded by a dome of beings encompassing it. The eels just before it lay substrate. All were watching intently. Some wondered how the monolith worked. Those that did know what the monolith was designed for only wondered about its strange shape.

It was a long cylinder, turned vertically, and domed at the top and bottom. At the bottom were the control systems, a complex of wires and computers that resembled a timer plugged into a stick of dynamite.

Once the monolith was secured in place at the center of the harvesting project, the eels were again darting here and there, plugging conduits into the monolith. As each conduit clicked into place, the assembly began to glow, getting brighter and brighter with each attachment.

Oddly, most of the eels remained lying down before it, although the monolith was now in-place.

When there were only two or three conduits left to install, the top dome of the monolith split and rolled open. With a loud whir a large cylinder protruded; Lead Caelin, Nick and Eanmund could have fit easily into the gun barrel-like shape.

The hum of the assembly became so loud it was disorienting. The water was vibrating with the noise waves from the assembly. Nick yelled, "I still think it's a weapon!"

"I agree!" said Lead Caelin again. He was contemplating what to do, ideally he needed proof it was a weapon before he could attack it.

"I think anyone with eyes and half a mind would agree." muttered Eanmund to himself.

Most the construction workers had joined into ranks with eels at attention before the monolith, just as though they were the professional military eels everyone suspected. Many of the eels in ranks were now swaying in unison, en masse, as the monolith gained power and brightness. The eels also seemed to be chanting themselves into a feverish frenzy as they swayed and the water around them grew warmer and brighter from the energy the monolith was collecting.

"Let's talk to their lead!" yelled Lead Caelin to Nick.

They left their post on the statue and began to swim towards the assembly. Eanmund went with them. This surprised Nick.

The water darkened with a shadow. Nick looked above him to see a squadron of roughly one dozen eels rocketing downward onto the three.

It was too late to do anything. Nick placed his hands over his breathing apparatus so that when the collision occurred it wouldn't be knocked from his mouth.

All three were slammed into by eels at attack speed. There were several eels assigned to each of them, as they were pushed towards the bottom.

Hundreds of eels broke off from the ground waving around the monolith, coming between them and Lead Caelin's team, who had rushed forward to assist their Lead. But the eel numbers were simply too great and Nick, Lead Caelin, and Eanmund were shoved down to the bottom and forcefully into the mud. No help could break through the wall of eels that had come between them and Lead Caelin's team.

Nick tried to think, "What can I possibly do right now?"

Suddenly he heard a slimy, "Let them up."

With all his appendages held, Nick was ripped to his feet, as were the others. The eel's teeth were mostly in his clothes, although a few were painfully piercing his skin.

The Foreman of the eel construction team was before them.

"What were you doing?!" he asked with a suspicious tone.

Lead Caelin yelled, "My job! I want to know what that monstrosity of a central assembly does!"

The eel laughed, and repeated, "monstrosity" to himself. He enjoyed the sound of the name Lead Caelin had given it.

The Foreman looked at Eanmund, and said disdainfully, "Why are you here Otter? Shouldn't you be on Enbala, practicing self-worship? For the Creator is surely from the imagination of your own minds."

Eanmund quietly replied, "All have a responsibility to oppose destruction, hatred and lies. I can't leave until I know my world, and my family, are safe from whatever it is you're doing here."

Then Foreman said, "You are fools! It is what we said, an energy harvester. The monolith simply gathers power from around it, then sends it to the depths."

Then the Foreman smiled. "But... this device will also tap into the natural energy in the atmosphere above the water too."

Lead Caelin said, "Energy harvester?! Not like one I've seen. I think it's a weapon. I know weapons."

The eel glared at the three of them.

The noise from the monolith was growing. The monolith emitted an intense and foreboding racket. All of them had only heard portions of what Lead Caelin said. The water seemed to be shaking with the noise of the monolith.

The last conduit was being secured in place.

The Foreman looked towards the eels preventing Lead Caelin's team from flying to the three's assistance. Then he looked back at Nick, Lead Caelin, and Eanmund, saying, "The 'monstrosity' shouldn't harvest some energy, it should harvest all of your energy, drawing the atmospheric energy your society is dependent on into the depths, leaving your filthy above-water civilizations completely destroyed and returned to their primitive state. We shall take our rightful place as rulers of the world! May the Great Shark conquer all!"

It was the confirmation they'd all been waiting for.

Nick noticed they were standing next to the crane controls he'd used earlier in the week. Something in his soul told him it was time to act. Using a quick jerking action and all his strength, Nick pulled away from his captors and scrambled to the controls. Nick snatched the controls, and in one motion tried to swing the crane towards the monolith.

It took the eels several seconds to realize that Nick had pulled away and what he was attempting to do.

A second before the eels, Lead Caelin realized what Nick was up to and forced his way between Nick and the impending rush.

The eels walloped Lead Caelin, trying to get through him and stop Nick's endeavors with the crane.

Nick spun the crane boom towards the monolith. The boom made contact but did nothing. The monolith was strong, its builders had already secured it in place.

Nick's mind raced.

Lead Caelin was fighting for his life, successfully stalling the eels alone, but he couldn't for long. The fight was so ferocious the growling, barking, and yells could be heard over the racket of the monolith. The water around Lead Caelin's battle was nothing but a blur of bubbles, mud and energy. The colors of seal and eel flashing intermittently through the roiling, spinning mass.

Nick considered the grabbing apparatus at the end of the boom; he thought, "If I can grab the conduits, maybe I can tear them off the monolith."

He struggled to lower the apparatus to a conduit. It neared his intended target. He struggled to get the grabber to catch on the conduit. Adrenalin was pumping through his veins, causing his control movements to be jerky.

"Catch... Catch... CATCH DANGIT!"

Violently, Nick was torn away from the crane controls. He was being held aloft by an eel's teeth, which had grabbed him right behind the neck, catching the neckline of his garments... and, from the pain and red haze, he guessed a little bit of his neck.

Nick flailed wildly, but he was like a crab which had been grabbed from behind. There was no point, he was subdued.

He looked towards Lead Caelin, who was now covered in eels, although Nick could still see Lead Caelin's body shaking in continued protest under the pile.

The Foreman was still standing where he'd been, but eyes were drawn into slits and his veins were red with pulsing blood.

"No more! Pull their breathing devices!"

Then the Foremen glanced around, and said, "Where is the third one?!"

Nick had also lost track of Eanmund. He couldn't remember when he'd last been with him.

They all scanned around. The eels temporarily forgot to pull Nick's breathing apparatus as they struggled to locate Eanmund. The eels began swimming to-and-fro feverishly in their search for him.

Then an eel yelled, "There, by the main assembly!"

Everyone looked towards the monolith.

Compared to the huge monolith, it was no wonder Eanmund had been hard to spot. Eanmund was diminutive in comparison. A small speck of grey against a loud, large, black monstrosity.

Eanmund was pulling something along with him. It appeared to be a small section of the explosive conduit.

Eanmund swam purposefully towards the barrel protruding from the monolith. Because no one had noticed him in a timely manner, he was almost there.

The Foreman screamed "Get him!"

The eels shot after him, but they were far too late.

As Eanmund entered the lip of the barrel, the monolith began the next stage of its energy-drawing process and began pulling energy into the barrel with Eanmund.

The effect on Eanmund was two-fold: the conduit he was carrying began glowing brightly, and he seemed to move into a tornado of energy, pulling him quickly into the barrel. From the audience's vantage, it seemed Eanmund disappeared into a blur of light and waves undulating into the barrel. This stream of energy into the barrel resembled a vein system, at the start only reaching into the nearby water but, as the energy draw increased, the veins grew towards the surface, then breached it and shot into the skies, reaching for the heavens. The very atmosphere bent towards the vein. Energy was being sucked into the barrel at an immense rate, and the vein leaving the monolith began to grow immensely bright, just as the monolith had done when it was first turned on.

Eanmund had disappeared into the contraption. As the energy draw grew, some form of internal dampers seemed to brace the frequencies and noise the monolith was putting out and a strange quiet descended on the arena of the construction site and surrounding onlookers.

It seemed Eanmund's quest was in vain. New veins and the large central trunk of energy continued to grow in size. The conduits leading to the surface, grew brighter and brighter. Several of the veins that had reached the surface became like lightning bolts, so bright you couldn't look directly at them. Their trunks were the size of large trees. The energy being pulled into the depths was beyond measure.

"Surely Eanmund must be electrocuted," thought Nick.

Several eels had tried to pursue Eanmund into the barrel. When they reached the tip of the barrel and came into contact with the energy vein there had been a loud flash. Nick thought of a bug zapper, as he closed his eyes to guard from the arc flash. When he opened his eyes again there were bits of eel flesh floating away from the barrel in a haze of red water, illuminated by the energy flow.

The Foreman turned towards Nick, Lead Caelin, the eels restraining Nick, and those giving their best to restrain Lead Caelin.

"Pull their breathers!" the Foreman said again.

Inside the monolith Eanmund had been pressed into a cavity between the barrel and the stream of energy flowing in. The energy was inducing some sort of field in the water, pushing Eanmund away from the stream and against the barrel. Eanmund could tell the energy was getting stronger because the force pushing him against the barrel was increasing. He knew what had to be done. With every bit of strength in his body he pushed the volatile conduit he held towards the energy stream. Closer. Closer… it was almost there. Eanmund grunted and pushed with all his might.

There was an odd rumbling. It was the type of rumbling where you know something is wrong; it didn't belong, at all. The rumbling didn't match any of the noises the monolith had previously made, and it was random, not like machinery. Faint, and mostly felt in the floor of the ocean at first, but the noise was growing. It was emanating out from the base of the monolith.

Everyone looked towards the monolith, through the vines and trunk of energy now sucking energy from the above-water atmosphere.

Near its bottom the monolith had started to glow. It grew brighter and brighter.

Then the bottom of the monolith exploded ferociously. A rushing wave of energy, from the first blast, shredded all those eels still laying prostrate before the structure. But that was just the beginning. It was apparent from a continued glow further up the monolith, and extending into the barrel, that the entire monstrosity was going to explode spectacularly. The second explosion was larger and sharper, and the energy wave moved away from the monolith fast, not fading as it passed into the nearby water. The wave washed through Nick and Lead Caelin's area just after the sound of the explosion and lifted them about thirty feet, then slammed them back down into the sea floor in rapid succession. The G forces both felt were immense, Nick especially struggled to not black out.

When they landed in the mud, Nick noticed Lead Caelin was near him. But Lead Caelin rolled towards a rock, putting it between him and what used-to-be the monolith. This was wise. A third explosion, and another wave passed through, again lifting and slamming Nick, but Lead Caelin's experience and action had shielded him from the effects of this wave.

When he landed, Nick tried to go to Lead Caelin, crawling towards the rock where Lead Caelin was sheltered. Lead Caelin was yelling at him but Nick's ears were overcome by the loudest roar, which was shaking the very bones of his skull and jaw. From the monolith's direction came a wall of fire, metal, eels, bubbles and carnage rushing at him, being pulled along in a vacuum created by a wave of unfolding energy.

The doctor was yelling, "His lungs are filled with water! He's drowning. Get a tap in there stat, Nurse!"

He looked towards Nick's dad, Mark, "I don't understand, this hasn't happened before!"

Only moments before they'd "pulled the plug" on Nick's life support; an overly dramatic saying, Mark now understood this meant only turning off the life support machines.

But Nick hadn't passed on. Suddenly he'd been fighting. He was coughing, sputtering and flailing as he drowned.

The doctor yelled, "Put him in a coma!", to the anesthesiologist.

Mark yelled, "Don't you dare do that again!"

The Doctor looked towards Mark, quickly considered his words, and then agreed.

"Disregard! The Dad's right. In this case, let's try to get him back. It's now or never!"

A nurse ran over with the EKG device for restarting the heart. They were desperately trying to get the pads on his chest as Nick shook and coughed wildly.

Mark grabbed one flailing arm as a nurse grabbed the other.

Nick's eyes were fluttering.

The cardiac device slammed Nick.

The doctor had forgotten to yell "Clear".

Mark and the nurse were both dropped to their knees.

"Aaaa!" the nurse screamed, when she caught her breath.

The doctor said, "They'll be fine, hit him again!"

Several hours later Mark sat next to Nick, staring at him like someone that had discovered a fairy tale character to be true, and refusing to let it out of their sight for fear of losing it forever.

Nick's eyes fluttered open.

"Son!"

Mark jumped up to hug Nick, attempting to embrace him through the maze of tubes and wires connected to him. An alarm started sounding in the monitoring equipment attached to Nick but Mark didn't notice. Mark's heart was bursting with joy.

Nick, too, was overcome with emotion. Was he really back? Was this Earth? How could it be trusted? Was this going to last? Nick grabbed the bed rails, in case he might be suddenly thrown back into that other world.

His father was grabbing a hand, prying it off the bars, and shaking it violently. Oddly, it was reassuring.

Nick tried to smile. It was odd, his face didn't work anymore. Maybe he managed a smile, but all of his muscles had become weak on Earth.

He whispered, as Mark shook him, "Yeah, Dad, it's me. It's good to see you too. Seems like it's been a long time."

"Holy crap, son, holy crap! You wouldn't believe it! They told me you had zero odds. None! It had to be the prayers! Only God could do this."

Nick thought about that. Considering his... dream?... it seemed likely.

"Yeah, yeah that might be."

"I've been praying son. Praying hard. Praying all sorts of things! Even prayed that you weren't bored. How silly is that?! Man, it's great to see your face. Unbelievable!"

Mark didn't really know what to say, but couldn't stop talking. Nick didn't have the energy or the muscle to respond quickly, so Mark kept filling in the holes with statements.

Nick's energy was little, but he did manage to whisper, "I wasn't bored Dad. I've got a story..."

And then Nick fell asleep. There'd be time. He couldn't help but sleep. His Earth body was too weak, and couldn't handle excitement yet. He'd tell his father all about Enbala, and Eanmund's sacrifice soon. His soul looked forward to it. He was glad to be back.

Made in the USA
Middletown, DE
24 September 2020

20240782R00172